AF594257

Kiss Away
YOUR PAIN
BOOK 2 IN THE WOUNDED HEARTS SERIES
DEBBIE
CROMACK

Printed in the United States of America

Book cover: Qamber Designs and Media (https://www.qamberdesignsandmedia.com/)

Developmental Editor: Susan Staudinger (https://www.stylisticediting.com/)

Copy Editor: Kat Wyeth (https://katsliteraryservices.com/)

Proofreader: Deb Richmond (https://katsliteraryservices.com/)

Interior Formatting: Qamber Designs and Media (https://www.qamberdesignsandmedia.com/)

ISBN 978-1-7923-8736-4 (pbk.)

ISBN 978-1-7923-8735-7 (eBook)

This book is dedicated to Lea Joan.
(Lea pronounced "Leigh" winky-face.)
We met on the Internet. A strange place to meet a new friend.
Our friendship grew over time.
You joined my teams and supported me and my journey from day one.
We've never met in person because we're half a world apart.
And yet, we've become such close friends.
This book wouldn't exist if it wasn't for you.

Thank you for all our brainstorming sessions, your constant support and encouragement, and your undying love of our friendship.

This book is also for my readers…
because you asked for it.

HUGS!

VISUAL RECOMMENDATION

I'm a very visual person. So, for each of my books, I create a Pinterest board that houses Pins of my hero, heroine, places they'll go, experiences they'll have, things from their past, and so on. To get a glimpse into the story of Enzo and Candi in Kiss Away Your Pain, I invite you to visit their Pinterest board here: https://www.pinterest.com/debbiecromackauthor/kiss-away-your-pain/.

PLAYLIST

Music is powerful. It can set my mood, help me change my mood, and/or intensify my mood. Along with being a visual person, I surround myself with music. When I write, I see my stories as though they're movies. And every movie has a soundtrack. I create a soundtrack for each of my books. Below is a list of songs you may want to check out as you read certain scenes and chapters in Kiss Away Your Pain. They'll bring you even deeper into the story. You can find most of them on my playlist on Spotify: https://open.spotify.com/playlist/1kAWoTA2LSgG8iBdSa0jMC. I hope you enjoy them!

Chapter 1 – "Canon in D" by Jean-Francois Paillard & Kanon Orchestre de Chambre

Chapter 2 – "Hero (Acoustic)" by Music Travel Love

Chapter 3 – "Stand Still" by Sabrina Claudio and "I'll Never Love Again" by Lady Gaga

Chapter 4 – "Pink Reprise" by Two Feet

Chapter 5 – "Ruby" by Paul Baker and "Love Your Voice" by JONY

Chapter 6 – "Are You Alright?" by Lucinda Williams, "Temptation" by Coté De Pablo, and "Fire for You" by Cannons

Chapter 7 – "Heartbeats" by Daniela Andrade & Dabin and "Paspatou" by Parra for Cuva

Chapter 8 – "Take Me Home" by Jess Glynne and "Wildest Moments" by Jessie Ware

Chapter 9 – "Sax – Sensual Music" by Smooth Jazz and "I'm There Too" by Michelle Featherstone

Chapter 10 – "It Never Entered My Mind" by Miles Davis and "The Nearness of You" by Nora Jones"

Chapter 11 – "In My Veins (feat. Erin McCarley)" by Andrew Belle, "The Lonely" by Christina Perry, and "Can't Get You Out of My Mind" by Sonya Kitchell

Chapter 12 – "My Confession (From "One Life to Live")" by Rie Sinclair & Friends and "Possibility" by Lykke Li

Chapter 13 – "From the Inside" by Alex Parks and "Gravity" by Sara Bareilles

Chapter 14 – "Here She Comes Again" by Röyksopp and "Love Me Like You Do" by Ellie Goulding

Chapter 15 – "Little Gem" by Euphoria and "The Distance" by Jamie Walters

Chapter 16 – "Unbound" by Robbie Robertson, "I Am the Fire" by Ghost Monroe, and "Make You Feel" by Alina Baraz & Galimatias

Chapter 17 – "Grace" by Kate Havnevik, "Broken" by Lifehouse, and "Unsteady" by X Ambassadors

Chapter 18 – "Ti Orero Miro" by Wildlife, "Silverline" by Omido, and "Gemini (feat. George Maple)" by What So Not

Chapter 19 – "Hurricane (feat. Fleurie)" by Tommee Profitt and "Here We Go / Quasar (Hybrid Remix)" by Hard Rock Sofa & Swanky Tunes

Chapter 20 – "Red Light" by Fast and Furious

Chapter 21 – "Never Let Me Go" by Florence + the Machine, "Repeat Until Death" by Novo Amor, and "Carry You" by Novo Amor

Chapter 22 – "Goodbye My Lover" by James Blunt and "Let Her Go" by Jasmine Thompson

Chapter 23 – "Run to You" by Lea Michele

Chapter 24 – "Stay (feat. Mikky Ekko)" by Rihanna and "I Can't Make You Love Me (Live)" by George Michael

Chapter 25 – "See You Again (feat. Charlie Puth)" by Wiz Khalifa, "Euphoria" by Loreen, and "Want My Love" by JES

Epilogue 1 – "Till The End" by Jessie Ware

Epilogue 2 – "I Get to Love You" by Ruelle

TRIGGER WARNINGS

This book contains some things that may be triggers for some readers. Those things include the mention of a car accident, grief, loss of loved ones, mention of drug addiction, and a parent leaving.

PROLOGUE

Candi

Lost love is the most painful, soul-crushing, gut-wrenching love of all. Trust me, I know. I was lucky enough to find my soul mate. And then he was gone…

"Niccolo Francesco Mancini, do you take Destiny to be your wedded wife, to live together in holy matrimony, to love her, to honor her, to comfort her, and to keep her in sickness and in health, forsaking all others, for as long as you both shall live?" asks the priest.

"I do," Nicco answers, his lips lifting into a smile that melts me. That man was head over heels for Destiny the moment he laid eyes on her.

"And do you, Destiny Louise Cardone, take Niccolo to be your husband, to live together in holy matrimony, to love him, to honor him, to comfort him, and to keep him in sickness and in health, forsaking all others, for as long as you both shall live?"

Standing behind Destiny, holding her bouquet, I can't see her face, but the gleam in Nicco's eyes as he focuses on her warms my heart.

"With all my heart, I do," she says.

"By the power vested in me, I pronounce you husband and wife. Nicco, you may kiss your bride."

As they seal their love with a kiss, I can't ignore the ache throbbing deep in the cavern of my soul at the loss of my once-in-a-lifetime love.

1

Enzo

"Enzo, is everything ready? They'll be starting soon." Tony's a worry-wart, an anal-retentive perfectionist, which, I have to admit, I admire. I've worked for him for two years now and he knows I have everything ready.

The bar top is immaculate, all the glassware is spotless, and the shelves are fully stocked with high-end liquor, including a Macallan whiskey that was requested by the groom. I've made sure everything in my ability to control is perfect for the high-profile ceremony. Typical southern California weather provides the perfect night for an outdoor wedding.

Guests are seated in their white folding chairs facing the baby's breath-covered arbor where the priest stands. Two men in tuxedos walk down the aisle and stand next to the priest.

Damn, I know that guy. He starred in Don Matteo. Holy shit. This is his wedding? I'd better be on my game tonight.

The prelude music from the harpist and two violinists stops, and everyone turns their attention toward the center aisle. The trio begins playing "Canon in D" and from behind the bar where I'm standing steps a woman with glowing Mediterranean skin and wavy, cotton-candy pink hair that flows down the center of her bare back. The backless floor-length dress she's wearing hugs every curve of her lush body and looks like a bottle of champagne that shimmers and sparkles with each step she takes. Like a moth to a flame, I can't take my eyes off her. When she reaches the arbor, she turns around, revealing the full effect of her tastefully sexy dress. Draped front exposing luscious cleavage and a slit up to almost the top of her left thigh. She's temptation wrapped in silk and sequins.

Fuck me.

Shit, rule number one: no fraternizing with the customers.

Next comes the bride. Beautiful. More understated than her maid of honor. Matron of honor? *Damn, I hope it's maid of honor. Reminder — rule number one.* During the quick thirty-minute ceremony, I watch every movement the pink-haired vixen makes. While the idea of "love at first sight" is a bunch of bullshit, I'm definitely captivated at first sight.

Once the formalities are over, guests head my way for drinks and hand-passed hors d'oeuvres while the photographer takes pictures of the bride and groom and their families. The venue staff breaks down the ceremony area and builds a dance floor. For being a high-profile wedding, I'm surprised to see so few guests. It looks like only about fifty.

Focusing my attention on serving the guests, I catch glimpses of the woman who I can't stop looking at. From here, it looks like she's giving directions to the photographer. She even took the camera from him at one point. Pretty damn bold. And kind of spunky, which I like. After the photo session, the wedding party makes their way to the bar.

Finally, I get a closer look at the pink-haired beauty, her eyes the color of melted dark chocolate. She walks up to the bar, her sultry aura ripples through me. Placing her elbows on the edge of the bar top, she extends her forearms across the surface. I steal a quick glance down, grazing past her breasts, at her hands. No wedding ring. *Nice.* It takes everything in me to not stare at her cleavage.

She and the bride share a look without a word. A huge smile spreads across the maid of honor's face, lifting her cheeks. Her beautiful brown eyes twinkle. She's exquisite.

The bride smiles and shakes her head. "One."

The maid of honor squeals then looks at me, with a peek at my name tag before meeting my eyes. A potent, invisible attraction saturates the atmosphere, encapsulating only us. Held in the moment, her eyes oscillate between mine, telling me she feels it too.

"Two slippery nipples please, Enzo," she says, her voice sultry and smooth. Raising her sexy shoulder to her chin, she shoots me a beaming smile.

Now I'm thinking about her nipples. "Coming right up —" I pause for her to tell me her name.

"Candi." The bride chimes in, breaking my gaze on Candi's eyes. "And I'm Destiny."

I shift my attention to the bride. "Congratulations, Destiny. Two slippery nipples coming right up."

I go about making their drinks. Standing in front of them, it's hard not to listen to their conversation.

"Mrs. Destiny Mancini." Candi squeals. "Girl, I'm so happy for you." She hugs Destiny then releases her. "Um, I have a confession."

"A confession? Why don't I like the sound of this?" She folds her arms across her chest.

"But you will." Mischief plays in the grin on Candi's lips.

"Out with it."

"I *may* have slightly orchestrated you and Nicco meeting the night of your birthday." She pulls her smile back into a grimace as the muscles in her neck tighten.

Destiny's posture drops as she jets her neck forward. "Candice Alessandra Gamal."

"What?" Her grimace retreats and is replaced with her beautiful smile again as she raises both shoulders.

"You are incorrigible." She laughs. "And why am I just learning this now?"

"Well, I figured that you can't be mad at me now." Candi raises her shoulders again and holds out her hands in surrender.

I set the slippery nipple shots on white cocktail napkins in front of them. They raise their shot glasses toward each other and say in unison, "Ride or die." Then they clink their glasses and toss back the shots.

More guests arrive at the bar and I turn my attention to serving them. It's not long before the dance floor is built and it's time for everyone to take their seats. Guest seating is arranged in a semi-circle with a smaller table of four facing the semi-circle. Down the center of the tables are simple, elegant garlands of vintage-looking roses with greens and baby's breath. White candles are tucked into the length of each garland.

Once everyone is seated, the best man gives his toast. Glasses are raised and he hands the microphone to Candi.

She stands next to Destiny, addressing the guests. "Hi, everyone. I'm Candi and I'm Destiny's maid of honor and best friend." Turning toward Destiny, she reaches out for her hand. "God answered my prayers for a sister when he brought your parents and you to be our neighbors. Being friends since we were five, we've been through so much together. From braces to bad perms, from pulling all-nighters studying to dancing our asses off, from celebrating accomplishments to sobbing over breakups." She pauses. "From losses." They each tilt their head to the side and pull their lips into pained smiles, looking like they may burst into tears.

Hmmm. The instant she said it, her mood shifted. I get the sense she's referring to something deeper than lost shoes.

Regaining her composure, Candi continues. "To incredible celebrations like today." She returns her attention to the guests. "I confessed to Destiny today that I kind of played a little bit of a matchmaker when she and Nicco first met." The crowd chuckles and she looks at the groom. "And that's because I knew enough about him to know he's a good man and he'd treat my best friend the way she deserves to be treated. I've watched your love blossom and strengthen and I'm enamored by it. There's something indescribable about soul mate love. It's magical. Unbreakable. Tonight, we're all here to honor you both and celebrate your love." She releases Destiny's hand, takes her champagne glass, and raises it. "To the bride and groom, wishing you endless years of love and happiness. Cheers."

With that, the guests raise their glasses, shout, "Cheers," and sit down for their meal. During dinner, people sporadically come to the bar to refresh their drinks. During lulls, I clean glasses and watch Candi because I can't seem to stop myself.

Bartending is the job that pays the bills between modeling gigs. With the industries I'm in, I see my share of hot women. They all pale in comparison to Candi. It doesn't matter though. The lifestyle I have doesn't lend itself well to a stable relationship. When I'm intimate with women, we both know it's a quick physical thing before we move on to our next gig. It's not like I get laid on every job I do, I just know when I do hook up with someone, that's all it is. Besides, any time I've tried to have a long-term relationship, they always ended up leaving me in the dirt.

There was a time I wanted to find the right girl, get married, have kids — the whole nine yards. But I had my heart stomped on enough that I learned to leave before they could. Now, I don't even bother.

After the wedding cake has been served, the bride and groom step onto the dance floor for their first dance. About halfway through the song, the DJ invites the maid of honor and best man to join them. He takes Candi in his arms and holds her close. *Lucky bastard.*

The music shifts to club music and guests disperse to the dance floor and to the bar. The second Candi starts walking toward me with her long, sexy legs alternately peeking out from the slit of her dress, a zap of electricity strikes my dick.

Stepping up to the bar, she rests her elbows on the edge. Some of her pink, mermaid-long hair slides around her shoulder and hugs the side of her breast. My dick twitches.

"What can I get you?" I ask.

"One Macallan and one chocolate martini, please."

"Whoo, rough night?"

She chuckles. "No, they're for the bride and groom."

"Ah." I start making their drinks, glancing in her direction a few times.

Her attention is fully on me.

"Here you go." I set the drinks in front of her. "Can I get you something?"

"I'll be back for mine." She smiles.

"What would you like?"

She pauses, staring directly into my eyes. "Surprise me." No smile. No smirk. No flirtation. She walks away, leaving me rattled. *This woman is so damn sexy.*

When she returns, I have a cocktail waiting for her.

She sits on one of the three white-leather bar stools we have on either side of the bar. Taking the drink in her hand, she asks, "What is it?"

"Taste it first. See if you like it. I took a chance. If you don't like it, I'll make you something else."

She takes the cherry stem in between her thumb and index finger. Gingerly placing the cherry into her mouth, she plucks off the stem, placing it on the cocktail napkin. The air scorches. Then she picks up the drink and takes a long sip from the tiny gold straw.

"Mmm." Tilting her head slightly, she sips again. "Good choice. I've heard bartenders match drinks with personalities. You don't know me, so why a whiskey sour?" Curiosity alight in her silky chocolate eyes, she looks up at me from under her long, dark lashes.

"Whiskey cocktail drinkers are a bit of a wildcard. They tend to live in the moment and tell it like they see it. No bullshit. They can be both the life of the party and also be found deep in conversation tucked into a corner booth. They have a discerning palate, hence the whiskey. For you, the sour of the lemon and lime juices highlights your sassiness while the simple syrup enhances your sweet side. And the cherry, well, it just wouldn't be complete without a cherry on top." Our gazes tangle as she processes my interpretation.

She gives me a nod with her sexy smile then raises her glass toward me and takes another sip. Sliding off the bar stool, she returns to the head table and sets down her drink before going to the dance floor. This woman is feisty as shit. A force to be reckoned with.

Reading the crowd, the DJ alternates between club music and slow songs. Between serving drinks and keeping the bar clean, I watch her dance. *Damn, she knows how to move her body.*

The sun dips below the horizon, coloring the sky with remnants of orange, yellow, and red. The DJ shifts the mood as a slow song fills the air. Candi walks up to the bar and sits on the stool where she was earlier.

"One of your whiskey sours, please." She smiles, sending a wave of heat through me.

Little vixen. I make the drink and set it in front of her. "Not dancing with your date?"

"My date?" Her brows pinch together.

"The best man."

She chuckles. "No, he's not my date. He's Nicco's brother and he's dancing with his wife." She points in their direction.

No date? Her?

Several guests step up to the bar. "Excuse me," I say to her and tend to the few who are on my side while Jake tends to the rest on his side. The slow song ends and more people are ready for refills. While they keep me busy, Candi sits on the bar stool, sipping her drink and watching people dance.

Another slow song comes on. The spurt of guests needing refills dwindles. Candi's gaze has moved above the dancing bodies to the stars in the clear night sky. The warm, gentle breeze tosses a few hairs around her face.

On a chain around her neck hangs a thick, silver ring with gold and silver Gothic-like filigree. Lost with her thoughts, she slides the ring up and down her middle finger. It's too big for any of her delicate fingers. Whatever or whoever she's thinking about, is a dark shadow looming over her spirit.

Taking a penny out of my pocket, I slide it across the bar toward her. So as not to startle her, I keep my voice quiet. "Penny for your thoughts?" I ask, wiping dry a martini glass.

Her trance broken, she turns her stool, setting sad eyes on me, sending the sadness beneath my skin.

"You look miles away."

Her vibrant smile I've seen most of the night is gone, replaced by a weight she's struggling against to push up the corners of her lips. "No. I'm here," she says softly, returning from miles away.

"I'm a good listener. It comes with the job. Being a traveling bartender is kind of like being a priest. People have a few drinks and confide in me. Probably because they know they'll never see me again. I hear all kinds of secrets." Leaning closer, I quiet my voice. "I'll keep yours safe," I promise.

Her beautiful face lifts then falls as she casts down her eyes. Lifting her head, she takes a long sip of her drink. "Sometimes the most wonderful celebrations are also reminders of those who are no longer here to celebrate with." Melancholy ridges the features of her face. Something in me yearns to take away her sadness.

Just then, Destiny comes over and stands in front of her. When Candi looks up at her, tears well in her eyes as her brows pinch together.

"I know." It's all Destiny says, then cradles Candi's face into her chest.

They release and Destiny cups Candi's face in her hands. Then she takes Candi's hand and nods toward the dance floor. "Come on," she says with a loving smile as she lightly tugs on her arm.

Candi smiles back at her as she wipes a tear from her cheek.

Standing, Candi hugs her and whispers into her ear. I watch her lips form the words, "I love you."

I don't know what just happened, but it's gnawing on my heart. Candi's been a mysterious, sexy firecracker the whole time. Seeing her hurting made my heart ache. But why? I don't even know her. And I'll never see her after tonight.

Unless I change that.

2

Candi

While I'm happy for my best friend, marrying the man of her dreams, and I know I should be celebrating them, it's hard not to think about Dominick. His ring keeps him close to me. It holds all our good memories.

I love Destiny and her huge heart. It's her wedding and she's dragging me to the dance floor so I won't be sad. God truly blessed me with her friendship.

Pushing away thoughts of Dom, I shift my focus to being present and dancing with Destiny. Even though she's not a party-girl, whenever she'd indulge me and go out to night clubs, we always had such a good time together. Those nights were for us only. Neither of us were ever there to meet guys. That's not our style. We were there to have fun with each other. And, boy, did we.

As we dance, I catch Enzo watching us, more than a few times. And Destiny catches me catching him. At each glance, a spark flickers inside me that I barely recognize.

Between songs, we take a break and sit back at the head table. We have a couple swigs of water and a few sips of our drinks.

"Enzo has the most brilliant green eyes I've ever seen." She grins at me then gives a quick glance in his direction.

"That he does. Like kryptonite, glowing from the inside," I say, ignoring the flickering spark.

"He seems nice. You guys were chatting a little, huh?"

"He is. I think being friendly is probably a prerequisite for being a bartender."

"I thought I sensed a little, chemistry maybe?" she prods with curiosity.

"Oh yeah?" I smile. "I dunno, Des. I don't even think about men anymore. You know, after Dom, that part of me died." I trace the rim of my glass with my finger.

"Can, there's no rule that says you only get one soul mate in life and that's it." She places a gentle hand on top of mine. "How often did you tell me that you believe in miracles and dreams can come true? I mean, our entire lives you've been saying it. You're not exempt from that," she says with such tenderness as she rubs my hand with her thumb.

"I know. It's just." I blow an exhale. "So much changed after Dom. God, he was my biggest fan and supported me in everything I wanted to do. Other than you, he was my best friend." My heart pulls with gravity. "He was my everything."

"I know."

"When he died, I had to figure out life. How to get through each day. How to survive. How to — live again." I pause. "I don't think the kind of love we had together is the kind of love you get to have twice. So, I just, don't bother. Y'know?" I look up into the sky that's now dark blue and splattered with tiny, glittery stars.

"I know it hurts. And I know that part of your life feels lost. But it isn't. Maybe..." She takes my hand in hers, causing me to look at her. "Maybe you're one of the lucky ones who gets to have love twice," she says as she squeezes my hand. "All I'm saying is, be open to it. Okay?"

Pain pinches my heart as I smile at her. "Okay." I take a deep breath and let it out. I'm not sure I'm ready. Ready to let Dom go. Ready to meet someone new. Ready to try to love again. I can't think about any of this right now. "Wanna dance?"

"Yes." Her cheeks raise, pulling her lips into a smile.

As we stand, I glance back to the bar. Nicco and Enzo are

talking and they both look our way. Destiny blows Nicco a kiss as we head back to the dance floor. Enzo gives me a nod. The tiniest current shimmies up my spine.

Destiny and I dance a couple more songs together and a few guests approach us to say goodbye to her. I go back to the head table to sit and finish whatever number whiskey sour Enzo made me.

The DJ announces the last two songs of the night. As Nicco brings his beautiful bride to the dance floor, my heart smiles. I'm glad I followed my instincts. He's a good man. And he's the perfect man for her.

The first song ends and "Hero" by Music Travel Love starts. I love their rendition of this song. As I watch couples on the dance floor, an olive-skinned hand appears in front of my face. I look up into Enzo's kryptonic eyes. Butterflies swirl in my stomach.

Putting my hand in his, the current that ran up my spine earlier floods my body.

One. Single. Touch.

His magnetic force pulls me out of my seat. I stand without a word. Holding my hand in his, he leads me to the dance floor. With gentle confidence, he wraps his arm around my waist and clasps his hand around mine. I draw a gulp of warm air into my lungs. I haven't been this close to a man since — since Dom.

Being in the arms of another man feels different, almost wrong. And yet, when I look into his eyes, I'm eased. I feel safe.

"Aren't you still on shift? Won't you get in trouble?"

"Jake's covering for me." He pauses. "Besides, if I do, it'll be worth it." The sincerity of his statement coupled with the intensity of his kryptonite-green gaze makes my heart beat a little faster.

Holding me against his hard chest, he leads our movements, languid and assured. The song lyrics float into me as the string lights draping from tree-to-tree glow against the dark sky and the chandeliers dangling from tree branches twinkle.

Releasing my hand, he gently sweeps my hair from the side of my face, sliding it over my shoulder. Leaning down, he moves his face toward mine. *It's been so long since I've been kissed.* Though my heart isn't sure I'm ready and my brain reminds me I don't even know him, my body responds. I take in a deep breath as my heart beats faster in my chest. He grazes past my cheek, placing his lips at my ear.

"You're exquisite." His words a shallow whisper, his warm breath travels down the curve of my neck, sending a chill down my spine, leaving a trail of goose bumps. I close my eyes and release the breath I'd been holding.

I don't usually react this way to men. I've been hit on plenty in my life and I know how to handle myself. Something about this man has my knees nearly buckling beneath me.

3

Candi

When the song ends, he releases me, bowing his head to kiss my hand.

"Thank you for the honor," he says, standing back to full height, looking down at me with a smile so sexy, it steals my voice.

It's the first time I truly take him in. Thick, dark hair, a little longer on top, but still neat. Groomed five o'clock shadow hugging his angled jaw. A small scar above his left eyebrow. Feeling his muscular back through his shirt when we danced, my mind sketches it.

"I realize we've just met and don't know each other, but I'd like to change that. Maybe tomorrow you'll let me take you out?" he asks, still holding my hand.

I know Destiny thinks I should be open, but I'm just not ready for anything, even a casual date. My life is busy with work. That's who I am now.

"Thank you for the dance, I enjoyed it. I have a project due, so I'll be working tomorrow. But you're so sweet to ask."

"Working on the weekend, huh?"

"Yeah, no days off in my line of work."

"Another time then?" His eyes shift back and forth between mine as one eyebrow raises slightly.

"My life's very busy right now with my work and I just don't have time for dating."

His lips pull into a weak smile as he lightly squeezes my hand.

"I get it. Well, it was nice meeting you, Candi." He lowers his head, cups my face in his free hand, and presses his lips to my cheek. Heat rushes through my chest. "Good night." With a slow, athletic jog, he goes back to the bar.

I take a deep breath and let it out, pushing away the attraction whirling through me.

That was the right thing to do, right? Yes, of course it was. Then why am I asking myself? It's true. I don't have time for dating and I certainly don't have time for a relationship. Plus, it's hard to imagine being with someone other than Dom.

As for the physical side of things, being in Enzo's strong arms aroused my senses in a temptation I haven't felt in a long time. Though my body is begging me to indulge, one-night romps aren't my thing. I'd long ago resigned myself to the fact that the rest of my orgasms would come from my trusty vibrator. Though nothing says he can't be my muse. *Stop thinking about him.*

Guests say their goodbyes to Destiny and Nicco. Nicco's brother, Marco, and his wife, Angelina, already went up to their room, so it's just the three of us left. Nicco thanks the bartenders and I give a wave to Enzo who nods back with a wink and a smile.

Breathe.

Together, we head inside to the elevators.

"I'm not quite ready for bed. I think I'll get a quick nightcap," I say, hoping to drown the sadness sitting in me. Though it's been years and I've healed, not having Dom here at the wedding with me is hitting hard.

"Are you sure?" Destiny asks.

"You'll be okay?" Nicco follows.

"Yes." I chuckle. "I'm sure. I'll be fine. Thank you for a lovely night. I'm so happy for you guys." I hold out my arms and Destiny comes in for a hug. We release and Nicco and I exchange cheek-kisses. "Love you guys." I turn and start walking toward the bar.

"Love you," Destiny calls out as the elevator bell dings.

As I walk through the open dark-wood and etched-glass bifold doors, the coziness wraps around me like a blanket. Like I stepped out of a time machine, I soak in the ambiance of a hundred years gone by. The bar top is a thick piece of dark wood and the ceiling is covered with old, refurbished tin tiles. Dim hanging lights, candles dotting the bar, and twinkling string lights woven through swags of greenery set the perfect tone for me to relax with my nightcap and try to ease my soul.

Though not crowded, there are quite a few people here. Some sitting at the bar, some in booths around the perimeter, and some on the small dance floor. I find an empty stool at the bar and slide onto the black snakeskin. They've done a little updating over the years.

"What can I get you, ma'am?" the bartender asks, adjusting his bowtie, reminding me of Enzo in his bartender uniform.

"A hot toddy, please." I push a smile to my lips.

"You got it."

He steps away to make my drink and I gaze around the room, letting the music soothe me. I check my phone for any messages or emails, hoping nothing urgent has come up for the project I need to finish tomorrow. The photo shoot went great and I want to edit all the best shots to send them back to Vanessa at Guess before my deadline.

Some days I still pinch myself to make sure this is all real. I've worked my ass off to build my fashion photography business to what it is today. I work with the most amazing people and iconic brands which blows my mind. I just wish Mom was here to see me. She'd be so proud of me. And someday, when I get my gig with Gucci, I know she'll be smiling down on me from heaven. I fiddle with Dom's ring hanging on my chain.

The bartender sets my hot toddy on a cocktail napkin and I stir it with the cinnamon stick, letting it cool so I don't burn my tongue. Watching the liquid swirl as the music caresses me, my thoughts drift to Dom. About once a month, we'd go to our favorite jazz club for a few hours to listen to live music, have some drinks, and spend time connecting with each other. I loved those nights.

"May I join you?" The low timbre of his voice shakes me from my reverie, causing the hairs on the back of my neck to stiffen.

Enzo.

"Oh. Hi. Um, sure." My heartbeat ticks up.

"I was heading out to my car and saw you in here as I was about to pass by. You sure?" He confirms my approval.

"Yes, please." I motion toward the open stool next to me.

He waves his hand at the bartender and points to my drink as he sits down. The bartender nods, confirming his order. "Nothing better than a hot toddy and some good music before bed." He looks around. "You here alone?"

"Yeah, I didn't feel ready to go to bed yet. I don't sleep great when I'm not in my own bed, so I thought this might help." I take a sip, the warm liquid flows down my throat.

"Oh, you have a room. So, you're not from around here then?"

"No, I am. L.A. I just knew I'd be drinking so I got a room to be safe."

"Mmm, good thinking." He pauses. "Your friends are very nice. They gave us a huge tip."

I smile and cock my head. "That's Nicco. The world has this weird view of him because of his role in Don Matteo and the tiny little bit they see on social media. They have no idea who he really is. He's such a good guy. He came from so little. Lost so much. And he's very humble. He knows how hard people work. Now that he has money, he does what he can to help others."

"That says a lot about his character," he says as the bartender places his drink in front of him.

"Yup, that's why I set them up." I sip my drink.

"Yeah, I heard that in your speech."

"You were listening to my speech?" *Didn't expect that.*

He takes a drink and tilts his head to the side. "You kinda caught my attention." His lips curl up at the edges.

"I did?" The hot toddy must be kicking in because heat warms my cheeks. It has to be the drink. I don't react like this when men say things like that to me. Of course, he *is* insanely attractive.

"From the second you walked down that aisle." One side of his mouth raises higher with his confession as his kryptonic gaze freezes me.

A frenzy swarms my blood at his words.

The sensual melody of "Stand Still" wisps through the air, silky ribbons of invitation. He offers me his hand. Mesmerized, I take it, following him to the small dance floor where several couples are dancing.

Firmly in his grip once again, I'm intoxicated by the moment. *What is it about this guy?* For most of the song, he holds my body against his, attraction billowing everywhere our bodies touch. His heart beats against my breasts. He moves us effortlessly, flowing with the music as the lyrics seduce us. My face at his neck, I inhale his clean, spicy scent with each breath.

He pulls back so we're face-to-face, close. Gazing into my eyes, he looks beyond them, deeper, entrancing me. His breath feathers hot across my cheek as his eyes flash to my lips. My heart beats wildly, flailing inside my chest, a lick of lust provoking me. I'm not thinking straight.

I slide my hand from resting on his shoulder up to his neck, pressing my fingers in slightly, pulling him toward me. Responding, he lowers his head, placing his warm, whiskey-laced lips on mine. *God, I forgot what this feels like.* All my thoughts are gone. All I can do is feel. I feel everything. I feel the heat of his skin touching mine. I feel the unhurried, hypnotizing circles of his tongue around mine. I feel the ache of desire I banished four years ago. I'm lost in him, consumed.

The song ends and we part our lips. Pangs of guilt thrash me. I shove apart our bodies. *What the fuck did I just do?*

"I — I have to go." Remorse stings my stomach. I dash to the bar and grab my clutch, passing by him on my way to the door.

He grabs my hand. "Candi, wait," he says gently, pain soaking his expression.

I look down at our hands. Acid curdles inside me. "I'm, I'm

sorry. I have to go." Withdrawing my hand, I walk quickly to the elevator. Frantically pressing the button, I look up at the lighted numbers. My pulse races. It's taking too long. I head to the stairs and start running up them, which isn't a great idea in this dress and these heels.

A few flights up, I hold onto the railing and turn myself around, sitting down on a step. Clutching my chest, panting, I grab Dom's ring around my neck as tears spill down my face. "I'm so sorry, Dom," I whisper to no one.

4

Enzo

I can't believe I asked her out. What was I even thinking? One date leads to more dates and that leads to a relationship. I don't want a relationship. It doesn't fit into my life. But when I caught a glimpse of her long, tanned legs at the bar, I flew straight for that flame. I had to talk to her again.

Cocooned together in the seduction of the moment, I stole a forbidden kiss, unable to resist her. It was a kiss that shouldn't have happened. A kiss I shouldn't have taken. A kiss she willingly gave me. Our hearts beat in unison to unspoken desire as our bodies heated against each other.

I've kissed plenty of women and nothing ever felt that intense. I'll hold onto that for a long time.

I feel bad I freaked her out. I have no idea what happened or what I did. She pulled me in and I took her lead. And then, in a flash, she was gone, leaving me rattled. It's for the best. She'd already turned me down anyway.

I have my career to focus on. I've gotta get some more modeling gigs. Thank God for the one I have this week, but there's nothing after it. I don't think my agent is even looking any more. It might be time to find new representation. What a pain in my fucking ass.

I pull into a parking spot at Hotel Bel-Air, walk past the lobby and through the stone archway that leads out to the pool. Today's my last scheduled shoot and it's for a swimwear line. I take pride in my reputation and always make sure I arrive early.

As I turn the corner, I see the unmistakable, mermaid-long pink hair. Candi. *What's she doing here?* She's unpacking cameras from their bags. I approach her and the group of people setting up for the shoot.

"Candi." I touch her lightly on her shoulder.

When she turns toward me, her torso darts back and her brows shoot up, crinkling her forehead. "Enzo." Surprise rides her voice. "What are you doing here? I'm sorry, I'm working right now. I don't have time to talk to you." An edge besieges her demeanor.

"I'm here for the Dive into Swim shoot. I'm one of the models. Are you —" I gesture to the cameras. "the photographer?"

"Yeah, I am. What do you mean you're one of the models? You're a bartender. And..." She grabs a piece of paper from the lounge chair. "You're not on the call sheet they sent me."

"I'm not?" I stand next to her and look over her shoulder at the paper. "There I am," I say, pointing to my name on the paper. "Lorenzo Cipriani."

"Oh." She looks up at me, her breaths shallow. "Enzo. Short for Lorenzo."

I give her a cheesy grin. "I bartend to pay the bills." I pause, nodding toward the cameras. "So, you're a photographer then."

"I am," she says, quickly shifting her eyes to the crew setting things up, then returning her gaze to me. "They called me in last-minute because their original photographer is sick and couldn't make it." She pauses, biting the side of her lower lip and crossing her arms at her chest. Unease afflicts every word, every movement. "Um, can I talk to you?" She starts walking away.

I follow her to the opposite side of the pool, thoroughly enjoying watching her ass swing from side to side.

When she turns to face me, her cheeks are pink, her eyes intense and stormy.

"Listen, um, I don't go around kissing strangers." She tucks her hair behind her ear. "My career is everything to me and I don't mix business with pleasure," she says, folding her arms across her chest again, building a barrier between us.

"Understood." I nod, slightly amused. "And don't worry, I didn't think that was typical for you."

"It wasn't." She interjects. "It's not," she confirms sternly, fixing her beautiful eyes on me.

"Hey, I'm sorry I upset you that night."

She softens, the edge dulling. "No, please don't apologize. You didn't. I —" She sighs. "I wasn't quite myself that night. I'm sorry for my behavior."

I shake my head. "No harm done."

She looks back toward the shoot set up. "I need to get back to work."

"Let's do this." I extend my arm out for her to lead the way back.

While she seemed guarded the night of the wedding, her armor just thickened a few more inches.

We head back to the setup and she tells each person what she needs them to do. Her confidence is so damn sexy. The two female models arrive and Candi asks us to follow her to the clothing racks of swimsuits we'll be wearing for the shoot. She walks us through her vision, including her thoughts on the mood and emotions she wants to convey. I've never had a photographer be so thorough and communicate to this level. She's impressive.

The models and I head into our separate tents to change into our first suits. I get changed and take off my necklace, tucking it safely into the front pocket of my jeans, then head back to the pool where Candi's helping move around the light fixtures.

"I'll be ready for you in just a sec," she says to us, refocusing her attention to the light fixture, with a quick glance back to me.

She twists her hair up on top of her head and secures it with a pen. "All right, Paulette and Trina, I want you lying here on the side of the pool, heads toward each other, holding yourselves up. Your arms will cross each other just above your wrists. Enzo, you're in the pool. I want your face above where their arms cross, like you're looking through them, and your hands will be folded together. Let's give it a try."

I get in the pool and get into the position she described. She looks through her camera lens.

"Roy, can you move that reflector to the left a little for me?"

He moves the reflector while she looks through the lens. "Yes, there. Perfect."

"Okay, I like this. Ladies, you're both looking out and away. Enzo, you're looking straight at me. You're serious, sophisticated."

I follow her direction with my expression.

"Yes, there." She clicks her camera several times then looks at the screen. "Now, I want you both looking down at Enzo. Even lean down a little toward him."

They move in.

"Oh yes, perfect." More clicks.

Several more poses in these suits. All of her directives are confident and clear, followed by praise and encouragement. We change into the next set of swimsuits.

"I want the three of you against this beautiful flower wall. I'm going to be on the other side of the pool so we get some water in the shot. Ladies, you're on either side of Enzo. There's no competition. You're happy to share him."

She approaches me.

"Can you stand with your legs spread a bit? You're confident, refined, worldly. Your arms by your side. First, I'm going to have you looking directly at me." The sun turns her eyes to hazelnut as she shifts them back and forth between mine. "Um, and then, I'm going to have you look at Paulette for a few shots, then Trina for a few shots." She turns her attention to Paulette. "Turn to the side for me? I want your hand on his chest."

Paulette's a little awkward and doesn't position herself the way Candi wants.

"No, not quite. Here, you stand where I am. I'll show you." She smiles with an encouraging nod.

She and Paulette switch places. Tucking her body into the side of mine, she places her hand on my pec muscle. Her breasts press against me, all I can think about is our kiss. I push it from my thoughts before I get hard.

"Just like this, okay?" she says, her breath feathering across my skin.

Paulette nods and they switch places again. Candi puts Paulette's hand on my pec. I clear my throat and Candi looks up at me. For a split second, we're frozen. She blinks then moves to Trina. "And also to the side with your hand here." She places Trina's hand at the top of my abs with a quick glance up to my eyes. "Let me go look through the lens." She walks quickly to the other side of the pool and clicks away.

She calls out position shifts and we move into place. After she's satisfied with her shots, we change into different suits. This time she's on a ladder, shooting down at us in the pool. It's inspiring watching her create her vision with requests of slight, subtle adjustments to body positioning and facial expressions. For the final swimsuit change, we're all in the water, including Candi.

She takes off her blue cotton dress, revealing her smokin' hot body in a tasteful black one-piece. My mind traipses to places it shouldn't go. Gritting my teeth, I have to focus on not getting hard. She gets into the pool and asks her assistant for her waterproof camera.

"Shawn, when I go under, can you hold me down so I can get the shots?"

"Yeah. Tap me when you want up."

Explaining her vision and letting us know what she wants from each of us, she sinks down into the water. That's some dedication.

When she pops up, she goes over to the side of the pool where her computer is. Her assistant knows the drill and flips through the images for her.

She moves through the water back toward us. "I want to try

one more thing. Enzo, you stay right where you are. Paulette and Trina, I want you angled out a little and leaning against the side of his body. Give me your top leg resting on the other with your knee bent slightly. Your foot at your ankle. I want to see the sexy curvature of your hips."

We assume our positions and Candi dunks beneath the water again, snapping away. She rises up once more.

"I think we got it. Let me just look. You guys okay?"

We each give some version of yes.

After looking at the shots on her screen for a few minutes, she raises her hands in the air. "Yes!" she cheers. "And that's a wrap. You guys were awesome. Thank you so much."

Break down begins as the female models and I get out of the pool. I head to my tent to dry off and get changed, thinking about Candi's glances I caught all day. While she remained professional, there's no denying our intensifying chemistry.

When I come out, much of the equipment is already packed up. I don't see Candi anywhere, but I do see one of the assistants.

"Wow, you guys are fast. Can I give you a hand?"

"Nah, but thanks. We've been doing this a while. Have it down to a science."

"You work with Candi?"

"With, for, yeah. She's pretty much the boss. A great one too. She's not all high-and-mighty about it. That woman rolls up her sleeves and gets dirty with us. We all make a good team together."

"It's good to work with great people. Hey, do you know where she is?"

"Mad respect for her," he says, hoisting a lighting fixture onto his shoulder and pointing to the other side of the pool. "Yeah, over there with Paulette. Great job today. Take care."

"Thanks, man. Yeah, take care."

As I make my way over to them, Paulette wraps her arms around Candi's neck. When she releases her, Candi takes her hands and she's looking at her intently, saying something. Now I'm close enough to see Candi gently shake Paulette's hands in hers. Another quick hug and Paulette walks out through the stone archway.

"Hey," I say, stepping over to face her. "Everything okay?" I angle my head in the direction Paulette left.

"Oh, yeah. She just doesn't have her confidence yet. I gave her some pointers and a little pep talk."

With everything I've witnessed today, I'm even more impressed by Candi. I know I shouldn't waste my time, but I can't stop myself.

"Look, I know you turned me down already, but I can't walk out of here without one more try. Is there any chance you'd let me take you out sometime?" I spread my most charming smile across my face. At least I get a chuckle out of her.

She tilts her head and smiles. I prepare myself for another rejection. "Enzo, you're so sweet, really."

"I know I felt something all day." I cock my head down and toward her. "And I think you felt it too." I pause, my chest heating. "But it's more than just attraction. I want to get to know you."

"Enzo, I, it's not." She has the confidence of a badass, alpha-chick, but right now, I'm feeling like I have the upper hand.

I take a step closer to her. "What is it?" What has her so resistant?

"I don't get involved with clients. It's my rule."

"Okay." I take a contemplative breath. "Our shoot is over. I'm not your client anymore. Although technically, I wasn't anyway. I was just a model. Dive into Swim is your client."

"I — don't get involved with people in my industry." Her eyes shift back and forth between mine as her posture stiffens. "I've worked very hard on my career to make it what it is and I'm not going to risk it for some —" She waves her hand up and down my body. "One-night stand with a hot guy."

At least I know she's attracted to me, though the gravitational pull between us already confirmed that.

I step in a little closer. "What if I'm looking for more than a one-night stand?" I ask, stunned by the words that just left my mouth. Holding her gaze captive, I watch her inhale and exhale.

She shakes her head slightly, not moving her eyes from mine.

"I'm sorry, Enzo. I just can't."

I lean in, hovering above her, our eyes rapt. It's taking everything in me not to pull that pen out of her wet hair and kiss her luscious lips.

"Candi!" one of her assistants shouts, breaking our trance.

She blinks and steps back. "Um, I've gotta go. Great job today." She looks down and then back up at me. Her shoulders relax, her voice softens. "It really was nice to see you."

With that, she turns and heads toward her assistant. And again, she's gone.

What the fuck am I thinking? This woman incapacitates my ability to think clearly.

I walk through the stone archway and into the lobby as I head out of the hotel. That's when I see Nicco. He points at me with an acknowledging smile.

"Hey, man," he says, extending his hand to shake mine.

"Hey, Nicco. How are you?"

"Great. I'm great. Just finishing up with a meeting. Are you working here tonight?"

"No. Actually, I just finished a shoot with Candi."

"A photo shoot?"

"Yeah. The bartending helps me pay the bills between modeling gigs. Unfortunately, this was my last one. At least until I can find a new agent." Frustration boils in me.

"Hard-working man." He purses his lips and nods toward the bar. "Hey, do you have time for a drink?"

I was heading home to an empty apartment. "Sure."

"So, tell me about your agent, what's going on?" he asks as we head to the bar.

"I can't put all the blame on him. It's my career and I probably should be after him more. He's a nice guy, I just don't feel like I'm a priority for him."

"It can be a challenging industry. A lot of success comes from who you know. You have to build your reputation with the right people."

We walk into the bar and sit on a curved, tan leather sofa next to a white marble fireplace. The plush carpet is soft under my steps. Enormous pictures of Hollywood's elite actors and actresses dress the walls.

"I don't know. Maybe I'm not cut out for modeling." A possible reality I've been ignoring.

"Nah, that's bullshit. Do you like it? Is it what you want to do?"

"It is. It feeds my creative side. I get to meet some truly inspirational people." I gesture toward the pool. "Like Candi." I pause. "It was incredible watching her work today. She has this vision and she's so clear about it. She's incredibly dedicated. I saw her do things I've never seen a photographer do. It was inspiring."

"Gentlemen," the waiter addresses us. "What can I get you?"

"This is on me," Nicco says to me. "Get anything you want. You like Macallan?" He raises his eyebrows.

"I mean, I do, but that's not necessary." Damn, he really is a generous guy. That stuff's expensive.

He smiles at me with an I-got-you nod. "Two Macallans, please."

"Two Macallans coming up." The waiter turns and leaves.

"Candi." He chuckles. "She's a firecracker." A broad smile spreads across his face.

"She sure is. Tough and beautiful too."

"Heh." He sniggers. "Was she giving you a hard time during the shoot?" A small crease forms between his eyebrows.

"No. It's just, I've asked her out twice and she turned me down both times."

Laughter billows from him. "I've seen her turn down lots of guys. Don't take it personally. She dresses sexy as hell and has a wild, sassy personality. I think men assume that she's easy which is the complete opposite. But she's a one-man kind of woman. She's deeply intellectual and smart-as-shit. One of the most dedicated, committed, and fiercely loyal people I've ever met. She's very selective when it comes to men."

"Here you go, gentlemen." The waiter places cocktail napkins in front of each of us and sets our drinks on them.

"Hmh. So, I have no chance in hell then." Well, that sucks.

He laughs again and picks up his drink, holding it out toward me. "You'll have to prove you're worthy of her."

I tap my glass to his and twist my lips to the side. "I'm not sure I'll ever get the chance."

"Prove it to me and I'll make sure you do." He sips his drink and leans back, crossing his ankle over his opposite knee. It's not a challenge, but more an invitation laced with protectiveness.

Ruminating on his words, I take a sip of my drink, letting the smooth liquid slide down my throat as soothing jazz music trickles into my ears. First, Candi's assistant spoke about her with a lot of respect. And now Nicco. I have to get to know this woman.

"Done." I hold out my glass toward him and he taps it with his.

"Now, tell me about what's going on with you and your agent."

I blow a puff of air, shaking my head. "I don't know, man. He was getting me pretty consistent gigs for a while, but now it's like I fell off his radar. My contract's up in a little over a month and I'm thinking of looking around."

Uncrossing his ankle and setting his foot on the floor, he leans forward, resting his forearms on his knees and holding his drink with both hands. "I'm a very fortunate man. Destiny's mom put me in touch with some of the top people in the acting and modeling industry. I'm where I am today because of her. Now I get to pay that kindness forward."

He proceeds to tell me how he's going to put me in touch with some top agents and agencies, making sure I understand that the rest is on me. I can't even believe what I'm hearing. Nicco Mancini is helping me further my career.

Not only that, but it sounds like, if I play my cards right, I might get another chance to see Candi.

5

Candi

The last couple months since Destiny's wedding have been so busy. I'm used to traveling for work, but it feels like it's been nonstop. I'm glad to be home for the week. I have a long-overdue girls' day scheduled with Destiny and I'm so excited. We're getting pedicures, facials, and having a gloriously healthy spa lunch.

When I open the door to Scrub & Honey, I'm instantly filled with calm as the gentle scent of lavender drifts into my nose. Harp and piano melodies enter my ears, relaxing me, my shoulders loosen. I check in and head to the sitting area. Sunlight filters through the tall windows of the long corridor that's dotted with large white urns filled with billowy peonies, heirloom roses, and hydrangeas in mixed hues of pastel pink.

When I reach the sitting area, Destiny's already there. She stands when she sees me and we hug, rocking back and forth a little.

"Girl, I've missed you," I say quietly, respecting the peacefulness of the spa, then release her, holding her hands in mine. "You look radiant. Married life must be treating you well."

Her smile lightens the room even more. "It is. Nicco's amazing. My writing feels incredible. And I'm just really happy."

"I'm so happy for you." I squeeze her hands.

"I'm also starving. Ready for lunch?"

"So ready."

We go to the locker room and change into our plush, white,

spa robes and slippers. The scent of eucalyptus continues relaxing me. When we enter the intimate dining area, we're seated at a reserved table. Almost as soon as we sit, a spa attendant comes over with lemon-infused waters followed by our plates of avocado and egg sandwich, fire-roasted shrimp, and pickled cucumber salad.

"You've been all over the place lately. Tell me about your adventures and the projects you've done," she says, picking up the sandwich and taking a big bite.

I pop off a shrimp tail. "Mmm, you and Nicco have to go to Zion National Park. It's beautiful and spiritual and just the most magical place I've ever been. I was doing a shoot for Elisabetta Frenchi and the energy was unreal. The colors were so vibrant and the way the sun lit everything at different times of the day, it was breathtaking. I swear even the models had an ethereal glow." I chuckle under my breath.

"That sounds amazing. I'll definitely mention it to him. Tell me more. Where else did you go?" she asks, practically shoveling food into her mouth.

I rattle off a few more of the beautiful locations I went to and share some of the funny things that happened during a couple of the shoots. Our time together always grounds me, filling me up and replenishing me.

"Oh hey, Nicco told me you had a shoot with the hot bartender before you left town after the wedding. I totally forgot to ask you about it. How'd that go?"

"How did Nicco know?" The mere mention of Enzo sends a bolt of energy thrumming through me. He and our hot kiss visited my thoughts many times over the past few months.

"They ran into each other after the shoot," she says, matter of fact.

"Girl." I squish my face and shake my head. Unease, mixed with a hint of craving, flits in my stomach.

"Okay, so tell me." She wiggles her shoulders.

"Well, I told you that I kissed him after the wedding and how fucking hot it was and then how awful and guilty I felt about it."

"Mhmm."

"And then, he turns out to be the male model of the Dive into Swim shoot I did. I was so uncomfortable at first, but he was actually really cool about it. I told him I don't kiss strangers. He said he figured as much. We did the shoot. And holy shit. His body. I mean, *damn*."

Her brows raise and she nods, hope filling her smile. "Uh-huh," she says with a prodding tone.

"You know I'm not one to get flustered by a guy. But after that kiss we had and working with him practically naked, girl, I was all sorts of flustered." I chuckle into my hand to hush my sound.

"Tell me more." Her eyes widen as she leans forward a little and takes another bite of her sandwich.

"There's not much more to tell. He asked me out again. I turned him down again. And that was that. I'll tell you what though, he's popped into my head more than a few times."

"Yeah?" There's that hopefulness again.

I sigh. "Yeah."

"That's okay, you know. It's kind of a good thing, don't you think?"

"I mean, I don't know. Dom was my person. He was everything I ever wanted in a life-partner. But you and I both know he was a little lacking in the passion department. I've *never* been kissed the way Enzo kissed me."

"Do you think maybe you freaked yourself out because Enzo looks a little like —"

"No, he doesn't." I cut her off. *Yes, he does.* Enzo looks a *lot* like Dom and I don't want to think about it.

"Okay," she says softly. The corners of her lips curl up slightly and she drops the subject. "So, I have a question for you."

"Hit me with it."

She finishes swallowing a bite of her salad and reaches her hand across the table.

I take her hand with mine as she sits quietly, looking at me.

Usually, I can read her eyes. Right now, I don't know what they're saying. "Are you all right?" I ask, leaning forward. "What's going on?"

"How would you feel about being a godmother?"

"Shit. You scared me for a second. I thought maybe something was wrong. I'd be honored to be a godmother to your baby someday."

Her smile reveals her secret and shivers skate across my body.

"Wait. What? You mean?"

She raises her shoulders and nods vigorously as the most beautiful smile lights up her face.

I spring from my seat, she rises from hers, and I wrap my arms around her, squealing.

The spa attendant clears her throat, shooting me a glare.

I release Destiny, dropping my voice to a whisper. "How could you tell me this in a place where I can't scream and jump around?" I wiggle my body that's bursting with joy for her.

"It just felt like the right moment." Her squinched face smiles with delight and she shakes her head as we sit back down.

"Oh this is amazing, Des." My excitement nudges a tear from my eye. "Congratulations. I have so many questions. How far along are you? Is it a boy or a girl? Do you have names yet? When are you due?"

Soft laughter rolls out of her. "I'm ten weeks. We don't have names yet or a due date. We *are* having a gender reveal party next month though. I hope you can come."

"Of course I'll be there, at my godchild's first party." I can't help but smile. My heart is so full.

Together, we wallow in the bliss of our spa day and her pregnancy news. It's one of the best days.

I took a red-eye from New York last night to make sure I could be here for Destiny and Nicco's gender reveal party. In their typical fashion, it's a small, private event for close friends and family.

I put my gift on the gift table. It's a basket of pampering mommy lotions and potions and the cutest "and baby makes three" onesie. Pastel blue, pink, and yellow balloons in varying sizes crawl up a wall of greenery behind the table and an adorable particle board elephant sits watch. On my way to Destiny, I pass the dessert table that's teaming with pink and blue treats like cotton candy cupcakes, macarons, and cake pops. A beautiful drip cake serves as the centerpiece.

Destiny's little belly is growing and she definitely has that pregnancy glow.

"Hey, how was your flight?" she asks, hugging me. "I know you got in so late, well early. You must be exhausted; I know you can't sleep on the plane. Thank you for being here." She holds my hands in hers.

"I wouldn't miss this." Though I'm tired, I'm so happy I could make this work and be here. I want to be part of every event in my godchild's life.

"Could you get me some water? I think everyone's here and I have a couple games I want to get started."

"Of course." I turn toward the bar and adrenaline floods me the instant I see him. Enzo. Tingles shock my skin as I stand frozen, watching him. Still hot as hell. He's making drinks and doesn't see me. I peek back over my shoulder and Destiny winks at me as her lips pull into a mischievous smile.

As I approach the bar, he looks up. Attraction bubbles between us, the same as it had the first time we saw each other. The sexiest smile spreads across his unforgivingly gorgeous face. My pulse quickens.

"Hi. I wondered if I'd see you," he says. Those green eyes hold me.

"I didn't expect to see you here." My breath catches in my throat.

"Yeah, Nicco requested me. You were right, he's a really good guy. He's helped me out a lot."

"So, you guys are friends now?" That could be good or bad.

"Yeah, you could say that." He smiles. "What can I get you? We have pink champagne with a puff of cotton candy." His wink pays homage to my hair. "A Tiffany-blue cosmopolitan. Or, anything you'd like."

"Destiny wants a bottle of water. And I'll have, um, I don't know."

"What do you think the baby will be?"

"They say if you carry low, it's a boy." I turn and look at Destiny then laugh and turn back to him. "Honestly, I can't tell if she's low or high or somewhere in the middle."

"I'll make you a bet." A devilish smile pulls at his lips.

"A bet? What kind of bet?" Okay, I'll play along.

"If it's a boy, you go out with me. If it's a girl, I'll stop asking." He cocks his head to the side with a wicked smirk.

He's certainly persistent. "You don't give up, do you?"

His smile vanishes. "Not when it comes to you."

The air stills as my skin warms.

He shrugs as he opens his hands toward me. "I only have a fifty-fifty chance," he says, grabbing a bottle of water and placing it in front of me.

Our hot kiss flashes through my mind. *I shouldn't do this.*

It's like his eyes have a spell on me. Kryptonite. I hold out my hand to shake his. "Pink champagne, please," I say, confirming the bet.

He nods with that sexy grin of his. "Pink champagne."

Destiny announces the gender guessing game and Enzo hands me her water and my champagne. I take a seat at a small round table where I can be involved in the party and sneak secret peeks at Enzo, even though I shouldn't. After several fun baby games, it's time to cut the cake and see what color's inside. A small part of me hopes it's blue.

6

Enzo

So I cheated a little. Nicco and I have become friends and he's told me a lot about Candi, making me all the more intrigued by her. Through our conversations, I must've proven myself to be worthy of at least seeing Candi again because it's true that he requested me for their party. He also told me that he accidentally found out the baby's gender when he dropped off the paper to the cake designer and it fell on the floor and he saw it. He wanted Destiny to be surprised so he kept the secret, but he told me when we were talking about the party. Hey, can't blame a guy for trying.

When I looked up and saw her in that pale, tan dress that wrapped across her breasts, accentuating her cleavage with the low neckline, ravenous hunger from our first kiss thundered through me. I knew I had to kiss her again.

As Nicco and Destiny pull out the slice of blue cake, I know there's a small chance I might get that opportunity. Candi turns in her seat toward me and raises her champagne glass then offers me a smile and finishes her drink.

The party winds down and guests begin leaving. Candi walks toward me, her tan legs so long and sexy with her short dress and high heels. Enough to drop a man to his knees. *Damn.*

"Well, it looks like I'll have the Tiffany-blue cosmopolitan." Her salacious smile strikes my dick as she sits on a bar stool.

I smile back and start making her drink. "So, we're on then?"

"On one condition." She holds up her slender finger.

Feisty vixen. "Name it." I don't care what it is, I'll do it.

"You may know Nicco, but I don't know you very well. We'll go on a double-date with Nicco and Destiny."

"Done." I crack a nod. "I know your schedule and Nicco's can be hectic. When do you want to get together?"

"I'm in town until Thursday and I think Nicco's around too. How does Tuesday sound to you?"

"I can do Tuesday." I'd rather it be tonight, but Nicco said she came in on a red-eye so she's probably tired.

"Okay, I'll check with them and let you know. Do you mind if I have your number?"

"Not at all." I set her drink in front of her and give her my number.

She punches it in and my phone chimes.

"Now you have mine."

I check my phone and see the smiley face emoji she sent. I edit and type in her name.

"I know you guys are cleaning up now. Is it okay for me to sit here and finish my drink?"

"Absolutely." I start loading dirty glasses into a glass-rack. "So, you were out of town?"

"Yeah, I was up in New York doing a shoot for Vogue," she says nonchalantly.

I stop and look at her then whistle. "Impressive. You really are big time."

"Well, I don't know about that," she says, taking a sip of her drink. "I mean, I have worked extremely hard to get here. I still haven't landed the one brand I've always wanted to work with. I will though. One of these days, I will."

Her tenacity is alluring. "I have no doubt about that. What's the brand?"

"Gucci." She takes a sip of her drink, looking up at me from under her thick, dark lashes. Determination cements her expression.

"Very high-end. Any specific reason?"

A chuckle lifts her chin, accentuating the sensual line from her jaw down to her neck. "When Destiny and I were little, we'd play dress-up. Her mom had the best magazines that we'd look through for our inspiration and I remember seeing an ad for Gucci. The setting was amazing, the model was beautiful, her outfit was stunning, and she was carrying the most magnificent Gucci bag." Her gaze drifted above me as she reminisced. Then she returns her eyes to me. "I grabbed my purple butterfly purse and drew a horrible Gucci logo on it with permanent black marker." She bursts into laughter making me laugh.

Destiny walks over to us. "What's going on over here?" she asks with a smile.

Candi catches her breath from laughing and holds one hand to her chest and the other out toward Destiny.

"Do you remember my purple butterfly purse?"

Destiny starts laughing. "The one you drew the mangled-looking Gucci logo on?" Candi nods with a huge smile pasted on her face. "Oh I remember it. An artist, you are not. Creative eye, yes. Artist no." She looks at me. "We were quite the little fashionistas." She turns and impersonates a model walking down a runway then turns and walks back, keeping her expression stone-like and exaggerating her steps.

Candi stands and struts toward her in her own sexy model-walk. As they pass each other, they nod, and continue walking, keeping serious expressions. When Candi reaches the point where Destiny turned around, she turns and walks back. Both of them erupt into bent-over laughter when Candi reaches us.

Once their laughter subsides, Candi sits back on her stool and sips her drink.

"Hey, what are you and Nicco doing Tuesday night? Is he in town?"

"I think he is. Why?"

"Well, it seems I've lost a bet with Enzo." When she glances at me, the corners of her lips curl up. "And we're going out. But I won't go without you and Nicco. What do you say? Are you up for a double-date?"

"Sounds like fun."

All the guests are now gone and Nicco joins us.

"Enzo, thank you, man. Great job today." He reaches over the bar to shake my hand.

"You got it." Gratitude fills me.

"Are we free to join Candi and Enzo on Tuesday night?" Destiny asks him.

He rubs his scruff with his hand. "Tuesday, yeah. Where are we going?"

Candi looks at me. "Someplace fun and casual?"

Nothing stuffy, got it. "I know a place. Great food and drinks. Cool atmosphere. Stage 2 Bar & Grill. Have you guys been there?"

"I've heard of it," Candi says. "But I've never been there."

Nicco and Destiny look at each other. "We haven't. Sounds great. What time?" Nicco asks.

"Meet you there at six?"

"See you then," Nicco says then looks at Destiny. I admire their adoration. I've never had a woman look at me the way she looks at him. Something tugs at me. "Are you ready to go?"

"Yup," she says. "Do you need a ride home?" she asks Candi.

"No. You guys are going in the opposite direction. I'm gonna grab an Uber home, get some pizza, and probably go to bed early. Thank you though."

Nicco leans in and kisses Candi on both cheeks then walks to the end of the bar and calls me over. He puts a hundred-dollar bill in my hand. "Thanks for today," he says, shaking my hand, then looks me square in the eyes. "I got you this far. You're on your own from here. Don't fuck it up." It's not a threat or even a warning, rather a devoted statement of protection like a big brother would say.

"I won't," I say, the words are a vow to myself. *Don't fuck this up.*

"See you Tuesday." He slaps a pat to my shoulder.

Destiny loops her arm through his. "Thank you, Enzo." She and her belly bounce happily off with Nicco.

I go back to cleaning up the bar. "Hey, how about I give you a ride home. I'd feel better than having you take an Uber," I say, taking her empty glass.

She doesn't answer right away. She just looks in my eyes.

"I'm a good guy. I promise. Nicco and Destiny trust me. Maybe you can too?"

She bites the corner of her lip. "Okay," she says softly. Utter temptation, this woman.

"I'm almost done here. I just need to bring these glass-racks back then I'll be ready to go."

"I'll wait here."

I bring the racks back and return to her. When I round the corner, she's still on the stool, her back partially toward me, gazing out above the thick green shrubbery at the clear blue sky. Miles away again, she holds the ring hanging around her neck and slides it back and forth on its chain. Melancholy veils her.

I walk over, keeping my steps slow, watching her, taking her in. My greedy hunger shifts to compassion for whatever is holding her hostage in that ring. "I'm ready."

Startled, she drops the ring to her chest and her head flickers toward me. "Great," she says, standing, looking up at me.

Desire hurls back into me as I look into her beautiful face. I want to kiss her. Right now.

"My car should be out front. I had the valet pull it around."

We walk in silence through the lobby and out to where my car is. I open the passenger door and she gets in, then adjusts her dress to cover her thighs as I close the door. She's killing me.

"Thank you for giving me a ride. I hope I'm not too far out of your way," she says when I get in.

"It's my pleasure. I'd feel much better knowing I got you home safely. Just tell me where to go."

"Yup. Turn right out of here then go through a few lights. I'll tell you where to turn."

When I put on my blinker, she looks at my dashboard then turns and looks behind us.

"Is everything okay?" I ask.

"Yeah. It's just, there's no one behind us and you turned on your blinker." She points her thumb behind us.

I chuckle, nerves trickle up my spine. "Yeah, habit. I was in a car crash a few years ago and it didn't have anything to do with not using blinkers, but it did make me a more conscious driver." I point to the scar above my left eyebrow. "This reminds me that I'm not the only person in the world and my only way to communicate to those around me is by following the rules of the road, whether or not anyone's watching. It's also my daily reminder that life is short and can be taken in the blink of an eye." My heart weighs in my chest as the devastation of the crash pummels my thoughts. I'm so damn lucky to be alive.

She doesn't say anything. She just nods as the corners of her lips barely lift. Her eyes darken and glaze. Unaware of her movement, she takes the ring on her chain between her fingers. What has her in its grip?

I bring her back from her dark place. "So, what got you into photography?"

Releasing the ring, she returns her gaze to me. "Actually, I think it was our fashion shows when we were little and her mom's magazines. I was drawn to the photographs. Fascinated by the lighting and shadows and the moods I could feel from the images. I think those magazines are what got me interested in the world of high fashion too. When I was in sixth grade, my mom got me a camera for my twelfth birthday. That was it. I was hooked."

"That's amazing that you knew what you wanted to do at such a young age. You followed your dream and now you're one of the top people in your field."

"How would you know that?"

"Nicco speaks highly of you and I also Googled you. You're very accomplished."

"Thanks. I've devoted myself to my craft and invested a lot in learning and equipment. Spent countless hours and late nights perfecting my images and almost always deliver before my deadlines. And it's all been worth it. This business is built on reputation and I make sure mine is world-class." She points to the upcoming traffic light. "Turn right up at that light."

"Is your mom a photographer too then?"

She hesitates, that darkness present. "No. She was a housewife. Given the chance though, she might've been. I think she would've been amazing at it." A bright smile lifts her cheeks then fades. "My dad's a little old-fashioned and didn't want her to work. I think part of why she encouraged me so much is because she wanted me to be able to have the dreams she couldn't."

"Jeez, that's too bad. I'm sure they're both proud of you and what you've achieved."

"Left here." Her energy lifts as her smile broadens. "My mom was. She was so happy for me. She was my biggest fan and I tried to make sure I told her how grateful I was for her constant support and love. She made me feel like I could conquer the world." Her cheeks lower. "My dad, not so much."

"Really?" Given what I've learned about her, I can't imagine a parent not being proud. She talks about her mom in past tense. Could she be the person behind the ring around her neck? The darkness looming over her?

"Right, up here. That's my building." She points. "That's a story for another day." Her gentle smile holds a sadness.

A chuckle drops out of me. "You're not going to believe this."

"What?"

"I'm two blocks over." I slant my head in the direction of my condo.

"What? That's crazy," she says and shakes her head. "Small world."

I pull up to the four-level condo and put on my flashers then get out and open her door, offering my hand.

"Thank you," she says, slipping her hand into mine. Warmth crawls up my arm from her touch.

"What floor are you on? I'll take you up."

"Second." She heads to the lobby and I follow her, catching a quick view of her ass swaggering. We get in the elevator and she hits the two button. I resist the temptation of trapping her against the back wall and kissing her delicious lips. "Thanks again for the ride home."

We ride the elevator in silence as I struggle to not get hard.

The elevator opens and she leads us to her door, 204. "This is me." She turns to face me and looks up at me with her beautiful brown eyes.

I want to keep talking to her. I want to share the pizza she's going to order. I want to kiss her. *Don't fuck it up.*

"Hey, since we live so close, how about I swing by on Tuesday and pick you up? You know, like a proper date?"

"Um." Her gaze flickers between my eyes. "Okay," she says softly.

I take a small step back when I want to step forward. "See you Tuesday. Five thirty?" I continue taking steps back to control myself.

Her nod is slow with the sexiest damn smile that makes me want to stalk forward, pin her against the door, and kiss her.

I wait until she's unlocked her door and steps inside before I turn and leave, hoping my car hasn't been towed.

Tuesday night. Two and half days until I get to see her again. No chance she won't be monopolizing my thoughts.

7

Candi

My heart's beating so fast. I enjoyed talking with him. I wanted to invite him in and ask him to stay for pizza. I wanted him to kiss me before he left. Whenever I'm near him, he consumes me. Logic wanes and my senses shift into overdrive.

I haven't felt this giddy about a guy since before Dom. He and I were friends for so long before we ever dated that we were like a comfortable pair of old sneakers. When I'm near Enzo, I have to keep catching my breath. His energy is magnetic; seductive, respectful, charismatic.

I shake the memory of our kiss out of my head and throw on shorts and a tank then order my pizza. Exhausted from work and the red-eye, I fall asleep about halfway through *The Wedding Planner*.

I see Enzo tonight. A strange mix of excitement and nervousness twists like a helix inside me. I don't know why I'm nervous. I get that it's our first actual date, but I've talked with him several times and already practically ambushed him into kissing me.

I pick out my coffee-colored, halter, cutout top; black skinny jeans; and black-leather moto jacket. Finishing off my outfit, I put on my gold hoop earrings and zip up my over-the-knee black-leather boots. Just as I'm finishing putting on my lipstick, the doorbell rings. A spurt of adrenaline rushes through my torso. I look at my phone, five twenty-nine. The man is prompt. A quick scrunch of my curls and I grab my mini Dior purse as I head to the door.

Deep breath, exhale. I open the door and…*wow*. Catching a quick glance of him, I suck in a sip of air. He's wearing jeans, an untucked crisp white button-down shirt, and a dark gray blazer with a lighter gray color creating a square-pattern on the fabric. He's strikingly handsome and I love his style.

"Hi. You look great. Am I too casual? Should I go change?"

"Thank you." He takes a step back and scans me from head to toe and back up then shakes his head and pulls his lips in. "Nope, you're just right. Perfect, actually." His pause devours me. "Are you ready?"

"I am." I lock my door and we go down to his black Jeep Grand Cherokee. He opens the passenger door to let me in and closes it once I'm settled in my seat. I'm digging his chivalry.

So far, our conversations have been heavily about me and I'm curious to know more about him.

"How's work been going for you?"

Staying focused on his driving, his enthusiasm lights up his eyes and lifts his cheeks. "Great actually. Nicco's a standup guy. He helped me get a new agent who's been consistently getting me modeling jobs, with some bigger brands too, and it's been great. I even signed a contract with Chapord and it's an honor to represent their brand." He releases his left hand from the steering wheel and reaches toward me, giving me a look at the striking, classy watch around his wrist. "Their company values and commitment to sustainability make me respect them so much."

"That's amazing. Yeah, I've done a couple shoots with them and I've always had great experiences. Have your gigs taken you anywhere interesting?"

As we drive, he tells me about some of the cool places he's been and brands he's worked with. He's definitely stepped up his career since we last saw each other and I'm thrilled for him.

When we arrive at Stage 2, Destiny and Nicco are there and

have already put in our name with the hostess. It's kind of like upscale-casual. The walls that aren't brick are painted a deep red. Dark, rustic-wood tables pair with black-leather, curved-back armchairs.

We're seated within five minutes and the hostess brings us to a slightly hidden booth near the back of the restaurant, likely to try to give Nicco some privacy from fans.

The chemistry between the four of us is relaxed and fun. With Destiny and I being friends, and Nicco and Enzo being friends, there aren't any weird, awkward silences like there can be when you're on a first date.

"So, from the story you two told me about your fashion modeling days when you were little and Candi's speech at your wedding, it sounds like you used to get into some mischief together," Enzo says to Destiny.

"With this one," she says, pointing at me, "always." Playfulness surfs the crest of our laughter. "So, I have to tell you this story. But I warn you, we may laugh so hard we pee ourselves," she says, chuckling again. "I don't even think you know this one." She looks at Nicco.

And now I know exactly the story she's about to tell. I squirm in my seat, ready to burst into laughter at the memory.

Enzo rubs his hands together with a huge smile on his face. "Oh I'm so ready for this." He focuses his attention on Destiny.

"Obviously Candi is the slightly wilder one of the two of us," she starts. Enzo glances at me with a frisky grin. "We were, I don't know, what? In our early twenties?" She looks at me and I bow my head in agreement. "And I let her talk me into a blind date with her and the guy she'd been dating for a while. She wasn't a very good matchmaker back then, let me tell you. Anyway, she starts telling this story of a time we were at a nightclub together and, in the story, she reverses our roles and makes *me* the wild one."

I can't help but chuckle, drawing Enzo's smoldering eyes to me.

"So, she goes on to tell him how we were dirty dancing together and I, really *her*, lifted up my top and flashed everyone."

We all bust out laughing.

She continues as I bubble inside.

"Now, at this point I'm thinking that she's never told the true story to the guy she's dating and I don't want to call her out on it, so I kind of go along, but I'm laughing so hard because I know the truth and now this guy thinks he's getting lucky with some wild chick."

We all erupt into laughter and tears squeeze out of my eyes as I rock back and forth, holding my hand to my chest.

"As the evening went on, he kept trying to get me to go out on a second date with him. He asked what kind of food I like to eat. I told him nothing spicy. He proceeded to tell me about a great Mexican place he knew of and an Indian place. Clearly, he hadn't bothered to listen to the fact that I don't like spicy food. Needless to say, there was no second date."

"I've improved my matchmaking since then," I chime in.

"You have." She cocks her head to the side with a sweet smile then kisses Nicco on the cheek.

"On our ride home, it was just the three of us and she confessed that she'd told her boyfriend the story, the *real* story, that it was *her* who flashed her boobs at everyone in the club. So, the entire time he knew the truth when I thought he didn't. The whole thing was so stinking funny. This one." She waggles her finger at me and I shrug.

We order desserts and the DJ announces that Karaoke is about to begin. As we eat, we're thoroughly entertained by some awful singers who are bravely singing their hearts out and enjoying every minute of it. There are also some who are surprisingly good.

As we finish our desserts, the DJ grabs the microphone and scans the room, "I believe I saw Mr. Enzo Cipriani in the house tonight." There's a small cheer from the crowd at the stage. "Where are you Enzo?" Claps and whistles fill the air.

"I guess you come here a bit?" I ask, intrigued and interested to see if he can sing or if he's so terrible, yet gorgeous, that they love him.

He hangs his head then lifts it and shrugs with a humble grin.

The crowd starts with a chant, "Enzo, Enzo," that grows

increasingly louder, coupled with more claps and whistles.

"Your fans await," I say, looking over at Destiny and Nicco who shake their heads and raise their shoulders, looking as stunned as I am.

He rises from our booth. "I apologize. I'll be right back." He winks at me and heads toward the stage.

As he makes his way up onto the stage, the cheers heighten to a clamor. Nicco pays our bill, we grab our drinks, and find a spot in the middle of the crowd to watch Enzo. The DJ moves a keyboard to the front of the stage along with a stool. Curiosity eats at me.

"Thank you, Brian," Enzo says into the microphone as he sits on the stool. Rows of vertical string lights serve as his backdrop. "Good evening, everyone. I see a lot of familiar faces here tonight."

Cheers, whistles, and howls erupt.

"This one's for someone special." His gaze searches the room as the crowd hushes.

Adrenaline rushes me. *Someone special?*

Destiny and Nicco look at me, presumption gleaming in their eyes. Could he mean *me*?

Enzo starts playing the keyboard and the lyrics to "Heartbeats" float out of his mouth, caressing the air. Piercing through the sea of bodies, his Kryptonite-green gaze finds *me*, possesses me. The audience is hypnotized, paralyzed. Slow and seductive, his words penetrate my soul. The crowd fades in a haze, only we exist.

Moments we shared flash through my head as his song envelopes me. Our hot kiss, dancing in his arms, the first touch of his hand on my skin. The images vanish as his eyes hold mine captive and he sings…to me.

With the last note sung, the crowd explodes with more cheers and howls. Every hair on my body stands on end as I'm shaken by the noise from my reverie. I clap and whistle. Destiny puts her arm around me and squeezes me.

"Thank you guys so much," he says, then bows his head and simpers.

As he jumps off the stage and weaves through the crowd toward us, people pat him on the back and shower him with compliments.

"Bro, what the fuck was that? You were incredible," Nicco says, extending his arms and hands in a what-the-fuck gesture, then throwing an arm around Enzo's shoulder and tugging him in.

Enzo, chuckles humbly. "Yeah, it's just, something I do for fun."

"For fun?" Destiny emphasizes. "Enzo, I mean, that was amazing. I had no idea you could sing like that, let alone play the keyboard. I, I have no words. That was awesome."

"Heh. Thank you, really, thank you so much."

He looks at me, intensity suspended in the air.

I'm still entranced and so overcome with emotions, I can't find the words to say. "That was beautiful," is all that comes out.

He moves, standing directly in front of me, and cups the side of my face in his hand then places his lips close to my opposite ear. I inhale a shallow breath. "That was for you," he whispers.

Tingles swarm my heating skin.

He uprights himself, leaving me in a melting puddle. "You wanna go up next?" he asks with a sly nod to the stage.

"Oh hell no," I say, taking a small step back with my head, my torso, my entire body.

A laugh bursts out of him.

"Not your thing, huh?"

"I know what I'm *good* at and what I'm *not* good at. No way in hell would I ever get on a stage and sing. No. Fucking. Way."

We all hurl into laughter. Crazy talk.

"Hey, you guys want to come back to our place for a drink? Or maybe s'mores?" Destiny asks.

"I'm in," Enzo shoots me that sultry smile.

"Yeah, absolutely. I just need to use the restroom before we go," I say. "Be right back."

I make my way to the restroom, slightly lightheaded from what just happened. Tucked into a stall, I overhear some women talking.

"Did you see the way he looked at her? It was like no one else was even in the room," says one voice.

"I know. I wish I could find a man who looked at me the way he looked at her," says another voice.

"With his looks that intense, I can't even imagine how mind-blowing he is in bed. Holy shit," says the first voice. They both chortle.

"That man is off the market. Hook, line, and sinker."

Still in my stall, I can't help but smile. It *was* kind of intense the way he looked at me as he sang. I'm not even going to think about what he's like in bed. I can't go there. I heave a sigh, trying to slow my pulse.

The clickety-clack of their footsteps fades. I shake my head to clear my thoughts and exit the stall. Meeting back up with Enzo, Destiny, and Nicco, we head to their house.

As we drive, I have to know more about this hidden talent of Enzo's.

"So, we were clearly blown away by you. How long have you played and when did you know you had such an incredible voice?"

"Nah, it's just something I do for fun. My friends are all pretty busy with their lives and their jobs so I don't see them that much. And my sister and her husband are busy. You know my previous agent wasn't getting me much work so I had some time on my hands and started fiddling around on the keyboard. Took some lessons online and enjoyed it so I kept learning new songs. Then I'd pop into Stage 2 here and there and sing a few songs. People seemed to like it."

He's so modest. "Like it? Did you hear that place?"

His chuckle is endearing.

"You're really good. Have you ever thought about singing professionally?"

"Nah, it's not my thing. I don't care much for the spotlight. Even a small crowd like tonight makes me nervous. But I enjoy singing so I do it sometimes. I try not to think about all those people watching me. Put me on a big stage and I'd crack."

"But you're a model. You're literally *in* the spotlight for your job."

"That's different though. I can't see when people's eyes are on me in a magazine ad or on a billboard somewhere. And photoshoots are usually only a few people and no one's looking at me specifically. Singing on stage in front of hundreds of people? No way. No thank you." He chuckles again then briefly looks over at me with that seductive smile of his. "But I'll serenade you any time you want."

The skin on my arms tingles as my core heats.

"Do you have any other secret talents I should know about?"

He pauses, looking left and right at the stop sign. "I'm a mean baker."

"Hah," torpedoes out of me. "You bake?"

"What?" He laughs at my stunned reaction. "I bake," he says, stern yet playful, and lifts his shoulders toward his ears.

"And when did you take up this hobby?" *What?* Hot as hell, makes me laugh, sweet, unbelievable singer, plays an instrument, and now he *bakes*? Who *is* this man?

"Well, I wouldn't go so far as to say it's a hobby. My sister baked a lot when we were kids and she'd always ask for my help so I would. I guess I picked up a few things along the way and now I'm a pretty mean baker." He shoots me that devilishly sexy grin.

"Your turn. Tell me something about you that most people either don't know or wouldn't guess."

It's a little personal and I probably shouldn't, but I share the first thing that comes to mind. "That as badass as I seem on the outside, a lot of times, I'm terrified on the inside. My mom always taught me to do it scared, whatever *it* happens to be. She used to tell me that people don't get anywhere in life by staying small and not taking chances. She would say that the worst that could happen is that it doesn't work out or they say no, and then I just keep trying until it does work out or they say yes."

"She sounds like an amazing woman." Respect lines his words.

I smile as he pulls into Destiny's driveway. They beat us back. When we go in, Nicco's out back starting a fire in the fire pit and

Destiny's in the kitchen gathering s'mores ingredients. I take off my boots and socks and Enzo follows my lead, removing his shoes and socks and rolling up his jeans a little. He takes off his blazer and hangs it on a hook above the weathered, light-gray shoe bench.

"This place is great, Destiny," he says, looking around the cozy beach cottage.

"Thank you. We love it here," she says, handing him a tray with the s'mores' ingredients on it. "Head out there." She points to the back door that leads out to the porch and beach. "You'll see Nicco. We'll be out with wine. Do you have a preference?"

"Okay. Nah, I'm easy."

As soon as he's off the porch and in the sand, Destiny hands me two wine glasses and a bottle of white wine.

"So, it's been an interesting night so far." One side of her mouth kicks up as she tilts her head a bit. "How was the ride here?"

She thinks she's being sly, but I know her too well. "It was nice. He's nice. I like him." I exhale and shake my head. "Des, I just don't know that I'm ready to date again. Shit, I don't know that I'll ever be ready."

Her sigh is filled with compassion. "Can, I know it's weird to think about and I know a part of you will always hurt for Dom." She pauses, drawing in her lips. "You're still young. And, you have so much love to give. You deserve to be loved again," she says gently, rubbing my arms and looking into my eyes.

Since Dom passed, the idea of falling in love again never entered my mind. He was my soul mate. That kind of love is tough to come by.

"Come on." I smile and tip my head toward the beach. "Let's go enjoy our night."

She grabs the other two wine glasses, a corkscrew, a bottle of red wine, and a small bottle of water for herself. When we reach the fire pit, the flames are starting to grow and the guys have pulled the white, weathered Adirondack chairs close to the round pit. The golden sun dips into the ocean, splaying colors of yellow, orange, pink, and even purple.

We spear our long forks into our marshmallows and float them above the flames. Nicco and Enzo talk about work and upcoming projects while Destiny sips her water and I sip my wine, watching the sun sink deeper into the ocean.

With s'mores filling my stomach, I sit back in my chair, ruminating on what a fun night it's been. Enzo finishes his last bite and stands up. *Does he want to leave already? I'm having such a good time with him.*

"Want to go for a walk?" he asks, those magnetic eyes pulling me in.

He doesn't want to leave. "Yeah, sure," I say, getting up from my chair, succumbing to his pull.

"We'll be back," he says to Nicco and Destiny as he turns toward the water.

"Have fun," Destiny says. "I'll be here eating s'mores." She holds up her long fork with a marshmallow perched on the tip. Pregnant lady with s'mores, watch out.

As Enzo and I head toward the water, he takes my hand in his. Though unexpected, it feels natural.

"This okay?" he asks, looking down at me and gently squeezing my hand.

Dom was a hand-holder. I've missed holding his hand. I like the feeling of Enzo holding mine. It's different, but nice. A warm contrast to the cool, grainy sand beneath my feet.

"Mhmm."

"Tonight was fun. Thank you for letting me take you out. Although, technically, I need to square up with Nicco before I can claim to have taken you out."

"Heh. That's Nicco."

"If you're feeling comfortable enough and you're up for it, I'd like to make you dinner sometime. Just you and me?" Anticipation cocoons his hopeful tone.

What is it about this man? Am I ready for him? Am I ready

to see if this could be something? Dom's gone. Why does it feel like I'm cheating on him? I'm drawn to Enzo in a way I can't seem to control. A powerful force that invades me.

"I'd like that," I say, a mix of fear and excitement commingle in my stomach.

"Great." He stops, facing the ocean. Moonlight skips atop the peaks of the undulating water. "Wanna go in?" He says, dipping his head toward the water.

"Now? But, we don't have suits."

"We don't need 'em."

8

Enzo

"I'm not wearing a bra," she says. I'd already noticed that and I've been focusing all night on keeping my arousal under control.

"Here, you put on my shirt," I say, unbuttoning it, taking it off, and handing it to her. "I'll go in the water and turn around, then you can take off your pretty top and put on my shirt."

She takes it from me and I strip off my jeans then walk into the cool water, gentle waves splash against my skin. When I turn to look at her, she's standing there, watching me.

"Ready? I'm going to turn around and you let me know when I can look again." I turn and wait, watching the moon as it hangs suspended against the darkening sky, anticipation simmering inside.

After a few minutes, her steps drop into the water, filling my ears with small sloshes. She's by my side, fermenting my energy.

"Can I look now?"

"Yes." Her voice is quiet, almost timid. "The water's colder than I thought."

"Do you want to get out?" I ask, turning toward her. I catch a glimpse of her sumptuous breasts and hard nipples as the water splashes against them just before she dips them below the surface.

"No, not yet."

"Come here. I've got you." I hold my arms out, not sure she'll come.

She steps toward me and I squat, giving her a place to sit. She wraps her legs around my waist and her arms loosely around my neck. Her breasts touch my chest through the wet fabric.

Her gaze moves slowly from my eyes down to my silver "S" emblem necklace and back up.

"Superman, huh? Was he your favorite superhero growing up?" Her eyes shift back and forth between mine as she awaits my answer.

Grief hooks into me, resurfacing from a place I try not to visit. No one's ever asked about my necklace before. Am I ready to share this with her? The way she looks at me makes me want to tell her. To share with her. To *trust* her.

"I had a few I liked." I pause, the salt air stealing my breath. "My dad gave this to me when my mom left us. I was nine and it hit me pretty hard." The words break the air like brittle as they leave my mouth. A crinkle forms between her brows, her eyes coalescing with my pain as memories engulf me. "He always told me that I was a hero. That I was brave and could do anything. That I was strong, but it was still okay to cry and feel hurt at the same time. Really, he was *my* hero. When my mom left, he became our dad *and* our mom. He sacrificed a lot and gave us everything he could, even through his own heartache." I shake my head slightly, my heart pinches. "He loved her. I don't think he ever stopped."

She listens intently as the waves lap against us. Her silence holding me with grace.

"To this day, my sister and I don't know what happened, why she left. But he never said one bad word about her. He tried to hold it together in front of us, but sometimes I'd hear him crying if I woke up late at night."

"I'm so sorry. He certainly sounds like a hero." She drapes me in her soothing tenderness. "If you're curious, would you ever ask him what happened? Or would that be too painful?"

"It would've been too painful and I never wanted to put him through that. Plus, I'd convinced myself it didn't matter. He was all we needed." I pause to take a breath. I've never shared this with a woman. Her curiosity and compassion compel me to continue. "He passed away a few years ago. I swear sometimes I wonder if it was heartbreak that finally took him." I swallow, trying to push down the lump pressing into my throat. "And I have no idea how to be a hero like him. I'm still trying to figure that out. But my necklace makes me feel like I have a small piece of him with me, giving me courage and strength."

"That's a lot of loss," she says with a tinge of melancholy, like she knows the pain of grieving.

"It looks like you keep someone close to your heart too." I look down at the ring on the chain around her neck and back into her eyes.

"I do." It's all she says. Nothing more.

Time moves fractionally as we stare at each other, sharing unspoken pain. Nothing exists outside us. Our souls connect through our eyes and the beating of our hearts.

A small swell of water splashes between us, breaking the moment.

"Ooo." She shivers in my arms. "I'm ready to go in."

"Come on, let's go," I say and start walking us toward the shore.

She unwraps from around me and we run out of the water to where our clothes are on the sand. I can't fucking stop myself from looking at her beautiful breasts and hard nipples behind my wet dress shirt that's clinging to every curve of her body. She's so damn sexy.

We scoop up our clothes and run back to the house. Destiny and Nicco are inside and have cleaned up around the fire pit. We grab the towels on the large porch swing and wipe the sand from our legs and feet before going inside.

"I'm grabbing shorts and a sweatshirt," Candi calls out as she runs through the living room and drops her clothes on the kitchen table then vanishes up the stairs.

Nicco and Destiny look at me, standing in their living room wearing my wet boxer briefs, holding my jeans.

"Bro, I'll give you shorts and a T-shirt, but there's no fucking way I'm giving you my underwear." Nicco jokes, making me laugh.

"Deal."

He brings down the clothes and I change in their downstairs bathroom. When I come out, Candi's come back down, her hair up on top of her head, wearing Destiny's clothes. Destiny's put our clothes in two separate plastic grocery bags.

Candi walks over and hugs her then gives her a kiss on the cheek. The same for Nicco. "Thank you, guys, for such a fun night."

I hold out my hand and Nicco shakes it. Then I lean down and kiss Destiny on the cheek. "Great night, guys. Thanks so much."

I slip on my dress shoes while Candi puts her tall boots into her bag and slides on a pair of Destiny's flipflops. She hands me my wet shirt and I put it in my bag. As we head out the door, it hits me that I've never been on a double-date before and I genuinely had a great time with everyone.

Given the hour, the traffic isn't bad and I get us back to Candi's faster than I'd like. I'm not ready for the night to be over.

I walk her to her door, wanting so badly to taste her lips again. After the intimacy of our conversation in the ocean, it doesn't feel right. I squelch my growing desire.

We stand facing each other. She looks so cute with her wet pink hair on top of her head and wearing Destiny's clothes.

"When can I make you dinner?" *I want to see you again, soon.*

The corners of her lips lift slightly. "How's Saturday night?"

"Okay. How about I pick you up at three-thirty and we can go to the farmer's market and pick out what we want?"

She nods. "Okay," she says softly. Her eyes flicker to my lips.

Fuck, I want to kiss her. "I should go." I lean down and kiss her forehead. "Good night." When I pull back, she opens her eyes, magnetism drawing us close. I love how her breaths tick up when I hover over her.

"Good night." She unlocks her door and steps in then turns around and smiles at me before closing the door. *Damn, this woman.*

Candi

I close the door and lock it then lean my back against it and look up at the ceiling. Exhale. *God, I wanted him to kiss me.* I haven't had feelings like this in so long. My heart ached when he told me about his Superman necklace and his mom leaving and then his dad dying. When I looked into his eyes as he spoke, the moonlight illuminated a mixture of innocence and pain, ensnaring me.

I had such a good time tonight. I was afraid I'd be thinking about Dom and feeling guilty. But I didn't think about him once. I was thoroughly consumed by Enzo and loved learning more about him.

And, *damn*, dude's got a body. When he stripped down to his underwear and the moonlight hit all the right spots, my mouth watered. Even though I'd already seen him half-naked at the photo shoot and in the pictures I took, something about his spontaneity and practically skinny-dipping in the ocean made for a whole different experience.

Now, all I can think about is seeing him again on Saturday.

9

Candi

Since we're having dinner in, I've picked a casual outfit; my white asymmetric-halter bodysuit, skinny jeans, and Gucci belt. Gotta keep the manifesting vibes going with my belt.

There's a knock on my door. Three twenty-nine. How does he do that? When I open the door, that subtle, spicy scent he wears drifts into my nose.

His eyes widen as they trail down my body. "Wow. Uh." He takes a small step back, his broad shoulders expanding. "You look incredible."

Warmth rushes through my cheeks. "Thank you."

"Are you ready? I thought I'd cook for you at my place since I know where everything is. But only if you're comfortable with that."

I love how respectful he is and always makes sure I'm okay with what he's thinking. "Yeah, that's fine." I grab my straw tote that I always bring to the farmer's market with me.

The market is right around the corner so we walk there, him holding my hand. We catch each other up on how the rest of our week went.

When we get to the market, we stroll up and down the aisles, taking in the scents of ripe fruits and vegetables, sweet baked goods, and fragrant flowers. I love that they always have jazz music playing, except at Christmastime when they play old-fashioned Christmas songs.

"What are you in the mood for?" he asks.

"How about fish? And a couple veggies?"

"Sounds good. Do you like orange roughy?"

"I haven't had it before. Is it really fishy tasting? I like fish, but I don't like it too fishy."

He smiles. "I think you'll like this then, it's very mild," he says, taking my hand. "Come on, this booth down here has the best fresh fish."

He pays for the orange roughy and we get avocados and asparagus at the next booth over.

"Do you want anything else?" he asks.

"How about dessert?" With all the sugar wafting through the air, I'm very much in the mood for something sweet.

"Oh I've got that covered." He winks as a coy smile dances on his lips. "I think we're done. Unless you want to look around at any of the other booths."

"I'll peek as we work our way out." Though I rarely get anything at the crafty booths, I do enjoy looking through them. Occasionally, I'll pick up a gift.

My bag filled with dinner ingredients and him holding my hand, we walk leisurely through the rest of the aisles. It's relaxing, comfortable, natural.

The booth next to the exit is billowing with dozens of tall containers of beautiful fresh flowers. I love flowers. There's something about them that always makes me happy.

"Pick some out," he says, nodding.

I pick a bundle of ranunculus in soft hues of coral, pink, and salmon and hand them to the young girl who works there. "I'll take these, please." She smiles and takes them from me, wrapping them in a thick brown sheet of paper. The total comes to $32.87.

He hands her a fifty-dollar bill, puts the bundle in my bag, takes my hand, and walks away. "Thank you," he calls out over his shoulder.

I turn to look back at her. She's holding the bill in her hand with her arm extended forward a bit and her lips are open. "But, sir…" She looks around, stunned, confusion painting her face. Then she curls her hand in toward her chest and drops her chin. When she lifts her head, her eyebrows are pinched together. She catches my gaze, puts her hand up at chest-height, and mouths, "Thank you."

My heart warmed by his gesture and her reaction; I smile at her.

"That was very kind of you."

"That girl works hard. She's here every time I come to the market. Hustles too. Her hands are dirty and nicked, her jeans are worn. Nicco paid forward to me the kindness Destiny's mom paid to him. I'm no millionaire — *yet*." A cheesy grin quirks at his lips. "But I have the ability to do things like that, so, when the opportunity is there, I take it. I've never had an occasion to buy flowers from her, but I always see her when I leave."

My heart just melted a little.

"Well, you didn't see it, but I looked back and I can tell you, she was very surprised and very grateful."

"Good. Hopefully someday, she can pay it forward to someone."

We walk back to his Jeep and he drives us to his condo a few blocks away. I'm curious to see what his place looks like.

When he opens the door and lets me in, I'm greeted by warm brown woods with accents of black and dark blues. It's kind of cozy-modern. It suits him.

"Can I get you a glass of wine? I have a nice white that'll pair well with our fish," he says, bringing my tote into the kitchen that's off to the left of the living room of the open floor-plan.

"That'd be great. Can I help you in there?" I follow him to the kitchen.

"Depends. Are you a good cook?" he asks, placing my bag on the black granite top of the island.

My laugh exposes my confession. "Not really. With my work and traveling so much, I don't cook very often so I'm not too good at it. My mom was an amazing cook. I didn't get that gene."

He laughs, taking our dinner ingredients out of my bag. "Let's let me do the cooking and you can observe," he says, opening the glass front black cabinet and getting out two white wine glasses. "Are you hungry? Want me to start dinner now?"

"Honestly, walking through that market always makes me hungry."

"Same." He chuckles, opening the bottle. He pours wine in both glasses then walks around the island and hands me a glass. Every time he's close to me, I feel his energy resound in my chest. "Thank you for being here," he says, looking down at me. The low timbre of his voice rumbles through my body. He clinks my glass and takes a sip of wine. "Mmm, that's good." Setting his glass on the island, he walks into the living room. "How about some music?"

"Sure."

He touches a few buttons on a black tower and smooth jazz music hums through the rooms. *He likes jazz?*

"This okay?"

"Yeah. I love this music."

He claps his hands together and rubs them briskly. "All right, let's get you fed. You can hang out in the living room, watch me cook, whatever you feel like."

"Okay." I grab my wine glass and wander through his living room. His wood and black-metal standing bookshelf is filled with books. Everything from success books, like *The 7 Habits of Highly Effective People* and *Rich Dad Poor Dad*, to cookbooks to espionage thrillers and crime action-adventure fiction books. "You read a lot," I say, looking back at him.

"When I have the time. I like to learn new things or read for pleasure."

On one shelf, there's a picture of him with a woman who shares his hair and eye color. "Is this your sister?"

"Yeah. That's me and Anastasia at a family wedding last year."

"She's beautiful."

"Tell me about it. I almost had to kick more than a few asses growing up. Guys would hit on her all the time. Thankfully, she ended up with a great guy."

"So, you like her husband?"

"I do. He's a great guy. Respects her, treats her right, takes care of her. They're good for each other."

Wine glass in hand, I walk back to the kitchen and sit on a black-leather-topped stool at the island to watch him cook. "Who's older?"

"She is," he says, turning on the heat under the pan with our fish in it. "By only two years. She's one of the strongest people I know, next to my dad." He sips his wine. "I think she felt like she had to sort of step in and try to be a mom to me. Our baking sessions were like her way of showing me love. And she's incredibly patient. I'd get so many things wrong and she'd never get upset with me. We'd either adjust or start over and she'd explain everything again." He pauses. "We were close growing up."

"Not anymore?"

"We are. I just don't get to see her as much. You know, we're older and have jobs and lives. They're trying for kids now." A broad smile spreads his scruffy cheeks. "Hopefully soon, I'll be an uncle."

"You like kids, huh?"

"Hell yeah. Though my love life hasn't led me down that path yet, I want a family someday. I want kids." He takes a sip of wine as he cuts the ends off the asparagus. "How about you? Do you want kids someday?"

An ache sits at the apex of my heart. "There was a time I thought I'd have kids," I say, running my finger across the base of my glass. "God seemed to have other plans though." After Dom died and I gave up on the idea of falling in love again or getting married, the idea of having kids got swept away with it all. I can't look up at him. I'll lose my shit. *Change the subject, fast.* "How're things going in there? Ready for help?"

"I think I've got things pretty well under control. I could use a little more wine."

I get up from my stool and pour more wine into both our glasses. "It smells delicious. I'm definitely hungry now."

"Good, it won't be much longer." He opens the glass-front

cabinets and takes out plates, then grabs silverware from a drawer. "Here, you can put the silverware on the table." He hands me the silverware and a fresh bottle of wine and nods toward the small table nestled into the corner of the room, where light streams in from two large windows. While I was wandering around his living room, he'd separated out the flowers into drinking glasses — such a bachelor — and put one on the island, one on the small dining table, and one on the coffee table in the living room. So cute.

Walking over to the table with me, he slides out my chair. "Here. I'll bring your plate over." Going back to the kitchen, he opens a door in the island and takes out napkins and a jar candle then grabs a long candle lighter and brings them over. Removing the lid from the candle, he lights the fresh wick.

"Smells nice," I say, taking a whiff of the vanilla aroma drifting into the air.

"I confess, I didn't pick it out." Embarrassment tints his chuckle. "When I told Anastasia I was making you dinner, she insisted I get a candle and told me that vanilla was a pretty safe scent." He pauses, glancing at me. "It's been a while since I've made dinner for anyone."

"Well, she gave you good guidance."

He comes back with our plated meals and sets mine in front of me then sits down with his. "Let's eat. I hope you like it."

I cut a piece of fish, hoping I like it because I don't want him to feel bad. "Mmm, it's good. Did you cook it in butter?"

"Nope, it's a naturally buttery-tasting fish. I used a very small spray of avocado oil in the pan just to help it not stick, but that's it. Mild, right? And kind of sweet?"

"Yes, it's really good."

"I'm glad you like it. This is a pretty simple meal. I think you could even make it." He delivers his words with encouragement and not judgement.

"I could probably give this one a try some time when I'm not traveling."

"You said earlier that your mom was an amazing cook. Did she pass?"

Instinctively, my hand goes to Dom's ring around my neck. I know this is typical get-to-know-you conversation that most people have on a date. It's been years since the accident. Sometimes it's still hard for me to talk about. I'm enjoying getting to know him and Destiny's right, it's probably time I let myself be open to at least the possibility of…something. *He let you in. Let him in.*

I take a breath. "She did." I push a weak smile onto my lips. "It was a car accident. About four years ago. She was the best." I take a sip of wine, hoping it will loosen the small lump in my throat. "I still miss her a lot. My dad's pretty overbearing and doused her dreams. He worked a lot and my mom and I kind of became friends as I grew up. She was always encouraging me to live life on my terms and never settle, never let anyone hold me back, and never take a handout. Earn my success." I breathe. "She was such a positive force in my life. I try to live by her words."

"It sounds like she had a great influence on you. I'm sorry you lost her." His words wrap around me in a comforting hug.

"I'm grateful for the time I had with her." Melancholy wrenches me as the truth of his mother leaving him and his family jumps to the forefront of my mind. "I'm sorry you didn't get that kind of chance with your mom."

Maybe he doesn't want to share more than he already has. This feels deep for a first official date. It also feels safe. Outside of Destiny, I don't talk about this stuff. He seems genuinely interested. I can't imagine what it must've been like for him being so young and having his mom up and leave. Will he share more with me?

10

Enzo

This isn't quite where I thought our night would go. I don't usually have conversations like this with women. Not that my conversations with other women are necessarily shallow, I guess I'm just not very invested in them. Candi consumes me, in every way. She's this beautiful web of independence and vulnerability, delicate yet strong, and sensual in a way that goes beyond sexy.

I don't talk about my mom with anyone other than Anastasia, and we don't talk about her much at all anymore. The uneasiness in Candi's eyes told me it was tough for her to share what she just did. I trust her.

"Yeah, it was weird at first. I was old enough to understand what was happening and also young enough that I was still pretty naïve. It was a confusing time. A part of me wanted to know why she left us and then another part of me was so angry that I didn't care why she left." I move my food around on my plate before spearing a piece of fish. "I had so many questions. Didn't she want our family anymore? Was she sick and didn't want us to watch her die? Did one of us do something wrong? Didn't she love us anymore?" Familiar knots twist inside my stomach.

She stops eating and focuses fully on me.

"Dad did his best to fill both roles and Anastasia tried to be a mom to me. But what eleven-year-old girl knows how to do that? I loved her for trying. After a while, it became normal. After years,

I stopped wondering." I put the bite of fish in my mouth, chew, and swallow. Candi waits patiently. "I found her. She didn't die. She went back to Greece. About five years ago, I hired someone to find her." My Adam's apple rubs up and down against my throat as I swallow.

"Did you see her?" she asks softly.

I hang my head, trying to force back the tears burning behind my eyes. "No. I — I've been waiting." I pause, tension clawing up my throat. "Waiting to be successful." I twist the ring on my finger, knowing I'm full of shit. "So I can show her who I've become without her." I shake my head as I draw in my lower lip. "It's been five years since I found her. And I don't know how much longer it'll be."

She sits still and listens, absorbing every word.

"And I know. I know that's filled with spite and anger." I look down into my hands, twisting my ring, ashamed at my admission. "And in some distorted way, it's like I want her to be proud of me. I want to shove it in her face that I didn't need her and I want her to be proud of me at the same time. It makes no sense." I pause, my heart floating like a cannonball. "I miss her," I confess, shaking my heavy head. "I shouldn't. She left us. But —" an awkward chuckle releases as I look up at her, a tear escapes down my face. "I do." I quickly wipe away the tear. "Shit, sorry about this."

She reaches over, placing her hand on top of mine. "Please don't apologize. I'm honored you're sharing this with me. And what you've felt and you're still feeling is all totally understandable."

I take a gulp of wine, trying to swallow the emotions that just vomited out of me. *What the fuck? I'm finally alone with her and I'm fucking crying. Get your shit together.*

"Not to point out the obvious," she says, her voice gentle. "But, you're already there. Look around you. You're pretty damn successful from what I can see." She pauses, the empathy in her eyes cradling me. "Maybe a little bit of fear is what's really stopping you." She shrugs. "And that's okay." Her brows come together as compassion coats her words and she squeezes my hand beneath hers.

Well, fuck if she doesn't see right through me and lay it on the table in front of me with loving grace.

"Heh," I force my lips into a half-assed smile that drops immediately. "I'm terrified."

She rubs the top of my hand with her thumb. "I would be too."

"Maybe I'll be ready someday." I clear my throat to keep myself from having an all-out fucking meltdown in front of this woman I'm dying to get to know more about. "We should eat up before our meals get cold."

A sweet smile lifts her face as she withdraws her hand. "So, tell me more about Anastasia. I always wanted a sibling. Destiny was the closest thing for me and I'm so grateful God brought us together."

As we finish our meal, I tell her some funny stories about me and Anastasia and what a great sister she is. The mood lightens. Although, I have to admit, she made me feel so comforted earlier.

"Do you want an after-dinner drink before we make dessert?" I ask.

"*Make* dessert?" Her eyes widen.

"Hell, yeah. I'm putting you to work." I chuckle. "Besides, nothing beats homemade."

"What're we having?" Curiosity sparkles in her big, brown eyes.

"I took a chance. Strawberry shortcake?"

"Oh that sounds enticing." The delicious groan that accompanies her words makes my dick stir.

"I already have the strawberries cut up and macerating so all we have to do is make the biscuits and whipped cream." I stand up and grab our plates. "Some whiskey while we bake?"

"Yes, please," she says, grabbing our wine glasses and napkins, following me into the kitchen.

I rinse off our dishes and load them into the dishwasher then put the frying pan and steamer into the sink and fill them with water.

"Need help?" she asks.

"Nah, I'm going to let these soak," I say, grabbing ice stones from the freezer. Setting the stones into two glass tumblers, I grab my whiskey decanter and fill the glasses with about two ounces each.

"What are those squares you put in there?"

"Trade secret." I give her a shrewd smile. "They make the whiskey cold without watering it down like regular ice cubes. That way, no matter how long it takes you to sip it, it still tastes the way it should by the end."

"Fancy. I like it."

"If it's too strong for you, let me know and I'll put ice in it." I bring over the glasses and hand one to her. "Thank you." I pause, grateful. "For earlier. I don't talk about that stuff."

"Any time," she says with a softness that matches her smile. "Cheers." She holds up her glass for me to clink.

"Cheers." I clink her glass and take a sip.

Placing the glass to her full lips, she sips hers and swallows. "Mmm, it's a little spicy with like, caramel?" Her eyes shift back and forth as she tries to confirm her guess.

"Yup, it can taste like caramel."

"I don't usually have it straight. It's nice."

"Okay, are you ready to make some biscuits?"

"Let's do it," she says, then looks down at her top.

"I've got you." I go to my bedroom and grab a T-shirt. "Here, put this on. I don't have aprons. This'll protect your top."

"Thank you." She puts on my T-shirt, lifting her long pink hair out of the collar.

She's still so sexy, even in my big shirt. "I like the way you look in my clothes."

Her cheeks lift in appreciation of my compliment. "What do I do?"

"We're going to start with the biscuits," I say, getting the ingredients and tools we need. "When they're baking, we'll make the whipped cream." I put everything on the island. "While I measure out the dry ingredients, you can cut the butter into chunks. You'll break them into smaller pieces with the pastry cutter when everything's in the bowl."

Putting the butter on the cutting board, she holds the stick delicately between her thumb and pointer finger and starts cutting it into chunks. Her fingers slip off. "Ooo, slippery little sucker."

"Don't be afraid to touch it. We might get messy. Hold it down with your hand. I don't want you cutting yourself."

She wraps her hand around the stick and keeps cutting. I have all the dry ingredients in the bowl by the time she's done.

"Now, scrape your butter into here and you can go at it a little more with this to break the chunks into even smaller pieces." I put the pastry tool next to the bowl.

She washes her hands and starts pushing the tool into the chunks of butter. "Like this? Am I doing it right?" While her usual badass self is sexy, in contrast, her baking insecurity is adorable.

"Yup, perfect. There's no right or wrong way. Keep going until the pieces are a little smaller."

Once it looks right, I add in the buttermilk and hand her a spatula. "Now stir it. It'll become more doughy soon."

She stirs and stirs.

I toss some flour onto the island top. "Scoop it out onto here."

She scoops out the crumbled mixture.

"Hold out your hands."

She does and I dust them with flour.

"Here's where it gets fun," I say.

"Oh yeah?" She chuckles like she has no faith in my statement.

"Work it with your hands until it's mixed together well, like a dough-ball. Then we're going to roll it out and fold it over, roll it out and fold it over. When we do that a couple times, the dough becomes nice and flakey." I take a sip of whiskey; it warms my throat on the way down.

When she has her dough-ball, I take some flour and coat the wooden rolling pin then hand it to her. "Try to make a rectangle if you can."

She takes the rolling pin from me, looks down at the ball of dough then back at me, and laughs. "What? It's round."

"You've got this. You're doing great. Give it a try."

She eyeballs the dough like she's giving it a warning then plops the rolling pin into its center. Fighting with it, she's got it lopsided and misshapen.

"I don't think this is right." She looks up at me. My eyes flicker to her twisted lips. I hold back from kissing her.

I can't help but laugh.

"Here, give me your hands." She does and I dust them with more flour, then dust mine and add a little more to the rolling pin. I tuck behind her, struggling to temper my desire. "Put your hands on the pin." She does and I put mine on top of hers, then I gently roll the dough. "It's more like a ballet than a wrestling match," I say, getting a whiff of her. She's sweet honey in warm milk.

"Hey," she retorts. "I told you I'm not good at this stuff." She lets out a pathetic little laugh.

I help her roll it out into a rectangular shape, focusing on the dough, baking, baking with Anastasia, baking biscuits, *not* my dick practically in between her ass cheeks. "Now, fold in each side and roll it out again." Still standing behind her, I place my hands on either side of her, watching her fold the dough. "Try it again. I've given you the basic shape."

She rolls the dough more slowly. "How's this?" she asks, turning her beautiful face to look up at me, our lips only inches apart, her breaths shallow.

Fuck me, I want to kiss her again, taste her. "Better." Remembering what happened after our kiss and not knowing why she ran away upset, I step back and lean my hip against the counter. "Do that one more time, then we're ready to cut 'em and bake 'em."

She rolls again while I wash my hands. I take the biscuit cutter and cut out the biscuits, placing them onto the parchment paper on the cookie sheet. She washes her hands as I put them into the oven.

Taking another sip of whiskey, she shakes her body. "Whoowh. That was stressful." I'd love to see that shake without my T-shirt on her.

I laugh at her cuteness. "What? It's supposed to be relaxing and fun."

"Okay, you relax and have fun while I tremble and drink." She laughs then swigs another sip.

I take out a clean bowl, hand mixer, and the ingredients for the whipped cream. "The hard part's over. Now we whip up some cream."

I pour heavy cream and vanilla into the bowl and add the powdered sugar. "If you've ever made at least a box cake, you can absolutely do this." I plug in the mixer and hand it to her.

"This one, I've got," she says confidently, placing the mixer in the bowl and flipping it on without checking the speed.

Poof! A cloud of powdered sugar explodes as the cream mixture whips out of the bowl, splattering her chest, face, hair, and arms, and the top of the island.

"Ahh!" she squeaks. Her eyes are squeezed shut, her lips are pursed together, and her hands are lifted and frozen still like a cop shouted, "Hands where I can see 'em."

I erupt into fold-over laughter.

"It's not funny." She laughs. "It's not funny. I don't understand. What happened?" she asks, opening one eye and then the other, turning to face me.

I temper my laughter. "You always have to check the speed before you turn it on. And you have to start slow." I drag out the last word, swiping my finger across her cheek to wipe off some splatter. I stick my finger in my mouth and watch her eyes follow the motion. Then I pull my finger out of my mouth and run my tongue along the edge of my lip, still watching her eyes follow my movement. "It tastes sweet," I say, cocking my head, then shrug and smile. I swipe more cream with my finger, placing it toward her lips, locking my gaze on her eyes. I give a small nod and she opens her lips, letting me in. Once my finger is in her mouth, she closes her lips around it, not breaking our gaze. As I pull it out, she sucks gently.

"It does."

Jesus, this woman.

"Let's clean you up and try again. Stay right there and let me grab a wash cloth." I go to the linen closet and get a wash cloth. When I come back, she's wiping the top of the island with the sponge from the sink.

I wet the cloth with warm water and gently wipe the cream off her face and arms. "The bathroom's down that hall in case you want to check my work and get your hair."

"Be right back." She grins and takes the cloth from me.

11

Candi

When I enter the bathroom, it's just as tidy as the rest of the house. He's definitely a minimalist. Matching soap dispenser and trash can, they look like they're from Bed Bath & Beyond. Hand towel that complements the brown, black, and gold shower curtain. I know it's wrong, but I have to peek inside his medicine chest. Is he honestly this neat or is he hiding his mess? I open it to find everything in order. No goo seeping out from his toothpaste, nothing weird or sketchy-looking.

I close it and look in the mirror. *Whew.* He's certainly perfected the art of seduction. The simple act of him putting his finger in my mouth made my nipples hard. I'm not used to a man being attentive on that side of things. Dom's idea of foreplay was touching my ass. One squeeze of my ass-cheek and he was ready to go. Then I did all the work. I didn't mind though. I loved him and that's how we worked. Enzo's energy is magnetic and powerfully sensual. *As much as he turns me on, am I ready for this?*

Seeing whipped cream splattered all over his T-shirt, I re-wet the cloth and wipe the spots then wet it again and wrap it around the bits that flew into my hair. One last look in the mirror. *There's no labels here. You're enjoying the company of a man. Who knows where it'll go? Maybe nowhere. And maybe, he'll help you let go of Dom.* I look at his ring on my chain.

I go back out to the kitchen and he's cleaned things up a little.

I peek at the bowl of fluffy whipped cream.

"I went ahead and whipped it up. The biscuits are almost done," he says, glancing at the oven.

"It's probably safer that you did." We both chuckle because it's true.

The timer dings and he gets mitts from a drawer then pulls out the cookie sheet, setting it on top of the stove. I sit at the island and sip my whiskey, watching him. He takes a bowl of strawberries out of the fridge, removes the plastic wrap, and stirs them. The sugary scent fills my nose.

"Can I have one?"

"Sure." He grabs a spoon, scoops a few strawberries into it, and leans across the island.

I open my mouth and he puts the spoon in, keeping his eyes on mine. The instant the sweet fruit hits my tongue, I close my eyes. "Mmm, so good." When I open my eyes, he's smiling. "Can we make them now?"

"Not yet. The biscuits need to cool." He grabs his whiskey glass. "Want more?"

"Just a little."

He takes my glass and goes to his cart. "I don't have the best view, but you can see some of the city lights from my terrace. Want to check it out while the biscuits cool?"

"Okay."

He hands me my glass and we go out to his terrace.

I take a sip of my whiskey and set it on the glass top of the small iron table of the bistro set. He has a decent view. With his condo being on a hill, I can see some of downtown L.A. and the twinkling lights of taller buildings. Walking to the railing, I stretch my arms across it and look up at the sky. Inhaling, my body warms from the whiskey.

His chest pressed lightly against my back, he grazes his hands past my waist and places them on the railing. "This city has its own energy, doesn't it?" he asks, his breath heating my ear.

"It does."

We stand quietly. Breathing. Listening to each other's breaths.

He kisses the top of my head and gets our drinks, handing me my glass. We take sips and return our attention to the view, resting our arms on the railing.

"I'm enjoying this," he says quietly, that low huskiness making the hairs on the back of my neck stand up. "I haven't wanted to spend time like this with anyone in a long time." He pauses, turning his body toward me. "What is it that you want right now, Candi?"

Our energies weave together, need baiting us. Respect growing deeper. Something unfamiliar, powerful, is creeping in.

"Right now? In this moment?" *As my heart rate is kicking up?* I can't stop my eyes from sweeping to his lips. A knot of desire twists inside me.

"Yeah." His gaze is tender, curious, and totally lacking in anything sexual.

All I can think is that I want him to kiss me. God, I loved the way he kissed me. *Not ready.*

I take a larger gulp of my whiskey. "Strawberry shortcake." I breathe, a little too loudly. "I want strawberry shortcake."

He chuckles. "Then let's go make 'em."

We grab our glasses and go back to the kitchen. He takes out plates and forks, putting them on the island. Then he grabs a spatula and places a biscuit on each plate.

"Careful, they might still be hot," he says, opening his biscuit. Steam swirls out of it and dissipates into the air.

I open mine. "The strawberries will cool it."

Before taking any, he pushes the bowl of strawberries toward me. "Load it up."

I dump two huge spoonfuls onto my biscuit and top them with the whipped cream. Then I push the bowl of strawberries back to him.

"It looks naked." He spoons two strawberries on top of my whipped cream then builds his shortcake. "Sofa?"

I nod and grab my drink. He grabs his and leads the way.

Nestling into the dark, slate-blue cushions, I tuck my legs under me and take my first bite.

"Oh, my God. This is unreal." I shovel another bite into my mouth. "Seriously so good. I mean, I've had strawberry shortcake before, in many different countries mind you, but this is next level."

"Well, you're very accomplished. It's kind of intimidating. I had to do something to try to impress you." His grin spreads across his face with pride.

"Wait, I'm intimidating?" Is that good or bad?

"A sexy kind of intimidating." He winks.

I'm thinking that's good? Doesn't really matter. I am who I am and I'm proud of what I've accomplished. I take a sip of whiskey and shove another bite into my mouth.

"Consider me impressed. This is amazing." I finish mine in a few more bites.

When he's done with his, he takes our plates into the kitchen then returns.

Standing close to me, he holds out his hand. "Dance with me?" His deep timbre travels my spine.

"You like dancing, huh?"

"It's the best way I know to get you in my arms." A coy grin sits on his lips.

I take a breath. I want to be in his arms again, curled between his wide shoulders. *What am I so afraid of?* The whiskey moves me. Putting my hand in his, I rise from the sofa.

He snakes his arm around my waist, pulling me gently to him. Heat radiates between us. Taking my hand in his, he sways our bodies to the lazy music saturating the air around us. As we move, he pulls our clasped hands close to my face and wraps one of my curls around his finger.

Then he draws back his face and lets out a sexy laugh, frowning at my lips. "You're kind of a mess with that whipped cream," he says, releasing my hand and running his thumb from the corner of my lip toward the center. Moving his gaze from my lips to my eyes, he licks the small trace of cream off his thumb, drawing my attention.

I inhale a shallow breath, my heart thumping in my ears.

Weaving his hand into my hair, he brushes his thumb across my cheek. "You got very upset when we kissed," he says softly. "And I don't want to upset you again —"

"No." I cut him off. My chest tightens. "You didn't upset me. I'm sorry you thought that all this time." Tighter. "I — it's —" I exhale. "It's just been a long time since I —"

"It's okay." He ceases my agony, cupping my face in his hands and shaking his head gently. "It's okay." Pressing his lips into my forehead, he holds me.

The music echoes in my head. I exhale against his chest. *Well, if this was going to go anywhere, I think I just fucked it up.* Silent loneliness bites at the hollow in my chest. My ghost exiled to loveless nights.

He releases me. "I'd better take you home." He pauses, tucking my hair behind my ear, searching my eyes.

Dread sinks me. *What's wrong with me?*

"I'm a little buzzed, will your feet be all right if we walk?"

"So am I. Yeah, I think so."

"I can always throw you over my shoulder if they start hurting." He smiles, easing the tension that's filled the room.

He holds my hand on the elevator ride down and on our walk home.

"It's crazy that we live so close to each other and never met," he says.

"I know, right? But I guess with both of us traveling for work, our paths just never crossed." A sudden feeling of desperation grasps me in its fist. I don't want this to be over.

"Or, we weren't meant to meet until now." He pulls our clasped hands up to his mouth and kisses the top of mine, giving me a small glimmer of hope.

When we get to my condo, I unlock the door and step inside, unsure of what to say.

"Thank you again for tonight. I'm glad you came." He pauses, giving me that sexy smile. "I had a really good time."

"So did I." I look down at his T-shirt. "I can wash this if you'd like." *Is he going to take his shirt and run?*

"If that means I get to see you again, then yes."

"I'd like that. I'm away next week for work. How about when I get back?"

"Definitely." He nods. "Good night."

"Night." I close the door and lock it.

He wants to see me again. Maybe I didn't screw things up.

What the fuck is wrong with me? I wanted him to kiss me. I did. My whole body did. I'm not cheating on Dom. Dom isn't fucking here. He's not here!

He's not here.

12

Enzo

What happened to her? I know she's attracted to me. There's fire between us. I see it in her eyes. I feel it when we're close. It's undeniable. She's whiskey running through my veins. Warm, soothing, intoxicating – erotic.

And then, I blink my eyes, and a wall slices between us. Some asshole must've really hurt her. Nicco said she's very selective when it comes to men. I'll show her I'm not another asshole.

I get to see her next week and I want to do something she'll find romantic. While I'm decent in the romance department, I think I need my sister on this one. I want to do it right. I grab my phone and call her.

"Hey, little brother. How'd the date go? Did you get the candle?"

I chuckle. "Yes, I got the candle. She liked it. It was good and…different."

"Different? What do you mean different?"

I pour whiskey into my glass. "Well, it wasn't like any kind of date I've been on before. It started out great. We went to the market, got food for dinner, some flowers. She opened up to me a little about her mom dying and, for some reason, I started talking more about Mom and ended up getting emotional."

"You did?" Her voice raises.

"Not sobbing or anything, but a tear got loose. I couldn't stop it. Trust me, I tried. She made me feel totally okay about it. With her mom dying and our mom leaving, it's like this weird thing that connects us. I don't know how to explain it. She's not like other women I've dated. The chemistry between us is unreal," I say, taking a swig of whiskey as our hot moments flash through my head.

"This all sounds encouraging so far. Well, maybe not the crying part. What else happened?"

"We were dancing and I wanted to kiss her, but remember I told you how she freaked out that time and ran off?" I pace between the living room and kitchen.

"Yeah."

"So, I told her I didn't want to upset her again and she said that I didn't upset her before. She said it's been a while for her. As soon as she said it, I felt it. I felt her shut down again. Wall up." I slice my hand through the air. "I think some dude hurt her, bad."

"Ugh. That's tough."

"I think I'm going to have to take things slow with her. And that works for me. There's something about this woman." I rake my hand through my hair. "I want to see her again."

"That's good. I see why you used the word different. Definitely a different kind of first date. But, hey, it sounds like you found some common ground, you had a nice night, you were able to connect emotionally. And, if you wanted to kiss her, that's a good sign." She hesitates. "Do you think she wanted you to kiss her?"

"Honestly, I don't know. I mean, that night, *she* pulled me in for the kiss. Though she was also a little tipsy. But, throughout the night tonight, I don't know, there was definitely attraction."

"Are you seeing each other again?"

I sit on the sofa and lean back. "Yeah, that's part of the reason I'm calling you. I want to do something romantic with her. Got any ideas for me?"

"That's great." The excitement in her voice makes me smile. "For a minute I thought you were going to say that was it. You don't do well at the first sign of trouble."

Ouch. She's not wrong. And she says it with compassion rather than judgement. She once told me she worried that my inability to stay with a woman might be because I have abandonment issues due to Mom. I have no idea whether she's right or wrong, but it did make me think about it. I'm not ready to give up with Candi. Not nearly.

"I know. Not this time. I'm telling you, there's something about her." I pause, sipping my whiskey. "So, whatcha got for me?"

"Something where you'll get a chance to talk and keep getting to know each other." She pauses. "Hey, I know. How about a picnic dinner and then the swan pedal boats at Echo Park? I'd think that was romantic."

"Hmh. Okay, I like the sound of that. Thanks. Hey, I gotta go. I want to wash the dishes before I go to bed."

"Someone taught you well," she quips. She never used to let me go to bed without helping her and Dad clean up the kitchen after dinner.

"Night. Love you." I hang up the phone and clean up the kitchen before going to bed.

My week is quiet for modeling so I take a few bartending shifts. Candi's been very busy with her shoot. We text a few times and I'm eager to set up our date.

Me: When do you want to get together?

Candi: I'll be useless by the time I get home on Friday. How about Saturday?

Me: That works. Pick you up at 6:00?

Candi: Okay. What are we doing? What should I wear?

Me: You okay with a surprise? Dress casual. Sneakers casual.

Figured I'd better specify since her last casual outfit was pretty dressed up...and sexy as hell.

Candi: I love surprises. :) Got it, casual.

Me: Have a safe trip back.

Around noon, my phone rings.

"Hey, how are you?" I ask.

"Enzo, I'm sorry. I think I caught a cold on the plane." She sniffs. "I was hoping to feel better by today because I don't want to cancel. But I feel like crap and I don't want to risk getting you sick. I'm so sorry," she says, then has a coughing fit.

She sounds awful.

Damn.

Hmm.

"It's okay. I understand. We'll reschedule when you're feeling better. Is there anything you need?"

"I don't think so," she mumbles.

"All right. Go get some rest."

"Okay. Bye." Her congested, nasally voice is adorably pathetic.

Nope. No way. I waited all week. She's sick? I'm going to go take care of her. I run down to the market and get ingredients for chicken soup. I also pick up crackers, vitamin C, tissues, peppermint tea, honey, and a small bunch of flowers.

I make the soup, pack up everything, and walk to her condo. When I arrive, I knock on the door. It's quiet. *Shit, she might be asleep.* I knock again. Then I see the light change behind her peephole.

"Enzo. What're you doing here?" Her alarmed voice comes from behind the door.

"I'm here to take care of you."

"You can't see me like this, I'm a mess." Her stuffy nose makes her m's sound like b's.

"I don't care." I wait. "I brought homemade chicken soup." I hold the bag up to the peephole, knowing she's looking at me. "You may as well let me in because I'm not leaving."

She opens the door with the saddest pout on her face and redness around her nostrils and under her nose.

She's right, she's a mess. She has no makeup on, her hair's in a wild pile on top of her head with pieces falling around her face, and she's wearing a cropped, light tan tank top, black cotton shorts, and thick fuzzy socks that go about halfway up her shins. She's the most beautiful thing I've ever seen.

Beautiful *and* the sexiest sick person I've ever seen. Her breasts are fucking magnificent. And her hard nipples poking through the thin fabric of her tank make it tough to keep my dick from ripping a hole in my jeans. *Simmer down, you're here to take care of her.*

"I don't want to get you sick." She leans her head and hand on the door.

"I have a strong immune system." I smile, ready to expose myself to her germs. "And if I do get sick, it'll be worth it."

"You're crazy," she says, opening the door to let me in.

I've only gotten to peek into her condo through the door a couple times. Stepping in, it doesn't feel quite like her. In fact, it almost feels the opposite. It's neutral on top of neutral. Very welcoming though, that part feels like her.

"Kitchen?"

She closes the door behind me and locks it. "This way," she says, grabbing an oversized, tan-and-brown plaid, flannel shirt off the sofa and putting it on over her tank top.

She rounds a wall into a vacant-looking kitchen. The only things on her countertop are a coffee maker and paper towel holder. This fits with the fact that she doesn't cook much and it makes me chuckle to myself.

"The soup should be pretty warm still. But I can heat it up if you want." I start unpacking the bags.

"No, I don't like things too hot. Are you having some with me?"

"So I can stay?" I ask, hoping it was an invitation.

She looks at me with a weak smile and moves her head lethargically up and down. From what I've learned so far, it's been a long time since anyone took care of her.

"Come on." I pick her up in my arms and she drapes her arms around my neck, resting her head on my shoulder. Carrying her to a very comfortable-looking cream-colored sofa that's loaded with puffy pillows, I set her down where it looks like she was under a blanket when I arrived.

She curls up her legs and I cover her with the heavy, fluffy blanket. Going back to the kitchen I hunt around for the things I need. I prepare our bowls of soup and bring them out, then go back for the crackers, water bottles, and flowers.

"I found this large glass. I hope it's okay I put these flowers in it."

She pushes a smile to her lips. "Mhm. They're beautiful. Thank you."

"I hope you like it." I hand a bowl to her.

She adjusts herself so she's sitting upright and takes the bowl from me. "It smells good," she says then swallows a spoonful. "Mmm. Perfect temperature too."

"Eat up. It'll help you feel better." I glance at the large TV hanging on the wall above an unlit fireplace. "What're we watching?"

"*Maid in Manhattan*. I love J.Lo."

"Want the fireplace on?"

"Sure."

I walk over to the fireplace and turn it on, eyeing a picture of a little girl with long, dark pigtails cuddled into a woman who shares her features. It's next to an old oil lamp. She has several around the living room. "Is this you?" I ask, holding up the picture.

"Yeah, that's me and my mom when I was around five years old."

"Cute. I like these lamps you have around," I say, putting the picture back down and returning to sit next to her.

"Thanks. They were hers. I got them when she passed. She loved these old lamps. She collected them. When I was little and I was allowed to stay up later on Saturday nights, she'd pick one and tell me it's story. Of course, I thought she actually knew the story behind each one. When I got older, she told me they were all made up." She giggles. "But I believed them. There were always so many elaborate details about who owned them and their journey in life and how the lamp played a role." She shakes her head with a sweet, reminiscent smile on her face. "She was a great storyteller." She pauses. "I went through a period of photographing some. I love the intricate ones. They're so pretty."

"They're really cool." I pause, looking around. "I like your place. It's not what I expected."

"No? What did you expect?" she asks, putting a spoonful of soup in her mouth.

"I don't know exactly. You're this bold, bright woman with a big, sassy personality. I guess I thought it would reflect that more. This is…subdued."

She rustles a chuckle. "Yeah. I'm all those things. With my on-on-on job and my traveling and adventures, when I come home, I want calm, cozy, serene. It's my haven to unwind."

"It's definitely that. I like it."

We watch the rest of the movie while we finish our soup.

"I brought some peppermint tea and honey. Can I make you some?"

"Oh I'd like that."

"You stay put."

I bring our bowls to the kitchen, rinse them, and put them into the dishwasher. Then I put the remaining soup into the fridge, heat up some water, and go back to get the crackers. When the water's done, I put in a teabag and bring it out to her with the honey and a teaspoon.

"I wasn't sure how much honey you wanted." I set the honey on the coffee table. "Another movie?"

"Yup." She pushes the blanket off her. "You wanna pick?" she asks going over to a cabinet next to the fireplace.

"Nope. Today is all about you and getting you better. You pick."

"I have mostly girly movies."

"One thing about growing up with your sister trying to be

your mother, you get used to a lot of girly things." I chuckle at the admission.

She ejects the disc, pulls out a leather case, puts away the first disc, and picks out another. The movie starts, *Runaway Bride*, a favorite of my sister.

Before getting back into her nest, she takes off her flannel shirt and squeezes honey into her tea. Then she tucks her legs up and secures the blanket around her chest.

"Comfortable?"

"Mhm." She sips her tea. "Enzo?"

"Yeah?"

"Thank you for this. For coming here and taking care of me." She inhales.

Something in the way she's looking at me and the tone of her voice tells me there's a "but" coming.

"There's something I feel like I should tell you." Unmistakable sorrow hovers in her eyes. Something that holds the reigns tight, imprisoning her.

Here we go. "Okay."

She scratches above her eyebrow. Her energy nervous, her posture rigid. "I know you must be wondering why I get all… freaked out when we're close."

"I mean, I'm curious. Figured some guy crushed your heart and you're hesitant. I get it. I'm pissed someone would hurt you so badly, but I get you being cautious."

She tilts her head as a weak smile barely lifts the corners of her lips. Melancholy encloses her. Pulling her lips in, she releases them and exhales. "Not quite." Her pause pained. "I dated a guy, for a long time. He was great. We had the best relationship." She exhales again. "He was my soul mate." Reaching for the ring on her chain, she slides it back and forth with her finger. Then she audibly inhales and blows it slowly out. "He died in a car accident several years ago."

My fucking heart drops to the pit of my stomach as my skin

pricks with white-hot needles. She closes and opens her eyes, her agony screaming through the air.

She inhales twice and exhales. Tears well in her eyes. When she looks down, one tear drops into her lap. "I found out after he died that he was on his way to buy me an engagement ring." She looks back up at me, shaking her head.

Holy fuck. Overwhelming torment pummels me. My chest collapses, squeezing the air from my lungs, crushing my heart with violent rampage. I'm covered in pins and needles. Fierce need wants to reach out and steal her sorrow. Banish it. Burn it.

"It rocked my world, losing him. And…and I…I haven't dated anyone since him and, I just…I don't know." The effort of every forced, anguish-cloaked word twists my heart. "This is going to sound crazy, but I feel like I'm cheating, somehow, on him. Which, I know I'm not. I'm sorry. You must think I'm nuts." She half-chuckles then sniffs.

I grab a tissue from her box on the coffee table and hand it to her.

"Thank you." She blows her nose. "I like you, a lot actually," she says, avoiding my eyes, looking down at the tissue then back at me. "I haven't felt like this about anyone in a long time." She pauses, looking up at the ceiling and shaking her head. "I didn't think I'd ever have feelings for another man after Dom. But, I don't…I don't know how to do this. And you're so great and I don't want to fuck this up and I don't want to hurt you." She sniffs, her words now coming out fast and chaotic. "I think, maybe, we should just save each other a lot of wasted time and emotional turmoil and not see each other anymore."

"No." I deadpan. She's out of her mind if she thinks I'm letting her go because of this. First sign of trouble? I'm not running. Not this time. Not from this woman.

"No?" She looks at me blankly.

"No." I move closer to her, put her mug on the coffee table, lean in, and kiss her forehead. "Candi, every person has a past, some more painful than others. A heart that doesn't know pain, doesn't know love. Your pain is deep. So, I know your love is deeper. You have such a huge capacity to love. I can feel it. And I'd like a chance to earn even the smallest piece of your heart." I pause, staring into her beautiful eyes. "I like you too much to let you go."

Her eyes dart back and forth between mine. After her stuffy-headed, rambling speech about why we shouldn't see each other, I don't think she expected my response.

"Oh."

I kiss her forehead again. "Get comfortable and give me your fuzzy feet."

She lies back, pulling the blanket up around her neck and slides her feet out toward me. I lift them and scoot closer to her, putting her feet on my thighs.

"Are your feet ticklish?"

"If you tickle-torture me they are." Her smile peeks out above the blanket.

"I'm going to rub some acupressure points on your feet that should help with your cold. Tell me if it's too hard or you don't like it."

"I will."

"Relax for me."

She rests her head back and closes her eyes. After a few minutes, I feel her release the tension in her feet and legs.

We watch the movie quietly as I rub her feet. The next time I look over at her, she's asleep. I should leave, but I don't have a way to lock her door and I'm not leaving her here alone with the door unlocked.

I watch her sleep. Watch her beautiful face. Watch the rise and fall of her chest. Then I scooch down and rest my head back to finish watching *Runaway Bride* with her feet in my lap.

13

Candi

The morning sun filters in through the windows, spilling warm, white light into the living room. It takes me a few seconds to orient myself. I rarely sleep on the sofa and my head's still stuffy from my cold. I look toward my feet, Enzo's lying on the chaise part of the sofa looking very uncomfortable. Arms folded at his chest, feet crossed, and head awkwardly propped on a sofa pillow. *He's still here.*

I can't believe he came to take care of me. I can't believe he still wants to see me after I told him about Dom. Says a lot about him that he's willing to take a chance with some chick who's still fucked up about her boyfriend dying years ago.

Maybe opening myself up isn't about finding the kind of love I had with Dom. It never occurred to me how much pressure I was putting on myself around that. Maybe opening myself up is about finding a companion, someone I can care about who cares about me. It doesn't have to be love.

Even though I'm still stuffy, I feel a lot better. I roll off my blanket, put on my flannel shirt, and go to the bathroom. Catching myself in the mirror, I'm a wreck. I don't have time to shower before he wakes up. So, I splash my face with water, get sleepy-goo out of my eyes, try to tidy my bun on my head, and quickly brush my teeth.

When I go into the kitchen to make coffee, there's very little evidence that he was there. No dishes in the sink, no mess on the counters. After seeing his place, this is just as I'd expect. I don't know if he's a coffee drinker, but I brew enough for both of us then check my phone for emails. Thank God I don't have a shoot today.

It's not long before the aromatic coffee penetrates the air. I get two ivory mugs out of the cabinet and Enzo rounds the corner into the kitchen, hair slightly disheveled.

"Good morning," he mumbles, then takes me in his arms and kisses the top of my head like it's the most natural thing. "How are you feeling?" he asks, releasing me.

"Actually, I feel a lot better. Are you some kind of shamanic healer?" I jest.

He chuckles, rubbing his neck. "No. I work out a lot and I like learning about the body and muscles and recovery. I got a book about acupuncture once. It's pretty fascinating." He moves his hand to his lower back and stretches to one side then the other. The features of his face contort with the movement.

My face squinches at his discomfort. "Not the best night's sleep?"

"Hah. No. It's okay though. I didn't have a way to lock your door if I left, so I stayed. Hope that's all right."

Hmh, thoughtful, protective. "Yeah, absolutely. I wish I knew how to do some of your voodoo magic on you."

He laughs. "I'll be okay. Hot shower, some stretching, I'll be fine. Coffee smells good."

"I made enough for both of us."

He pours coffee into our mugs. Quietly, we each scoop in sugar and pour in creamer. I walk over to my dinette and he follows me like it's our daily routine.

"I'm glad you're feeling better," he says, sitting at the table. "Do you get to rest today?"

I sit next to him. "I do. And I'm looking forward to eating more of the soup you made me," I say, taking a sip of coffee. "I have a shoot downtown tomorrow, so I'm going to take a steamy shower and be lazy so I can feel a hundred percent by the morning."

"That sounds like the perfect thing to do. If you need anything, let me know and I'll bring it to you."

I smile and shake my head slightly. "You don't have to do that."

"I know I don't have to. I want to. I know how independent and capable you are, and I love that about you. I also know you're not used to being taken care of. But you're going to have to get used to that with me because I plan on taking care of you, even when you're not sick." He sips his coffee.

Well, that was very matter-of-fact. And I kind of like it. But I have no idea what to say to that.

A silly chuckle releases from me. "Okay."

"Listen, I'm out of town tomorrow through Wednesday for a shoot. What're you doing Thursday night? Can we reschedule for then?"

"Yeah, I'll be in town. I'd like that." Excitement rises in my chest.

"Good." He takes a gulp of coffee. "I'm gonna get going. I want to hit the gym and I have a few things to do before I pack. Got an early flight tomorrow."

"Okay." I walk him to the door where he puts on his shoes.

When he stands back up, he faces me, ticking up my pulse.

"Thank you again for coming over and taking care of me."

"Anytime," he says quietly, holding my face in his hands, weaving his fingers into the loose hair at the nape of my neck. Staring down at me with his beautiful green eyes, his inhale is audible. After his exhale, a low growl rumbles deep in his chest. "You're tough to leave," he says in a hoarse whisper, holding my gaze and shaking his head slowly from left to right with a quick lick of his lips. He presses his fingers lightly into the back of my head and exhales again.

My pulse quickens. *God, I want to kiss him again.*

He leans in, presses his lips to my forehead, then pulls back. "Get some rest."

My phone rings in the pocket of my flannel shirt, breaking the moment.

I pull it out to see who it is.

"It's Destiny."

He smiles. "Put in a good word for me. I know how important it is to impress the best friend. At least that's what my sister tells me. And, for the record, you're the most beautiful sick person I've ever seen." He winks, kisses my forehead again, and leaves.

I close and lock the door then answer the phone.

"Hey. Feeling any better today?"

"Um, I am." I pause, dumbstruck. "And that's mostly due to Enzo."

"Enzo? I thought you canceled because you're sick."

"I did. And he showed up at my door with homemade chicken soup, crackers, tea, honey, flowers," I say, punctuating each word as I say it. "I…I was blown away." I put my hand on my forehead.

"Oh really," she says, with a playful, accusatory tone.

I grab my coffee from my dinette. "I know. I tried to tell him to go away because I didn't want to get him sick, plus I looked like a train wreck, but he said he wasn't leaving." I walk over to the sofa and curl up in my fuzzy blanket.

"Can, that's so sweet." Her voice singsongs.

"It was." I pause, struck with a tinge of repentance. "Of course, I think my cold made me delirious and I ended up telling him about Dom."

"You…you did?"

I knew she'd be a little surprised. Hell, I was surprised.

"How…did that go?" Her words come out in hesitant concern. "Are you okay?"

"It didn't go how I thought it would. You know I haven't been ready for anyone. I'm lucky, I had my true love. And then he died. And some days I'm still so messed up about it. So, I told him I didn't think we should see each other again."

"Oh, Can." Her compassion always comforts me. If she was sitting next to me, one hand would be on her heart and the other reaching out to touch and console me.

"But he wouldn't accept that. He basically said we all have our crap and he's too into me to let me go. He said the most beautiful things to me."

"Aw. That's great. So, you'll see each other again?" Hopefulness raises her voice.

"Yeah, next week." I pause, sipping my coffee. "It's crazy, Des. I don't know what happens to me when I'm with him. He's like that dizzy feeling when you get up too fast and have to hold onto something so you don't fall over. He's this intriguing combination of witty and sensitive and hot…as…fuck." We both burst into laughter.

"Well, I'm very happy to hear this. Hey, Nicco's taking me to brunch. Want to join us?"

"No, thanks. I'm gonna lay low and keep resting. I have a shoot tomorrow and I want to make sure I'm better."

"Okay. Keep feeling better and let me know if you need anything. And I want updates. Love you."

"I will." I chuckle. "Love you. Bye."

By morning, I'm almost feeling back to a hundred percent. When we break for a fast lunch at my shoot, I check my phone.

Enzo: How are you feeling today?

The text came in twelve minutes ago. He might be busy now, but I text back.

Me: So much better, thanks. How was your flight?

I see the three dots. He's there.

Enzo: I'm glad to hear it. Good flight. Uneventful.

Me: In my delirium, I forgot to ask where your shoot is.

Enzo: We're in Rock Canyon Park in Provo, Utah. It's pretty. I think you'd like it. Wish you were here with me.

He does? That's sweet.

Me: Gotta get back to work. Send me pictures.

When I get home and check my phone, he's sent me some breathtaking pictures. I have meetings the next few days and projects to get back to people so time flies by. We text back and forth a little while he's away. It's nice to have someone thinking about me.

By Thursday, I'm excited to see him. Sneakers casual, hmm. I put on black skinny jeans and my sleeveless light gray top that plunges in the front and has ruching from under the bust down to the waist. I turn in the mirror and nod. "Sneakers casual."

At five fifty-nine, there's a knock on my door. *Does he get here early and wait until one minute before his expected arrival time before he knocks?*

Sneakers on, I open the door.

Damn, he looks hot.

He chuckles, blowing air through his nose. "How do you manage to make casual look stunning?"

I look down, holding back my hair. "Too dressy?" I ask, looking back up at him.

Shaking his head, he chuckles again. "Nope. You're perfect." He leans in and kisses my forehead. "Ready?"

"Yup." I close and lock my door. "Do I get to know where we're going yet?"

"No. It's a surprise."

As he drives, we catch each other up on our last couple of days.

"We're here," he says, pulling into a parking spot at Echo Park Lake.

"I love this place. I haven't been here in years."

"Are you hungry?"

"I am."

"Good. I have dinner for us." He gets out and grabs a large picnic basket and a plaid yellow, black, red, and white blanket from the back seat. Then he comes around to me. "Will you take this?" he asks, handing me the blanket.

I tuck it under my arm and he takes my other hand in his then starts walking. "Let's find a spot under some shade. You okay with a picnic dinner?"

"Absolutely. I can honestly say I've never had a picnic dinner."

We find a grassy spot under a cluster of trees and I lay out the blanket. He sets the basket on a corner, opens the lid, and starts pulling out all these little containers. They're filled with rolled up meats and cheeses, fruit, crackers, cut up pieces of bread, hummus, and one looks like it has chocolate sauce in it. It's like a charcuterie on-the-go. Then he takes out a bottle of white wine, two stemless wine glasses, and a battery-operated candle. This is seriously romantic and I'm in awe.

"I brought a variety because I wasn't sure what you'd like, so I hope there's something here you want."

"Are you kidding? I want to eat all of it." He continues to surprise me with his thoughtfulness.

"Well dig in," he says, tapping on his phone. Jazz music swirls into the air.

I help him take the lids off the containers then take a cracker and piece of cheese. He pours wine into the glasses and hands me one.

"Is there a story behind your butterfly tattoo?" he asks with a nod to my wrist.

I turn my forearm and look down at the small butterfly, brightly colored with shades of pink, purple, and orange, on the inside of my left wrist. "I got it because of my mom. Ever since I can remember, she told me I could be anything I wanted. She told me how a caterpillar becomes a butterfly. She made me believe that miracles can happen just like how a fuzzy little bug can turn into a magnificent creature that can spread its wings and fly. That fascinated me. Hence, my purple butterfly purse that I destroyed with the Gucci logo." I break into a laugh that he joins.

"Any other tattoos?"

"No, just this one. My dad was so pissed at me when he saw it."

"From the little you've told me, sounds like he was kind of tough." He tosses a few grapes into his mouth.

"He didn't approve of me."

"Too rebellious?" His smile teases.

My mind briefly jumps back to a conversation with Mom when I was around ten years old.

"Mommy, why does Daddy hate me so much?"

She put her arm around me, tucking me into her side. "Oh, my precious girl, Daddy doesn't hate you." She lifted my face to hers. "Your daddy is a traditional man. He wanted a son. To follow in his footsteps. To carry on the family name. But it doesn't mean he doesn't love you. He does. In his own way, he does." She held me so tightly to her chest and dropped her head to mine.

I swallow, coming back. "No. Although I was pretty rebellious, but I never got into any real trouble. No, I just couldn't be what he wanted."

Confusion shakes his head and he shrugs his shoulders. "But, you're incredibly successful in your career, you're independent, you're smart, you're kind, you're beautiful." Holding out his hand, he extends a finger for each characteristic he names. "What more could a parent possibly want of their child?"

I tilt my head and pull in my lips. "I'm not a boy."

His features sag. "Oh."

I raise my eyebrows. "There's no changing that. No way I could ever be what he wanted. They tried for another child, but it never happened. So, I've always been this big disappointment for him."

"Whoo." A puff of air shoots through his lips. "I'm so sorry, Candi." His tone is tender. "That's a lot to carry through life."

I lift my shoulders. "It kind of is what it is. I try not to let it get to me. I mean, there's literally nothing I can do about it."

"I take it you don't see each other much."

"Not really. Not after my mom died. Going to see her was the only reason I'd see him." I pause, Mom dropping into my thoughts. "It's weird. I know my mom's gone, but I want to show her that I did it. I followed my dreams. And, I know it shouldn't even matter, but, there's a part of me that wants my dad to be proud of me."

He looks me square in the eyes. "I don't think that's weird at all. And I have to believe that, on some level, he is."

"Maybe." I grab a rolled-up piece of ham and a square of cheese. "Any entertaining stories behind your tattoos?" I recall our night in the ocean, seeing the birds that begin below the waistband of his underwear at his right V-line and travel around his torso, about halfway up the right side of his back.

"I wish I did. I saw the birds on some guy and thought they looked cool. I was young and dumb." He dips a cube of bread into the hummus and pops it in his mouth. "Oh, I do have this one that means something to me." He pushes the sleeve of his black T-shirt over his sculpted left bicep. The tattoo reads, "Faith and Desire." "My dad had a saying. Let faith hold you, let desire move you. I got it after he passed."

Goose bumps spring out on my arms. "I like that."

"I wish he could've met you. He'd have liked you." The earnestness of his words enmeshes me, drawing me deeper to him.

We finish most of the food he'd brought, including the strawberries dipped in chocolate. Then we bring the basket back to his Jeep and he takes the blanket from me, tucking it under his arm. Him holding my hand, we walk to the booth to rent a swan pedal boat.

He places the folded blanket on my seat of our lit-up swan and we sit and pedal out into the lake.

"Thank you for making sure I wore sneakers. Some of my typical shoes would *not* have done well here." I chuckle with a quick survey of my shoes in my head.

He winks at me. "I picked up on that pretty fast, though you do have great taste in shoes."

"Tell me more about your dad." I'm enjoying getting to know more about him.

"He was great. He tried so hard, especially with Anastasia. He'd watch YouTube videos to learn how to braid her hair and I don't even want to know what he did about her period. I hope to God I don't have to help my daughter out with that someday." He shakes his head and hurls a terrified growling sound.

I can't help but laugh. In that instant, I picture him braiding a little girl's long, dark hair. Ardor sweeps through my core.

"So, here's what I know about you. You're a highly successful fashion photographer. You're respected by everyone around you. You're smart, independent. You're dedicated and very loyal. You're beautiful. Feisty. And you're fierce in the sexiest way."

Heat rushes to my chest at his compliments.

"What *don't* I know about you?"

This one may surprise him. "Hmm. I race my car on the racetrack."

"You what?" He whips his head toward me, shock skirting the edge of his voice, brow shooting to his hairline.

"High performance racing," I specify in explanation.

"Yeah, I know what it *is*. So, let's add dangerous to the list."

A laugh rolls out of me. "No, not if you follow the rules. It's very controlled and you go through serious training and education. They have a lot of safety protocols you have to abide by. And it's not like Indy racing where you're two inches from each other's bumpers and the smallest tap could send everyone spinning and flying all over the track."

"What got you started in that?" His curiosity amuses me.

"A guy I dated in college, his dad raced in the circuit. We'd go watch sometimes and I got the itch. The ability to control a car at a high rate of speed just seemed...*exhilarating*." I release a low, growling purr. "Okay, maybe it felt a little dangerous at first and that might've been what I was drawn to." I shrug and purse my lips. "Sure, there's still a little bit of risk involved, but once you know how to handle the car, it's a blast."

"Dangerous and sassy as hell." He shakes his head with a huge smile spreading across his handsome, scruffy face. "This, I gotta see." It's more of an expression than a request to watch.

So, I go there. "You should come with me sometime."

"Yeah?" Even though I'd just invited him, the tone of his question asks permission, like he's checking to make sure he's not infringing on something that's me-time.

"Yeah," I confirm.

After college, when I was out on my own, working on my photography career, I'd go to the track events and learn and practice. It was my hobby, my fun. I admit, the danger was kind of a thrill, a rush. When Dom and I met, he wasn't into it, *at all.* It scared him too much. He wasn't into driving and he wasn't into watching. So, I stopped doing it, which was fine because we had a lot of other things in common that we enjoyed doing together.

About six months after he passed, I ran into one of the guys from the track and we caught up over coffee. He said I was welcome back anytime. So I started going to the events I could make it to when they fit into my crazy schedule. It's been great to get back into it.

With both of us needing to work tomorrow, he makes sure to have us back to my house by nine o'clock. As usual, he walks me to my door.

"This was a fun surprise." My back to my door, I look up into his eyes.

"I'm glad you liked it." His kryptonic eyes move back and forth, seizing me in place.

Kiss me.

He extends his arm above me, leaning it against the door, close to my face. With his other hand, he takes some of my curls in his fingers. I sip a shallow breath and let the door brace my back. He leans in, our faces inches apart. Lust coils itself through my core.

"I'm not going to kiss you until you tell me to kiss you." His warm breath crosses my lips. He leans back a little and presses his lips into my forehead. "Good night."

I stop holding my breath. "Good night." It's all I can say. *Is my jaw on the floor?*

He takes my chin in his hand and rubs his thumb along my jaw. Exhaling audibly through his nose, his eyes flicker to my lips then he steps back. "I'll leave once you're in."

I unlock the door and step inside then turn around. He gives me that sexy smile of his, bows his head, and turns to leave.

Closing the door, I lock it behind me, and breathe. *Holy shit that was intense.* God, I wanted to feel his lips again. I don't know if I was more turned on by him *almost* kissing me or his complete respect for me by *not* kissing me, given what I shared with him. What I do know is that I have to kiss this man again…soon.

14

Enzo

I need to kiss her again, balls-aching need. And, Jesus, what a weight to carry. Her dad basically didn't want her because she wasn't a boy? What the fuck is that? While I have compassion for her, and I'd never admit this to her, I'm also pissed at him. I can't believe all she's been through. She is one strong woman.

I want to see her again, soon. And we don't have anything set up. I'm not one to chase a woman. I don't know what it is about her. Her heart, her essence, her soul. I'm addicted.

I pick up my phone and call her.

"Hi. Everything okay?" she asks.

"Yeah. Sorry. You're not in bed already, are you?"

"Not yet. I'm going to get washed up soon. What's going on?"

I sit on my sofa. "I realized we don't have another date set up yet."

She chuckles that sweet sound that makes me picture her beautiful smile that accompanies it. "You're right we don't. I have a client project due tomorrow, but what're you doing tomorrow night?"

"Can't tomorrow night." *Shit.* "I'm doing a bartending favor for a friend of mine who owns Sterling's Cognac Bar starting at six. He's down two employees who are sick. Saturday?"

"Saturday. Six o'clock?"

"Four o'clock." Time goes by too fast when it's six o'clock.

"Okay. What're we doing?"

"Decide then?"
"Okay. G'night."

I met Sterling at a high-end yacht party I was working about five years ago. We hit it off and we've been friends ever since. He has an upscale clientele and his place brings in steady business. Tonight's hoppin' as usual, everyone dressed to the nines.

A little after 7:30, I look up and see her walking toward me in the amber glow of the room. Candi. A sleeveless, dark brown, satiny-looking dress, with a plunge that dips a few inches below her magnificent breasts, hugs her body. Through her torso, it's a corset-type thing and the slit goes straight up to the top of her thigh. Unquenchable thirst rages.

Each delicate step toward me morphs to a thunderous quake, practically shaking the ground, knocking the wind from my lungs. Lust slashes me, fueling my hunger for her.

Pink hair flowing below her breasts, she ignores the dozens of eyes ogling her and locks her gaze on me as she saunters up to the bar. Hunger pivots to ravenous greed. I want to devour every inch of her.

Fuck me.

Sliding herself into a cognac-colored, leather bar stool, she puts her brown, satiny purse on the bar top that's a translucent golden-yellow and brown marble, illuminated from the inside.

"Make me something I'll like?" she asks, folding her arms on the bar and tilting her head in a subtle flirtation.

"You've got it." I rumble, balls aching.

I pour a sweeter cognac I think she might like and bring it over to her, placing it on a white cocktail napkin. "Take a sip."

Placing her lips on the rim, she tilts the glass, letting the liquid enter her mouth, eyes on mine as she does. "Mmm, it's tasty. A little sweet, kind of fruity."

"What're you doing here?" Desire flashes as I rake my gaze over her.

"I sent in my project so I thought I'd come check this place out and watch you work for a little while. Is that okay? If it's going to make you uncomfortable, I can go."

"Looking like that?" I focus my eyes on hers and force myself not to look at her mouth-watering cleavage. "You're not going anywhere." I smile.

She glances down and then back up at me. Her elbows on the bar, she clasps her hands together and rests her chin on them. "Then I'll stay." The corners of her mouth curl up.

A few people have come up to the bar. "Excuse me," I say, and tend to my customers.

The flow of people is consistent so I don't get much of a chance to talk to her, but our eyes meet often. When there's a small break, our chats are quick.

The next time I look in her direction, I see Anastasia and Gino standing next to her. Walking over to them, I throw my hands up.

"Hey, what're you guys doing here?" I reach my hand across the bar to shake Gino's hand.

"We just finished eating dinner and were on our way out. Gino spotted you. What are *you* doing here?"

"Sterling's in a bind. He's got two employees out so he asked for my help."

"Always giving the shirt off your back." She smiles. She'd do the exact same for a friend in need.

"Hey, this is Candi." I point to her.

They both turn.

"What?" Anastasia gleams. "This is Candi? Hi, I'm Enzo's sister, Anastasia." She takes Candi's hand in hers and clasps her other hand around it, shaking them. "It's so nice to meet you. I've heard a lot about you."

Am I ready for them to meet? Is Candi ready to meet my sister? I guess it's too late now.

Candi smiles. "It's nice to meet you too. Enzo told me some fun stories about the two of you."

Anastasia releases Candi's hand and Gino reaches over and shakes her hand. "Gino. Nice to meet you, Candi."

"You too."

"You guys want drinks?" I ask.

"No, we're heading home. Hey, we never get to see you. How about you guys come over for dinner tomorrow?" She turns to Candi then back to me.

I look at Candi, worried she's feeling like she's in an awkward and uncomfortable situation. She raises her eyebrows and nods. "Yeah, that sounds fun." She smiles at them.

"Great. We'll see you tomorrow night, say six-ish?" she asks.

I nod and lift my hand in an agreeable gesture.

She blows me a kiss and puts her hand on Candi's arm. "See you guys tomorrow."

Gino gives us a wave as they turn and walk away. Then he slides his arm around her. It's nice how affectionate he is with her. Anastasia is a walking bundle of love and affection. I think it rubs off on the people around her, including me.

With their spot at the bar open, a customer steps in and orders a drink. Then it's one after another after another. As I'm making a drink further down the bar, I see a guy in a suit walk over to Candi and start talking to her. *Back off, dude.* Making drinks, I keep my eye on him. I don't like his body language, leaning toward her the way he is. Did that asshole just look at her chest? He picks up her almost-empty glass and waves to the other bartender who's closer to them. *No fucking way are you buying her a drink.* Steam spewing out of my ears, I stalk out from behind the bar and head toward them, ready to kiss her right here if I need to. As I get closer to them, approaching Candi's back, I hear her.

"Actually, I'm seeing someone, but thank you for asking. I enjoyed our conversation."

"So did I," he says. "Have a good night." He takes his drinks and walks away.

Trying to hide the fury boiling in me, I tuck in next to her.

"Hi. What're doing on this side?" She takes a sip of her drink.

"Are you all right? Was he bothering you?" My questions are rapid-fire.

She cocks her head as one side of her mouth kicks up. "Enzo Cipriani, were you trying to save a damsel in distress?" she teases.

"If I had to, yeah." I nod, adrenaline still heating my blood.

"You don't need to worry. I know how to handle myself."

"I don't doubt that, I just —"

"Were you jealous?" She draws her head back, her eyebrows pinching together.

"No," torpedoes out of me. "I was being protective. It comes from being a brother to a pretty sister." *Was I jealous?*

Why was I ready to kiss her? Claiming her like some raving Tarzan. She's not my girlfriend, we're just hanging out so far. Are we even dating? Anastasia's always told me that when it comes to women, I should trust my first instinct. And my first instincts with Candi have been intrigue, an interest to know more, and hot-as-fuck chemistry. When that guy was talking to her, all I wanted was for her to be mine. So far in my dating life, I've never felt like this.

Did she mean what she said to him? Is she feeling anything like what I'm feeling? Or is her heart still with her dead, almost-fiancé she wears around her neck? There's something between us. Something I'm not willing to let go of. I'd better watch my step. If I come on too strong, I might just drive her away.

She swallows the last of her drink. "I'm going to get an Uber and head home," she says, taking her phone out of her purse.

"I'd rather be the one to take you home."

She smiles politely. "Thank you, but I don't think I can hang until two AM anymore."

"I know. I wouldn't ask you to. I have a tough time myself these days," I confess with a chuckle. "Hey, I didn't take my break yet. Let me make sure the other bartenders are okay with me taking it now and I'll walk you out."

"I'll wait here."

I check with the other bartenders and they're fine with it so I go back to Candi. She stands when she sees me and I get to take in all of her once again. Fucking luscious. Desire licks my skin, blistering through me.

"She'll be here in three minutes."

"She?"

"Yeah. If I get anyone creepy-looking, I cancel it. And I always have my pepper spray with me."

"Okay, good." I walk her to the entrance. "Hey, we don't have to go to my sister's tomorrow night. I'm sorry if you felt ambushed by her excitement."

"She was very excited." She raises her eyebrows and laughs. "But no, I think it'll be fun. Are you okay with it?"

"Yeah, completely. I just wanted to make sure you didn't feel pressured into it."

"Not at all. She seems sweet."

The Uber pulls up out front and I walk her out. Opening the door, I pop my head in quickly. I don't love her taking Ubers. Before she gets in, I take her in my arms.

"You look beautiful," I whisper in her ear then kiss her forehead and release her, that soft scent of honey lingers in the air between us. "Text me when you're inside your house and your door is locked."

When she looks up at me, moonlight glows in her eyes. "I will. Good night." She gets in and the driver takes off. About half an hour later, I receive her text.

Candi: Home safe. See you tomorrow.

Me: Thanks for letting me know. Yup, see you tomorrow. 4:00.

My phone chimes around two o'clock.

Candi: I have an urgent issue to address for work. Can I push our time to 5:30? I'm so sorry.

Damn. I know how dedicated she is to her work. I hope she doesn't have to cancel our date.

Me: No problem at all. Let me know if you end up needing more time.

Candi: I'll get it done.

Candi

I don't even know what drove me to go to the bar last night. All I know is that I wanted to see him. He seemed pleased to see me. And, even though he denied it, I'm pretty sure there was a hint of jealousy when that guy was talking to me. I know we aren't exclusive and I have no idea if he's seeing other women. And, at this point, it's probably none of my business. But I don't do the whole see-multiple-people-at-the-same-time thing. I need to let him know that tonight. Even if it sends him packing, that's not something I'm willing to compromise on.

At five twenty-eight, there's a knock on my door. I smile inside and open the door.

"Hi. Did I give you enough time? I told Anastasia I'd let her know if you needed more time."

"Nope. I'm good."

We go down to his Jeep, he opens my door, and then we're off.

"Thank you for being flexible. This came out of the blue."

"Of course, no problem. I know the business. It can be demanding."

"Yeah, I worked my ass off to get it straightened out. My client changed their mind and I had to scramble through pictures and make some adjustments in order to fulfill what they wanted. It was tight, but I managed to get it done and be on time for you."

"Aw, I feel bad. We could've canceled with my sister. That must've felt like a lot of pressure."

"Nah. I'm used to it. Besides, I'm looking forward to tonight."

"Yeah? It's not too much, dinner with my sister?"

"Not at all. Now I'll get some real scoop on you." I raise my eyebrows and grin.

"Why do I suddenly feel nervous?" He laughs that husky laugh of his.

We arrive at his sister's house and he hands a bottle of red wine to Gino as Anastasia wraps her arms around me in a hug like we've been friends for years.

"Hi. Welcome. Come on in," she says brightly.

As I step further into their home, the air entering my nostrils is coated in butter, garlic, and parmesan cheese. My stomach starts preparing for what smells like a delicious meal. The décor is shabby chic which suits her personality.

"Enzo said you got some last-minute work plopped in your lap. Did you get it all done?" she asks, leading us toward the kitchen.

"I did. I wasn't expecting it, but it's also not unusual in my line of work. Thankfully it doesn't happen too frequently to me. But when it does, I jump on it. I've built myself a solid reputation and I work hard to keep it that way. I never want my clients disappointed."

"So, you're available to them all the time? You don't take any time for yourself?" she asks, getting dinner plates out of the cabinets.

"I haven't had much in my life other than work for quite a while." I glance over at Enzo. "I could probably set better boundaries, like on weekends. I just love my work."

"It's important to love what you do." She smiles and gets out four wine glasses.

Gino opens the wine and pours it into the four glasses.

"What do you do?" I ask her.

"I'm a teacher." She beams. "I teach third-grade math and I

have the best students." She sips her wine. "Are you guys hungry? I made spaghetti and meatballs with garlic bread."

"My stomach's been ready since we walked in and I took a whiff," I say.

"Here, grab a plate and load up what you want. I'll put the bread on the table." She hands each of us a plate and puts the garlic bread on the natural-wood top of the dining table.

Enzo extends his arm for me to go first. Using the pasta fork, I scoop out my spaghetti from the bowl and take a few meatballs. Then I sprinkle on some grated parmesan cheese from the vintage-looking silver bowl and spoon set and head to the table.

"Sit anywhere," Gino says.

I pull out a chippy, light blue chalk-painted chair and wait for them. Enzo's not far behind me and takes the seat next to me at the round table. Anastasia and Gino join us and Gino goes back to the kitchen, returning with another bottle of wine.

"I like your parmesan dish. My mom loved vintage things," I say.

"Thank you. It was our grandmother's. She was an amazing cook," Anastasia says with a reminiscent smile.

"From the look and smell of this dinner, so are you. And you taught your brother a thing or two." I look at Enzo and he almost looks bashful.

"She taught me everything I know about cooking and baking." He winks at her and she smiles warmly.

"Oh, save room for dessert. I have chocolate fondue for us." I'm loving her already.

As we eat, Enzo and Anastasia share stories from their childhood and they talk about how great their dad was. I love how close they are and the respect they have for each other. Neither mentions their mom. Gino chimes in every now and then and I just soak it all in.

"It took a lot of patience teaching him how to cook. Things were either exploding, or tipping over, or horribly lopsided," she says, shaking her head with a giggle.

"Kind of like someone I know." A shit-eating grin spreads across Enzo's face as he tilts his head a few times in my direction.

"No, really?" Anastasia's hand flies to her mouth in unfiltered alarm.

"I'm a disaster in the kitchen." I hang my head in feigned shame. We all burst into laughter.

Finishing our meal, we bring our dinner plates into the kitchen and pitch in to bring out the fixings for the chocolate fondue.

"Enzo's told us about some of the high-end brands you shoot with. That has to be exciting."

"It is. I've worked hard and I've been very fortunate. There's just one brand I haven't gotten yet, but I will."

"What brand is it?" Gino asks.

"Gucci."

Enzo smiles at me in a way that makes me feel his belief in me.

"Enzo said you're good friends with Niccolo Mancini. Surely he can pull some strings for you." Anastasia says.

"Oh, he would, without a doubt. But, that's not me. I need to earn it on my own."

"Then I believe you will." A confident smile spreads across her face.

Gino gives me an approving nod.

After indulging in the deliciousness of the fondue, I offer to help Anastasia clean up.

"Thank you for such a great dinner," I say, carrying in the plate of crumbs from the garlic bread along with the pile of empty fondue plates.

"You're welcome. I'm so glad you came. Enzo doesn't usually let me meet anyone he's dating." She rinses a plate and puts it into the dishwasher.

"No?" *Hmmm.*

"Honestly? I don't think he's ever been all that interested in any of them. When he started asking my advice about you, I knew you were special." A sweet smile lifts her cheeks.

"Thank you. That's nice of you to say."

"I've kind of been like a mother hen most of his life and I want him to find someone who's good for him. None of us are getting any younger. And he's such a great guy. I want him to be happy. I mean, obviously there's no pressure here at all. I just, I really like you." Her shoulders raise toward her ears and the biggest smile lights up her face, making me smile.

"Well thank you. I like you too. And Enzo. He *is* a great guy. I can see what a big impact you've had on him. He has a sensitive, nurturing side you don't see in many men these days. I think he gets that from you."

"Well, he missed out on the truest form of having a mom, so, I did my best as his sister." She shrugs one shoulder.

I touch her arm. "You did an amazing job."

Her brows pinch together and the energy of her pushing her lips to form a smile overwhelms me. Pain sits behind her eyes, making my heart hurt.

She shakes her head like she's shaking away bad memories and exhales. "You two going out after this?"

"I'm not sure. We didn't think that far ahead."

We finish loading the dishwasher and join the guys who are drinking wine out on the deck.

"I think we're going to head out," Enzo says, approaching Anastasia and hugging her.

"Thank you for such a nice night," I say to Gino.

"We enjoyed having you here," he returns.

Enzo and Gino do the man-pat hug as Anastasia and I hug and say good night.

We get in his Jeep and head out.

"What do you feel like?" he asks. "Want to go out or do you feel like going home?"

"I'm so full from all that good food. How about we go home?"

"Home it is," he says. "Anastasia really likes you."

"I had such a nice time with them. You guys have some great

stories. I particularly enjoyed listening to her talk about how you'd pull her around on your bathrobe across the wood floors and she'd beg you to do it again and again. You were strong even when you were little."

"I think that's what started my journey into lifting weights." He laughs that hearty laugh that warms my insides.

On the rest of the drive home, he shares more with me about his childhood. I thoroughly enjoyed the night and seeing him interact with his family. I especially loved how they welcomed me with open arms.

Holding my hand, he walks me to my door.

Tonight, when I look into his eyes, there's a connection, beyond the electric attraction I've felt intensifying between us. Something deeper. Something I want more of. Does he feel it?

"Do you want to come in for a drink? I don't have whiskey, but I have wine."

He doesn't say a word. He just tips his head up and down slowly, pulling in his lips.

I open the door, locking it behind us. "I'll be right back." I go to my bedroom to take off my shoes and leave my purse.

When I come back out, he's in the kitchen getting wine glasses out of the cabinet.

"Stick with red?" he asks.

"Sure." I don't have much of a selection.

He grabs the one red bottle I have and opens it then pours it into our glasses. I go to the living room and turn on some jazz. Handing me my glass, he takes a sip of his then sets it on the coffee table.

"I like this one. Dance with me?"

"I know what you're doing." I tease, thoroughly wanting to be in his strong arms again.

I want to feel his energy intertwine with mine once more. I also don't want to be one of several women who might also be in his arms. I need to tell him. *Not now.* Now, I want to feel his body against mine, even if it's just for a little while. I want to feel the rush that powers through me when he holds me. I crave it.

Taking a sip of my wine, I set it down then enter his awaiting arms, draping my arm across his shoulder and resting my hand on the back of his neck. With one arm around my waist, he holds my hand in his and sways us back and forth, slowly spinning us. His magnetic energy permeates me. Invades me. Eclipses me.

"I overheard you talking to that guy at the bar last night. Did you mean what you said, about seeing someone? Or is that your standard line?"

"It's something I've said before. I don't play games. I don't give out fake numbers. I don't say I'm going to the bathroom and never come back. I'd rather be polite and straightforward than give them false hope. It takes guts to walk up to a stranger and start talking to them."

"That's considerate."

"Why? Is that what you want? For us to be exclusive?" He stops spinning us, puts his other arm around my waist, and holds me. Moving both of my hands down around his arms, I take a breath, unsure of how he's going to receive what I'm about to say. My stomach clenches. *Here we go.* "I mean, I don't want to force labels onto anything and I also have to be honest with you. I don't see multiple men at the same time. That's just not who I am. And I get it if you're not ready for only one person." *Please don't walk away.*

He locks me in place with his gaze. "Let me be perfectly clear." His voice deep and deliberate, he lowers his face closer to mine, sending electricity through me. "I don't want to see any other women. I only want to see you." His eyes shift back and forth between mine. "I only want to kiss *you.*" He doesn't move any closer.

My senses pique in increasing intensity with each word that comes out of his mouth, his last sentence sending chills racing over my flesh. My breaths are heavy, wanting. Whether it's his words or the wine or my body no longer able to resist him, I don't know and I don't care. I move my hands to the back of his neck and tug him gently toward me.

"Kiss me," I whisper.

Digging his fingers into my lower back, a growl hums deep in his chest, vibrating against me. He bends his head lower. Heat rages through my pumping blood the instant our lips meet.

I grip harder around his neck, lifting onto the balls of my feet. Our tongues dance in unison with the sexy jazz music circling our bodies like ribbons of smoke.

My heart beats frantically with each desperate probe of my tongue, wanting more. He pulls back, holding my face once again, his hot breath skimming my lips.

"I've been dying to kiss you again," he says, shaking his head, hard breaths accompanying his words.

I open my lips, craving him. In stark contrast to my pounding heart, he moves his lips, unhurried, toward mine, making my heart beat faster. Controlling my frantic desire, he seduces my mouth with his masterful tongue, baiting me with each movement.

Leaving my mouth begging for more, he drills his kryptonic gaze into me as he presses his hard-on into my abdomen. Breaking our gaze, he nuzzles his mouth into my neck, trailing down, sucking lightly. Tingles cover my body as I tilt back my head in the bliss of his journey. He continues down to my clavicle, dragging his tongue along it, then focusing kisses on the hollow just above it. I whimper, heaving uncontrolled breaths.

"Mmm." His sound tells me he's enjoying his seductive torment.

Adrenaline and desire intoxicate me. I need his mouth on mine again. I've never experienced passion like this from kissing. I'm out of my mind. I want more. I bring his face back to mine. Fire burns in his eyes as he claims my mouth again, probing deep with his tongue, dominating me. He circles my waist with his arm and holds my head in his hand. Snaking my hands behind his head, I tug. He groans, tilting his pelvis into me as he holds me against him.

"Jesus, Candi," he breathes, moving his hands to cradle my face. "I'm running low on willpower." He places a sweet kiss on my lips. "But I'll take this as slow as you want."

"Okay." I nod. *I'm not ready for more. Am I?*

He takes a deep breath and lets it out, then releases my face and holds me to his chest. His heart pounds against my face, matching my own erratic heartbeat. Lust licks between us. "I'm gonna go and let you get some sleep," he says, then kisses the top of my head.

Untangling from each other, we walk to my door.

"Call you tomorrow?" he asks.

Speechless and unable to slow my heart, I nod.

"Good night."

I close and lock my door…my breaths stilted.

My heart might not be ready, but my body sure as fuck is.

Will my heart ever be ready? I want to believe it has the capacity to move on. Can I let go?

15

Enzo

When the words left my mouth, nothing felt more true. For the first time in my life, I'm ready to give myself fully and completely to one woman. Her tenacity, her values, her integrity, her beautiful face, her fucking body. She's unlike any woman I've ever met. And I can't get enough.

The next week is busy for both of us. I have shoots lined up and a couple bartending jobs. She's out of town again. We both receive a group text from Destiny.

> **Destiny:** Hey! You guys want to come over for dinner on Sunday around 6:00?
>
> **Candi:** I get back home Saturday night so Sunday works.
>
> **Me:** I'm working but should be done by 5:00. Candi, meet you there? Destiny, what can I bring?
>
> **Candi:** Yup.
>
> **Nicco:** We're having filet mignon. Enzo, want to pick out the wine?
>
> **Me:** Done. See you all then.

The rest of the week passes quickly and I'm looking forward to seeing Candi. Our kiss has been taunting me. I want my hands, my mouth, on her body. My heart and my head are willing to wait because I respect her and what she's been through and I don't want to push her. My body, on the other hand, wants to be deep inside her, devouring her and making her come undone.

Pulling into their driveway, the last house on the left at the end of the street, I park next to Candi's BMW M3. Wine in hand, I ring the doorbell. When the door opens, Candi's standing there wearing a long-sleeve, cabernet-colored top that's open down to her waist, exposing the inner swells of her breasts. Her long legs extend from below her black-leather mini skirt down to her black-leather stilettos that strap around her ankles. *Holy fuck.* She obviously has no idea what she does to me.

After grabbing a quick eyeful, without hesitation, I wrap my arm around her waist and pull her in for a kiss, wishing we weren't standing in the foyer of Destiny and Nicco's house. I've missed her succulent lips.

Struggling not to get lost in her, I pull back. "Hi. It's good to see you."

"Hi." Her eyes sparkle when she smiles. In her heels, she's only a couple inches shorter than me. "It's good to see you too. Come on in."

We all stand in the kitchen, catching up and drinking wine while Destiny and Nicco finish cooking. Then we sit around their four-person dining table, telling stories and sharing laughs. After dinner, we gather in their cozy living room in front of the fire and continue our conversations. Around nine o'clock, Candi yawns.

"Oh, I'm so sorry, you guys," she says, yawning again. "I think it's the different time changes lately. They're kicking my ass."

"Come on." I stand up. "Let's get you home." I reach out my hand.

Taking my hand, she stands up.

Destiny and Nicco get up and we all go to the kitchen. Candi and I put our wine glasses in the sink and we say our goodbyes.

Holding her hand, I walk her to her car. She puts her back toward the car door and faces me.

"I'm sorry I'm so tired. Did you want to stay longer?"

"No. I wanted to come out here and kiss you," I say, taking her face in my hand.

"I'd like that," she says softly.

Dropping my head, I cover her sweet lips with mine and barely slide my tongue between them. She opens them a little. I deepen my slide. She whimpers, driving me deeper. I back her flush against her car door, teasing her mouth with my tongue. The way she tugs my neck to her makes my pulse increase.

I break our kiss. "I wish I was taking you home tonight."

"Yeah?" she asks, tucking her fingers into my front jeans pocket.

"Mhm." I trail my finger along the fabric of her top, following it with my eyes. I skim gradually down, following the curve of her breast. Touching her silky skin already has me getting hard.

She inhales, drawing my eyes back to her face. Holding her gaze, I continue gliding my finger along the seam down to her stomach. When I reach the waist of her skirt, I slide my finger to the other side, moving it more slowly up that side. Up her stomach, over the swell of her breast. Her eyes close as her chest rises with a stilted breath. I keep sliding my finger along the seam, indulging in touching her, hardening even more at her response.

"You have no idea what you do to me, do you?" I ask, my willpower a taught, fraying thread.

"No." She breathes. "I don't think I do."

Grabbing her waist with both hands, I tilt up into her. She sucks in a sharp breath. I kiss her, long and deep, then break the kiss. Her eyes oscillate between mine. Moving my hand to her breast, I circle her nipple with my middle finger on the silky fabric of her top. Her back arches as her nipple tightens and she whimpers. Circling slowly, over and over, I watch her body respond. As she tilts back her head and pulls at my pocket, I drink in her sounds.

Moving to the other nipple, I watch her responses heighten as she pulls hard on my neck, her eyes opening and closing, her tongue licking her lips. Taking my other hand, I slide it between her legs, not too high. Her eyes fly open.

"Tell me to stop and I will," I say, despite my desperate need for more.

Her eyes dart back and forth frantically between mine.

I inch my hand higher. "I'll stop when you tell me to."

She licks her lips, her breaths hard and heavy as her chest moves out and in.

I inch higher. She tips her pelvis forward.

One more inch. "Tell me to stop."

She shakes her head. "Don't stop," she whispers, pulling my forehead to hers, moving her pelvis back and then forward to meet my fingers.

Still paying attention to her nipple, I slide my fingers across the wet fabric of her panties. "You're so wet." Using a light touch, I continue teasing her with my fingers, never dipping beneath her soaked panties.

She gyrates her pelvis back and forth against my fingers, tugging at my neck, pulling at my pocket, whimpering. Then she opens her legs a little wider. I move the fabric of her panties and slide my fingers into her. *Jesus, she's tight.* She gasps. The sound rattles through me. I'm so turned on I can hardly breathe.

Gliding my fingers in and out, I kiss her, cupping her breast in my other hand and matching the probe of my tongue with the insertion of my fingers. She rocks her pelvis to my rhythm. When I rub my thumb into her nub, she breaks our kiss, looking at me with wild eyes. I rub harder, moving my fingers inside her. Her moans drive my desire, quaking the earth beneath us, vibrating up my legs.

Working her with my fingers, I move the fabric of her top across her nipple, exposing her magnificent breast. As I lift it, taking her nipple into my mouth, I lengthen the stroke of my fingers to include her nub. I suck her nipple and she arches her back, moaning quietly. Keeping my strokes long between her wet folds and rubbing her nub at the end, I increase my speed with each stroke.

She's panting and I'm loving her sounds, her movements. When her breaths become rapid, I focus my fingers fully on her nub, working her, rubbing faster and faster, her whimpers filling my ears. She yanks my neck as her legs slam shut around my hand, trembling. Her head hurls back against the car and she throws her hand over her mouth, trying to muffle her sounds. The muscles of her inner thighs squeeze my hand like a vice as she curls her body and head into me, breathing heavily. She drapes her arm around my neck like she's trying to hold her body up from collapsing.

When her thighs relax, I withdraw my hand and cover her breast with her top. She lifts her head, looking into my eyes, hers blazing with pleasure.

"Yeah, I wish I was taking you home tonight," I say, sticking my fingers in my mouth, tasting her. Greed grapples inside me.

Taking her face in my hand, I stroke her cheek with my thumb. "Come on. Let's get you home," I say, then kiss her forehead.

"Okay. Good night."

She adjusts herself and we get in our cars and drive home. Trying to deflate my dick as I drive, I follow her to her condo and park out front, putting on my hazard lights.

When I walk up behind her at her door, she startles. "I thought you were going home."

"I am. After I make sure you're in." I lean in and kiss her. "Good night."

She unlocks her door and goes inside, smiling and peering at me as she closes it. When I hear the lock click, I go back to my car.

Holy fuck does she turn me on. I'm going to need to jack off when I get home. I can't fucking take it anymore.

Business taken care of; I get into bed. My phone chimes.

Candi: Tonight was wild. I've never done anything like that. Never felt anything like that.

Me: No?

Candi: No.

Me: How's that possible?

Candi: I've just never been with anyone so attentive.

What? Her body should be worshiped.

Me: That changes starting now.

I'm going to give her pleasure like she's never felt before.

Candi: I can't stop thinking about it. You had me out of my mind.

Me: I had to leave you with something to think about. We're both so busy the next few weeks.

Candi: I know. We'll stay in touch and figure out when we're both home again. I need to get some sleep. I fly out again tomorrow.

Me: Safe travels. Sweet dreams.

Candi: Good night.

Wednesday afternoon, I get a call from my agent. "Vance, hey, what's up?"

"Are you sitting down? I have a big one for you." There's an edge of pride in his tone.

A quick spurt of adrenaline shoots through me. "Yeah, what is it?" I ask.

"If you have something going on, you're gonna want to clear your schedule for this."

"Shit, man, what is it?" My curiosity is piqued.

"Next Tuesday, you're going to be in Italy, shooting for Gucci."

"Did you say Gucci?" I ask, stressing the last word, making sure I didn't mishear it. *No fucking way.*

He bellows a laugh. "That I did."

"This is unbelievable. Thank you so much."

"We're getting you there, man. You're on your way."

"Holy shit." I rake my hand through my hair. "I can't believe this." I also can't let this opportunity pass me by. But how do I position it? "Hey, this is gonna sound crazy, but can I make a request?" I ask, wrapping my hand around the back of my neck and pacing.

"What kind of request?"

"I'd like them to consider a specific photographer for the shoot."

He chuckles almost nervously. "I'm not sure I can do that, Enzo. I mean, I can ask, but..." He pauses. "What's this about?"

"I know a photographer, she's phenomenal. She's bid for gigs with them before, but it never worked out. I know I can't demand they use her, but I want to ask them to at least take a look at her for the job."

"It's important to you?"

"It is."

He's silent for a few seconds. "Let me see if I can get Tommaso back on the phone."

"Can I be on the line?"

"Sure. Hold on."

The phone rings.

"Hello, Giana. It's Vance again for Tommaso. Is he still available?"

"Yes, he is. Please hold for me."

"Vance, hello again."

"Hey Tommaso, I have Enzo on the line with us."

"Enzo, welcome to the project. We like your work and we're looking forward to seeing what you bring to the campaign."

"Thank you, Tommaso. I appreciate the opportunity."

"Enzo has a request on the photographer. Do you have anyone booked yet?"

"We had someone in mind, but there was a scheduling conflict so now we're scrambling to find a new one. Who do you have in mind?"

"Her name is Candice Gamal," I say. "I've worked with her before and she's incredible. She has a distinctive, creative eye and stops at nothing to get the perfect shot. She has a vision I've never seen in another photographer and her work ethic is outstanding."

"Hmm. Where can I find her work?"

"She's done Fendi, Guess, Versace, Dolce and Gabbana. She even submitted to Gucci before so someone there may have something for you to look at. She's also on Instagram."

"Really? Okay, I'll have a look."

"That's all I'm asking. Please consider her. You won't regret it."

"You speak with great conviction. I'll give her serious consideration," Tommaso says.

"Thank you. I appreciate it. If you decide to move forward with her, please keep our conversation between us."

"Yes, of course." He promises.

We hang up and I'm so excited. Obviously for myself, but also for Candi. This would be her dream come true, and I'll be the one who helped make it happen, not that she'll ever find that out.

With long days and time differences, Candi and I don't text much. My Thursday night, Candi's Friday morning, I get a call from her.

"Hey, how are you? I wasn't expecting to hear from you," I say.

"I had to call you. I had to tell you. I'm gonna pee my pants." Her words hurl out of her mouth, faster and higher in pitch with each sentence.

"What? Tell me. What?"

"Gucci!" she shouts with the joy of a child who's been waiting for this moment her entire life.

A chill washes over me. I wish I could see her face right now. I wish I could be with her to share in her happiness in person.

"What?" I return, mimicking her excitement. "That's incredible. Congratulations. I'm so happy for you." A hint of guilt flushes through me that quickly washes away with how excited she is.

"Thank you. I just had to tell you. I can't believe it. I'm still pinching myself."

"When you're home next, we'll go out for a celebratory dinner."

"Definitely. Hey, I gotta go."

"Okay. You did it! Bye."

"Eeee! Bye."

Arriving on set, I'm excited to see Candi and to work with her again. I'm also a little nervous about how she'll react to my being here and not having told her.

It's going to be hard to be with her for hours and not kiss her. The shoot is scheduled for two days. Even though we're both here, these types of shoots are typically fourteen- to sixteen-hour days. I'm sure we'll need to sleep tonight and stay focused on the job.

Though I'm early, Candi was earlier. She's walking around the breathtaking garden where we'll be shooting. From where I stand, I can see her creating her vision. Walls of greenery surround a lake that boasts tall grasses and lily pads. Tucked into the greenery are life-size, white marble statues of goddesses with long, flowing hair like hers.

After a few minutes, the stylist arrives as well as hair and makeup artists. Candi's team is here, running cords and setting up lighting.

Three female models arrive and introduce themselves to me. Candi starts walking toward us. When she sees me, the biggest smile spreads across her beautiful face and she picks up her pace.

She wraps her arms around my neck and all I want to do is kiss her. This obviously isn't the place for that.

"Hi. What in the world are you doing here?" she asks, releasing me.

"Things have been so busy; I didn't get a chance to tell you. I got a call from Vance about this job and then days flew by and I thought I'd just surprise you."

"I'm surprised." She pauses and looks over at the models. "Let's get started."

From that moment, she turns into the badass, visionary photographer I admire. Around one o'clock, Gucci's has lunch brought in. We work for another hour and a half before breaking because Candi likes the natural light we have. During our quick break to refuel, Candi shares with us her thoughts for the next round of pictures.

"Enzo." A deep male voice comes from behind me.

I turn around to see a gentleman who looks to be a little older than me. He extends his hand.

"I'm Tommaso." He's shorter and wider than me with a thick, bushy mustache.

Meeting his hand, I shake it. "Tommaso. I didn't expect to meet you. This is great."

"I don't often come to the shoots, but every now and then I do, if the timing works out. I was so curious to meet the photographer you spoke so highly of."

Candi stops talking to the female models and turns to us.

"Ms. Gamal, I'm Tommaso Moretti from Gucci," he says, extending his hand.

"Hello." She shakes his hand. "It's so nice to meet you. Thank you again for this opportunity. The shoot is going very well."

"Yes, I can see that. I've been watching your work from over there." He points to the green-vine covered veranda of a small white building on the property. "Very inspiring. You have a keen eye. I've enjoyed watching you marry our concept with your vision and make it come to life."

"Thank you so much. I'm pleased with how the shots are coming out. I'll do my best for you. I'm grateful to be here."

He pats me on the back. "You were right about her."

Fuck. My heart freefalls in my chest.

As he turns to leave, Candi speaks.

"I'm sorry, what do you mean he was right about me?" Leaning toward him, her eyes shift from me to him.

He stops and turns back to face us.

"He told me we had to hire you. I almost thought he wasn't going to do the job if we didn't." Heaving a laugh, he pats me on the back again. "I'm glad I listened to him. I have to get going. It was a pleasure watching you all work. I'm looking forward to seeing the final campaign." He turns and leaves.

Blood drains from my face and there's a high-pitched ringing in my ears.

Her eyes shift from him back to me. Expecting anger, what I see is far worse. The hurt veiling her eyes lacerates my heart. Her jaw clenches as creases form between her brows. I feel her fighting back tears, and it rips at me.

I fucked up…big time.

And I don't know how to fix it. Even if I did, I can't do it right now.

Keeping her eyes boring into mine, she speaks. "Everyone ready to get back to work?" The slight quiver in her voice shimmies across my skin. Without another word, she turns and goes to where we're shooting the next set of pictures.

The rest of the afternoon and into the night, a frigid edge vexes her. Her presence stiff. A steel cage erected. I'm desperate to talk to her, to explain. But, it's impossible.

By eleven-thirty, we call it a night. I don't know what hotel she's staying at, but I can't let her leave without talking to her. She's helping her team gather cameras, lights, and cords. I say good night to the models and beeline for Candi.

"Can I talk to you please?" I beg.

She doesn't look at me. "Not right now. If you want to help, grab those lights on the other side of the pond." She points, still not looking at me.

I gather the lights and bring them back for her team to pack up.

I touch her arm. "Candi, please. I need to talk to you."

She recoils her arm, finally looking at me. "I'm working right now, Enzo," she says, ice coating her words. "I'm at Bernini Palace Hotel. If you want to talk to me there, that's fine. But plan to be quick because I need to get some sleep before tomorrow." Apprehension gusts the air.

"What room?"

"Twelve thirty-seven. Excuse me." She turns and goes back to helping her team pack things up.

I drive straight to her hotel and wait outside her door. And wait.

When she comes down the hall, I lift my back from the wall. We don't greet each other. She slides in her key and opens the door, tension riding her movements.

Barely into the living area of her suite she turns to me.

"This." She points furiously back and forth between us with fire in her eyes. "This is why I don't date people in my industry. Eventually something like this happens and it ruins everything." Her words barreling out of her, she starts pacing. "My work is impacted which means my reputation is impacted. I need to be fully and completely in my work," she says, pointing to her chest. She stops pacing and stands in front of me. "And today, my heart hurt so bad I couldn't even see straight." These words come out slower, pained, as she places her hand on her heart. Her eyes search mine frantically as her brows pinch together.

My heart pounds in my chest. Her hurt drowning me, suffocating my core.

"This is my dream job. The thing I've wanted since I was a little girl. And you've tainted it. My mind is so distracted right now. I'm doing the most important, most meaningful job of my career and I can't even focus." Her hand still on her heart, her neck jets forward as she raises her other arm with her hand extended. "Did you think…" She places her other hand on her heart like she's trying to suppress the pain. Her voice softens as she chokes out her next words. "I couldn't land Gucci on my own?"

As I go to speak, she starts again.

"Never mind," she says, putting her hands up in surrender. "I don't want to know. It doesn't matter." When she shakes her head, a tear falls from her eye.

I reach out to wipe it, but she turns her head away. "Please just go," she says, taking Dom's ring in her fingers. His ghost always with us. She turns away from me, walks into her bedroom, and closes the door.

I didn't even say a word. I didn't know what to say. All I wanted to do was make her dream come true. And in one unintentional moment, I stripped away her opportunity to earn her dream job on her own and I managed to have her think I didn't believe she could. On top of that, she can't even enjoy her dream job because I fucked it up. My heart squeezes unbearably tight in my chest. *Some hero.*

I text Anastasia to call me and go to my hotel. About an hour later, my phone rings, waking me.

"Hey." I rub my eyes, lying in bed.

"Are you sleeping?"

"Yeah, it's about one AM here."

"Enzo, I didn't realize the time difference. I'm sorry."

"No, no. I asked you to call. I wanted you to call. I need to talk to you."

"Why? What's going on? Are you okay?"

"I fucked up."

"On your job? What happened?"

"No. With Candi. I thought I was doing something good and it blew up in my face. And I don't know what to do." I sit up in my bed.

"Oh, Enzo. Tell me what happened."

"I told you I got this Gucci job and you know getting a Gucci gig is Candi's dream."

"Yeah."

"Well, I suggested they hire her for the job and they did."

"Enzo." Disappointment drapes her tone.

"I know. I know. She ended up finding out and now she's hurt. She thinks I don't believe in her and she's so tense when she should be enjoying every second of this experience." I rub my face with my hand. "How do I fix this?"

She sighs. "You have to talk to her."

"I tried. She doesn't want to hear what I have to say. I'm not even sure I know what to say except, I'm an asshole."

"You're not an asshole. You were trying to do something nice. You just…went about it the wrong way."

"Tell me what to do. Please."

"She's hurt. Give her some space. You have one more day there, right?"

"Yeah."

"I know it's going to be awkward, but just do your job. Be your professional self and try to make it easy on her. You're the model and she's the photographer. For now, nothing outside of that exists. Don't try to talk about it on the job."

"No, I won't."

"Just be the model," she reemphasizes. "Try to let her have this. Will there be time for you to talk when the shoot is over?"

I yawn. "I'm not sure how late we'll go. Maybe. And I'm guessing she'll leave the next morning."

"Then you either talk to her before she leaves or when you're both back in town. You have to do it in person. Don't do it over the phone."

"What do I say?"

"Say what's in your heart. Tell her the truth. That's all you can really do."

I blow a long puff of air out my mouth. Say what's in my heart. What *is* in my heart?

HER.

"And Enzo?"

"Yeah?"

"I'm proud of you for fighting for her and not giving up."

"I like her, Anastasia. I don't want this to be what ends us. She's worth fighting for."

"She is."

I yawn.

"Go get some sleep."

"Okay. Thanks for talking through this with me."

"I'm always here for you. You know that."

"I do. I love you. Bye."

This isn't how it ends for us. I'm going to fix this. I don't know how, but I'm going to fix this. I can't lose her.

16

Candi

I knew I shouldn't have let myself get involved with him. It was foolish of me. Careless. Especially knowing he's in the industry. I got so wrapped up. Wrapped up in feeling. For the first time in so long, my heart felt something. Something I never thought I'd feel again. Something I longed for and didn't know it until him.

And now it's all fucked up.

My dream job, marred. My trust, broken. My heart, shattered.

It's late, I'm exhausted, and I need sleep.

My heart hurts, my mind is racing, and I can't sleep.

I need my best friend. I grab my phone and call Destiny.

"Hi. I didn't think I'd hear from you. How's it going? How does it feel to be fulfilling your life-long dream?" Joy dances with her words.

Joy I should share, but can't.

Pent-up tears burst — uncontrolled — out of me.

"Can, what's wrong?" Concern coats her voice.

All I can do is cry. I can't form coherent words.

"Can, are you okay?" Her concern shifts quickly to panic.

I inhale sharp breaths and try to speak. "Not even a little bit."

"Do I need to come get you? What's going on? Talk to me."

"I didn't get my dream job." I suck in choppy breaths.

"I don't understand. What do you mean? You're there, aren't you?"

I temper my sobs and get out of bed to get a tissue. "I'm here. But *I* didn't get it. *Enzo* talked them into hiring me." Bitterness seethes inside me like a beast.

"What? What does Enzo have to do with it?"

"Turns out, he got the gig and something about how he wouldn't take it unless they hired me too." My chest sags, disappointment and confusion whirling.

"He said that?"

"That's what it sounded like, according to Tomasso."

"Oof. Okay."

"How could he *do* this to me?" Acid sours my stomach as unease brittles my bones. "He fucking went behind my back and he doesn't even believe in me. Here I was starting to feel something for him and he fucking goes and does *this*. And this whole shoot that's supposed to be the most magical, most amazing campaign of my life, is a fucking train wreck because I'm so twisted and hurt." I blow my nose.

"I want you to take a deep breath with me." She inhales.

I inhale.

She exhales.

I exhale.

"Let's talk this through. What did he say when you asked him about it?"

"I didn't ask him about it. I found out in the middle of the shoot and had to finish out the day. He came to my room after to talk to me, but, well, I basically shut him down and came into my bedroom and closed the door. I'm pretty sure he left. Or he's out on the sofa. I don't even know." I climb back into bed and lean my back against the headboard.

Guilt clashes with fury knowing I didn't give him a chance to say anything. What could he possibly have said that would've made it okay? Nothing.

"Okay. First, I don't think he was trying to deceive you or undermine you." She takes a breath. "His dad gave him that

Superman necklace and he's trying to figure out how to be a hero. Heroes don't do what they do because they want recognition. They wear a mask because they want to do good things anonymously. I think he *does* believe in you, *and* I think he wanted to be your secret hero and make your biggest dream come true. He cares about you."

"That's *not* his place. *I* earn my way. I would've gotten Gucci on my own." My chest burns.

"I know you would have. And, no, it's not his place. But, he's a guy. You and I both know that guys don't always think things through. I think he saw an opportunity and took it. And I doubt he thought any further beyond that. Besides, Gucci wouldn't have hired you because he told them to. He doesn't have that kind of pull. Your work speaks for itself, that's why they hired you, because you're exceptional at what you do."

I look up at the ceiling, my neck tight, and blow a huge puff of air out through my mouth. Thoughts and emotions tangle and swirl, a raging twister fuming inside.

"You two need to talk to each other and clear the air. I know you want to be mad and that's okay. What he did was shitty, but I think it was well-meaning shitty." She's silent, and so am I. "Do you think maybe you're scared of what you're feeling for him? And maybe that's really what has you wanting to push him away?" she asks with that sweet tone of knowing she's right.

"Ugh. Do you have to be so logical and call me on my bullshit?" I tease.

"That's what I'm here for." She lovingly reminds me.

"Okay, I'll listen to what he has to say."

"Good." She pauses. "I'm also happy to know your feelings for him are growing."

I sigh and scooch my body back under the covers, wrestling with the deception gnawing at me and the yearning for him compounding. "He reminds me so much of Dom. It scares me. And then, in other ways, he's so different. Different in ways that I like. And that scares me."

"It's okay to be scared. After Dom, you never thought you'd feel something similar for another man. And now that you are, it *is* scary. But scary doesn't mean wrong or bad." She takes a breath. "What's in your heart?" Her voice is soft.

That's a loaded question. A question I'm not sure I know the answer to. A question I'm afraid to answer.

"Right now, my heart's all mixed up. When I'm with him, he makes me feel alive, desired. The intensity of our conversations is, I don't know, it's intoxicating. He's this totally hot, masculine guy and he's also not afraid to show his emotions. The energy between us is…fucking wild, Des. It's so powerful. And passion, holy shit. I've never been with someone so sensual and in tune with my body. It's like he took lessons or something." I rub my palm into my forehead. A flash of tingles shoots between my legs.

We both chuckle and my heart lightens. I needed this. She's my level head, my rock.

"Wow. Well, that's certainly promising."

A yawn reminds me how tired I am and that I need to get some sleep. "Thank you for talking with me."

"Any time. Get some rest. *Enjoy* yourself tomorrow. You're shooting for fucking Gucci!" she shouts with joy.

"Eeeee!" bursts out of me.

She's reignited my excitement from when I first got the call from Gucci. I'm myself again and ready to tackle tomorrow.

"And talk to Enzo. Give him a chance to explain himself."

"I will. I love you. Good night."

"Night."

Destiny always makes me feel better. I *am* mad and hurt. But I should at least hear him out.

Excitement fueling me again, I arrive at the shoot site early. I'm tired as shit, but looking forward to the day ahead.

When Enzo and the female models arrive, they go straight to makeup. I head over to join them.

"Good morning, everyone." I take one look at Enzo. *Oof.* "Helena, do you have some depuffing patches for under Enzo's eyes?"

"Yes," she says. "I have something for the dark circles too. Sit for me?" She finds her eye patches, opens them, and starts applying them under Enzo's eyes. "Look up for me?"

When he does, he looks up at me. "I didn't get much sleep last night." A sheepish smile forms on his face, tugging at me.

"Close your eyes and rest here," Helena says, then goes over to work on one of the female models.

"Come to my room tonight after we wrap," I say, keeping my tone businesslike. "I can't talk to you now. I have to stay focused on this campaign and give it my complete attention." I soften. "I didn't give you a chance to talk last night and I want to hear what you have to say."

He sits up straighter and nods. "Okay."

I push back my emotions from yesterday and put everything I have into making this campaign phenomenal. Though it's tough to do the shoot with Enzo in every shot, after about an hour, I'm fully in my zone and loving the outcome.

With barely a break for lunch, we shoot into the night. A little after nine o'clock, I'm confident I've captured Gucci's vision and I'll be able to deliver them a quality product that's exactly what they want. Enzo helps me and my team collect all the equipment and we leave the majestic garden.

When I get to my room, Enzo's waiting by the door. Without a word from either of us, I unlock the door and we both step inside. Anxiety twists my stomach. He's usually my comfort, my desire. Right now, he's anything but.

"I'll be right back." I go to my bedroom and change into sweatpants and a sweatshirt.

When I return to the living area, Enzo stands from the sofa.

I sit in the adjacent chair, my nerves on edge, and tuck my legs under me.

He sits back down and rests his forearms across his knees, leaning his body toward me. He drops his gaze from my eyes to his folded hands. When he looks back up at me, he shakes his head. Tension permeates the room.

"I'm so sorry, Candi." He draws in his lips. "I, heh." He swallows. "I wanted to help you get your dream job. I thought I was going to make you happy." Gazing down, he rubs the palm of his hand with his thumb. Then he raises his head. "Not for a second did I stop and think that that wasn't how you'd want to land your dream job. Not with your integrity. I just…I didn't think. And honestly, there's nothing more I can say to try to redeem myself." He shakes his head. Regret shadows his eyes when he looks at me. "I didn't think. What I did was wrong. And I'm so sorry. I should've told you about it to begin with. I just got carried away. I hope you can find a way to forgive me." A remorseful line dents his brow as he searches my face. "And I need you to know, I didn't give them that ultimatum. I just asked Tommaso to consider you. You know a brand like Gucci wouldn't offer you a campaign unless they researched you and saw how talented you are."

I take a deep breath and exhale, letting his apology seep into me, cradle me, ease me.

"Much of my adult life, I've pushed people away. I run before they can. I don't want to run from you. I don't want to be alone anymore." His Adam's apple moves up and down. "I don't want to lose you." He begs, wearing at my fury, prying at the steel bars of my cage.

Though wounded, my heart speaks. *I don't want to lose him either.* My nerves settle. I get up from the chair and sit on his lap, facing him. He rests his hands on my hips. I want him to feel my energy and look straight in my eyes. He needs to feel my words. "You hurt me." I pause, letting my words hang in the air. "On a few levels."

Remorse darkens his narrowing eyes as his brows pull together. "I know." He drops his head.

I reach under his chin and lift his head so our eyes meet. "I don't have to be a damsel in distress for you to be my hero."

His eyes squeeze shut. "I know that," he says, taking a sharp inhale. "I'm so sorry," he whispers, then buries his head between my neck and collarbone and wraps his arms around my waist.

We stay cradled in one another's arms for a few minutes, healing ourselves and each other. Unspoken understanding silking a web between us. When we retract our embrace, his eyes volley between mine.

"Can you forgive me?" he asks.

My pain subsides with his sincere apology. I nod gently. "I forgive you," I hush.

He wraps his arms around me and buries his head into me again, holding me so tightly.

When he releases me, the sparkle has returned to his beautiful green eyes. I lean forward and kiss him. Hot air from his nose brushes across my cheek like he's releasing his pent-up anguish from the last couple days. He weaves his hands into my hair as his shoulders raise and he deepens our kiss.

Our tongues intertwine like they've been waltzing together for years, but with heightened desire. God, I love the way he kisses me, the way he taunts and teases me with his masterful tongue, like it's making love to my mouth and he's savoring every movement.

He moves his lips to my neck and I tilt back my head, breathing as he kisses a trail down my neck. He's getting hard beneath me. My body responds before my head can think and I grind down into him.

He groans.

Am I ready for this? *Yes, I'm ready.* I want this. I want it with him.

I put my hands on his shoulders and grind again. Exhaling loudly, he stops kissing my neck and locks his eyes on mine. Fire burns behind them. Desire scorches the air.

I pull my sweatshirt off over my head and toss it onto the chair, sitting on him in my black lace bra and gray sweatpants.

"Jesus, you're beautiful." He cups my breasts in his hands, sits forward, and kisses the skin that's not covered by lace. His delicate kisses send shivers quaking through me.

Reaching down, I grab the hem of his shirt and start rolling it up. He lifts his arms over his head and I tug it off, tossing it onto the chair. He rests his hands on my hips as I smooth my hands across his broad shoulders, down his muscular arms and back up. I graze my palms down the flesh of his chest, pausing and circling his hardening nipples. He grunts, digging his fingers into my skin.

"Stand up," I say as I get off of him.

He stands and I unbuckle his belt then unbutton and unzip his pants as he watches me. I slide his pants down his legs and remove them, one leg at a time. Then I go back for his boxer briefs. Moving the waistband over his hard-on, I slide them off. His body is incredible. Flat, hard pecs tensed above ridges of abs. Strong arms I want wrapped around me. And toned, powerful legs. My blood races, heat gathers in my chest.

I give him a nudge, pressing my fingers into his chest, and he sits back on the sofa. With his eyes salacious on my body, I put my thumbs into the waist of my sweatpants and move them down my legs, stepping out of them. Slowly dropping between his knees, I take him in my hand and stroke. A groan rumbles in his chest, traveling into mine. Then I lean forward and circle his head with my tongue, eliciting a delicious sound from him. Popping the tip of his head into my mouth, I pull it out and flick my tongue against the sensitive V. His body tenses as another begging sound releases, buzzing the room.

I repeat the motion a few more times, then wrap my lips over my teeth and take him into my mouth. A groan roars from the abyss of his expansive chest. When I look up at him, his eyes are wild, his mouth drops open. He watches me. My heart races, greed mixes with need. I return my attention to his dick. With my hand and mouth working in unison, I get my rhythm, pumping up and down him. His breaths grow louder, faster.

"Candi, wait." His breath intense, ragged. Lust careening.

"Jesus. You're gonna make me come." Another hard breath hurls. "Come up here. It's my turn."

I want him. I want him inside me. I want to *feel* him inside me.

Releasing him, I stand then straddle myself above his lap. Covering his lips with mine, I move my panties aside and slide myself onto him, releasing a moan of pleasure, sucking a controlled breath as he fills me.

"Fuck," he grunts a breath, gripping my hips. "What are you doing? Are you sure?"

"I'm sure," I say, rocking my hips.

He groans. "I don't have a condom."

"I'm on the pill." I continue rocking my hips, clenching my walls around his girth.

He moves his hands to my breasts, palming them and squeezing them. Sliding one strap of my bra down over my shoulder, exposing my breast, he leans forward, taking my nipple into his mouth, circling it with his tongue. Then he slides his hand between my legs and rubs my nub. My body ablaze with fire. The sensation is too much. I remove his hand from between my legs. Without a word, he takes my guidance. Leaning back, I put my hands on his knees, letting my body rock back and forth on him. He moves his hands to my lower back, joining my motion and pumping up into me. I want to feel him slide in and out of me.

Lifting myself off of him, I turn around so my back is facing him and I spread my knees outside of his. Then I take him in my hand and guide him inside me again. He growls on an exhale. Using my legs, I lift myself up and release back down on him. Up and down, up and down. He puts one hand on my hip and grabs my hair with the other, tugging.

His heightening sounds drive my desire. A groan rumbles, vibrating my body, shaking the ground under my feet. "You feel too good this way," he says, heaving breaths.

Time to do what I know how to do. I lift off of him again and straddle him, facing him once more. His eyes flicker rapidly between mine. Then he leans forward and kisses me. As we kiss, I push him against the sofa and grab the top of the sofa for leverage. Working my body and pelvis in a wavelike motion, I ride him, unbridled passion driving me.

"Fuck," he says under his trembling breath. Grabbing my hips with his hands, he matches my rhythm as he pulls me down onto him. "Candi. You're gonna make me come." The harder his breaths, the louder his groans, the more relentless my gyrating. "I don't wanna come yet. Not before you." Leaning back and continuing my movements, I slide my hand between his legs and rub the length of skin between his balls and his butthole. "Oh, Jesus, Candi."

Finally, his body tenses over and over as he releases loud, animalistic growls. He holds my hips still as he pulses inside me and shudders, his head pressed back into the sofa. As he chases his breath, I squeeze my walls around him, causing a flinch and groan as he digs his fingers into my skin.

When his shudders subside and his breathing normalizes, he lifts his head from the sofa. Taking my face in his hands, his eyes voracious, he kisses me tenderly.

"I gotta pee. I'll be right back. Don't go anywhere." I lift off of him.

"Don't worry, I won't. I don't think I can move."

I walk quickly to my bathroom and clean myself up. Then I grab a washcloth and get it wet with warm water, looking at myself in the mirror. *Holy shit that was incredible. He felt so good inside me.* I wring out the washcloth and go back out to the living area. He's right where I left him, head resting back, arms splayed out next to him, knees resting open.

I kneel between his legs and wipe him off. He watches me, gratitude abound in his gaze.

"Thank you."

Resting my elbows on his knees, I cradle my chin in my hands. "I'm starving. Are you hungry?"

A chuckle rolls out of him. "Yeah, I could eat. What do you want?"

"After that? I'm ready for a cheeseburger and fries, chocolate cake, and champagne."

"Done," he says, flashing me that sexy smile of his that makes my knees wiggle.

Taking the washcloth, I grab my sweatpants and sweatshirt and go to the bathroom again. When I go back out, he's wearing his boxer briefs.

"It'll be about twenty minutes. Do you mind if I take a shower?"

"Not at all."

Room service arrives before he's out of the bathroom. I wheel the cart into the bedroom and turn on the TV. When he comes out of the bathroom, he helps me put the plates on the bed for our feast. Leaving the chocolate cake on the cart, we climb onto the bed and sit cross-legged, angled toward each other.

"This is unacceptable, you know," he says.

"What's unacceptable?" I ask, taking a bite of my burger.

"You didn't come."

"I know. I don't usually come. That night at Destiny's." I shake my head and widen my eyes, recalling the wild night. "I don't know what happened to me. You had me out of my mind. That rarely happens."

"Well, you'd better get used to that happening. Next time, you're mine. You're going to see how attentive I am." His words move through me with the promise of seduction, flooding me with a rush of anticipation. "Tonight wasn't at all what I expected. I kind of thought you were going to kick me out. That was —" He bugs out his eyes and cocks his head. "Something else. You're like...a goddess."

My cheeks heat at the compliment. "I'll have to take your word for that." I put a few fries in my mouth.

"So, you don't date, but you're on the pill?"

"Yeah, I have cysts and fibroids in my uterus and the pill helps keep them minimized."

"Jeez, I'm sorry. Do they hurt?" he asks, putting his burger on his plate and focusing on me.

"They used to, but the pill helps."

"Okay. I don't want to hurt you." His compassion blows me away.

We finish our meals and get our pieces of chocolate cake. He pours champagne into our glasses and we climb back onto the bed.

"This may not have been how I pictured my first Gucci gig going, but I still want to celebrate." I hold up my glass. "To Gucci."

He clinks my glass. "To Gucci."

"You know, we're not far from Greece. I was only heading home. I don't know if you were, but what do you think about rearranging our plans and going there tomorrow? Maybe we can find your mom." I glance over to see his expression, hoping I'm not being too bold with my suggestion.

His eyes open wide and his head draws back. "Uh…uh." He lifts his hand to his chin and rubs the scruff. "I, uh, um. I hadn't, uh, thought about that," he stammers.

Obviously, I've caught him off guard. Maybe that's too much for him. "We don't have to. I just thought, we're so close, you know?"

"No, yeah," he says, rubbing the back of his neck. "Wow, um. You have me a little tongue-tied here." Discomfort fringes his aura.

"I'm sorry. There's no pressure," I say gently. "I just thought that, we're here together and, I could go with you. You know, moral support if you need it."

He sits quietly, rubbing his finger across the top of his lip, his thumb anchored into his cheek. Then he looks at me. "If there's anyone I'd want by my side to do that, it's you." He locks his eyes on mine as he breathes me in. "Okay," he says hesitantly, and nods his head slightly.

"Okay." I reach out my hand and squeeze his hand tenderly. "Let's finish this cake and look up flights."

17

Enzo

Flights and hotel room booked, it's late. My nerves are wired at the thought of possibly seeing my mom tomorrow. I don't want to be alone. I want to be with Candi.

Together, we put the plates and glasses on the room service cart.

I take her in my arms, looking down into her beautiful brown eyes. "Can I stay?"

"Yes, you can stay." Stretching up onto her toes, she kisses me.

While she washes up for bed, I wheel the cart out and put it outside her door. With my toothbrush back in my room, I can't brush my teeth so I lie down in bed and wait for her.

I wasn't sure she'd forgive me. I'm so thankful she did. And then she rode me like a fucking goddess. I didn't see that coming. I'd planned to make her come undone the first time we had sex, and every time after that. Her body, the way she moves, the way she fucking feels, all I could do was watch her, feel her, so tight around my dick. Unrelenting passion, capsizing me in slow motion. If I was standing, she would've brought me to my knees.

Now she wants to go with me to see my mom. I'm scared shitless. I know the name of the café where she works, but I don't know if she'll be there. If she is, I don't know what to do. Shit, I don't know what to say. Knowing Candi will be there with me eases me a little.

Our first night together. I'm looking forward to holding her in my arms. Before she comes out of the bathroom, I fall asleep.

I wake before the alarm. Candi's spooned into me, her body molding perfectly to mine, her long, pink hair falling around her. I listen to her breaths. The faint smell of her sweet honey fills my nose. I want to stay like this forever.

Even after last night and our physical connection, I know I have some earning to do with her. I have to earn back her trust. To prove to her that I *do* believe in her, with every fiber of my being. She holds a pain I can't even imagine. I want to protect her from pain, not be the cause of it. I have to earn her heart.

As quietly as I can, I get out of bed and put on my clothes. On a piece of hotel notebook paper, I write a note telling her I'll meet her at the airport. I have to get back to my hotel and pack up my things.

Before heading to the airport, I email the private investigator to see if he's able to verify that my mom is still working and living in the same place as when he originally found her for me.

Meeting at the gate an hour ahead of our boarding time, we grab a snack.

"Have you thought about what you'll say to her?"

"I have. A lot actually, through the years. My thoughts always seem to end up scrambled. I know the little kid in me wants to be angry and yell at her. And adult-me knows that sometimes we have to do things in life that hurt other people and we never fully feel the impact of our decisions and actions. I guess, really, I just have questions. Well, one question, why?"

She puts down her chocolate-filled cornetto and places her hand on top of mine. "I think when you see her, the right words will come to you." With her words, her touch, she weaves herself into my soul.

She always knows how to comfort me.

When we land, we get a taxi to Canaves Oia Suites to check in. With our bags in our room, I check my email.

"Hmm, that guy I hired can't verify my mom's location. He said he'd need more time."

She takes both of my hands in hers and looks up at me, sweet and confident. "Then we take a chance and go find out on our own."

Cupping her face in my hands, I kiss her full lips, trying to soak in some of her calm.

Nerves rock through me and I blow a loud sigh. "That's what we came here for, whether I'm ready or not." I say on an exhale, my words gravelly. "Let's do it." Butterflies mix with acid in my stomach.

We head down to the lobby and get into a taxi.

"Ambrosia Café, please." I hold Candi's hand tightly on the ten-minute ride.

I try to distract my thoughts by taking in the scenery. A hallmark of this area, loulaki-blue domed roofs top bright white buildings and colorful flowers scale the walls and fill large pots at entrances to storefronts.

The taxi driver pulls up to the café and we get out. Candi holds my hand, despite the fact that it's wet with sweat. The outdoor cobblestone patio is filled with quaint, mismatched tables and chairs that sit under a canopy of purple jacaranda branches.

Unable to move, I stand staring at the little café. My hand in hers, she stands still by my side.

"I suppose I should go in and see if she's here. That *is* why we came here." My chest clutches as I struggle for air.

She squeezes my hand. "Whenever you're ready."

I take a deep breath, disquiet rattling me. It trembles out of me, shaking my skin.

"I'll be right here." Her softness, her care, are stones grounding me.

As I release her hand and begin to move, I see a woman step onto the patio. My blood freezes in my veins. Fear stakes my heart in panic and I almost turn and run. Candi's by my side again holding my arm, she must've sensed it.

The sun dances on her facial features, delicate, pretty, like how I remember my mom. Grayish-white hair is pulled back into a braid that falls below her shoulders. She's carrying a tray of drinks and a black apron is tied around her waist. She looks like the woman in the pictures the private investigator sent me.

Candi rubs her hand across my back. "Go to her," she says softly, encouragement nudging me.

Hyper-aware of every step I take toward her, trembling in my core, I move at a leaden pace. Dense air steals my breath. *Am I ready for this?* The closer to her I get, the heavier my steps. A high-pitched ringing echoes in my ears. I watch her as I move closer.

With a soft smile on her face, she serves drinks to the couple sitting at a table and engages in a pleasant exchange. Looking up from them as I approach, she sees me, and searches my face for a second. When recognition hits, her eyes widen. Dropping the tray with a clatter to the ground, one hand flies to her chest and the other around her stomach as she gasps and steps back.

Electric bumps scatter across my skin. I pick up the tray. "Do you — know who I am?" I ask quietly, searching her eyes. Green eyes I remember so vividly from our talks on the rickety wooden bench, eating black raspberry ice cream with chocolate sprinkles at Nelson's Ice Cream Shoppe when she'd take me for mother-son dates. Eyes that are now weathered by time and begin filling with tears.

"Yes." Her voice barely above a whisper, she pauses, taking a shallow breath. "You're my son…Lorenzo," she chokes out as her brows squeeze together, forming deeper creases.

A rash of chills swarm me. "Yes, I'm Lorenzo. I, I came here to find you. I'm sorry, I didn't mean to startle you." My stomach churns, turbulence unsettles me.

"You did, but it's okay," she says, moving one hand to cover her mouth. She looks at my face like she's studying me. Then she extends her hand and cups my cheek. So gentle. Unexpected.

My eyes squeeze shut and my pulse hammers. When I open my eyes, she withdraws her hand, curling it into her body.

"Would it be all right if we talked?" I ask, terrified I'll be rejected once again.

"Yes, I would like that very much." She takes the tray from me and looks at her watch as her hand shivers. "My shift is over in ten minutes. You can sit at one of the tables." She points to several open tables. "Can I bring you anything?"

"No, I'm fine, thank you. I'll wait for you."

As she turns away from me, she holds the tray to her chest and lifts her hand to her mouth, walking with labored steps back into the café. I go back to Candi who's seated on an iron bench beneath bright pink flowering trees.

She stands when I approach. "How did it go?"

I strain a sigh. "She's finishing up her shift in about ten minutes and then we're going to sit and talk." I rub my callouses with my thumb, nerves pulsing at me.

"That's great." She pauses. "She's pretty."

"She is. She's just how I remember her, except with gray hair and wrinkles." I weakly smile. "I'm going to go sit and wait for her and try to think about what to say." My mind — blank.

"Okay. I'll go find some shops and keep myself occupied. Call me whenever you're done. I won't be far."

"Okay." I blow a puff of air and give her a quick kiss then sit at a small bistro table on the patio. Given the time of day, it's pretty empty. Each minute that passes doesn't bring words, only heightens my tension.

About ten minutes later, my mom comes out to the patio. As she walks toward me, she tucks a few hairs that have come loose from her braid back behind her ear. Sitting down across from me, her movements are hesitant.

"It's nice to see you." She strains a smile, her posture stiff. "I, I watched you grow up on your social media." The statement knocks me.

"You did?" *Why?*

"Yes, I follow you on Instagram." She lifts her shoulder as the corner of her mouth tilts up. "Anastasia too." Her eyes roam my face. "You've done well for yourself. And you're so handsome." She pauses, with a proud, but weak smile. "I know it's not my place to say…" Tears form in the wells of her eyes. "I'm so proud of you." She leans slightly toward me as her eyes squint.

I process her words. *She's been watching me? She's proud of me?* My heart pounds, confusion throngs, adrenaline gusts.

"I — have a question I hope you'll answer." A lump swells in my throat, practically closing off the air.

"Okay." Hands cupped together in her lap, knees together, and ankles crossed, she quietly waits for my question.

I swallow hard, rubbing my calloused hand. "Why…" My lower lip trembles. I pull in my lips, trying to make it stop. "Why did you leave us? Didn't you love us anymore? Did we do something wrong?" My nine-year-old self is desperate for the answer. Desperate to know if I'd done something somehow. Broken pieces desperate to be put back together by knowledge. To understand. Wondering all these years if I was too broken to love.

Leaning forward again, she touches her hand to my cheek as tears trail down her face and pain coats her eyes. "Oh, my dear boy. I loved you all very much. You didn't do anything wrong. I left *because* I loved you. I left because I wanted you to have a better life than I could give you." She pauses, looking down, shaking her head. "I struggled with drug addiction for many years. I tried to get help, and your dad did everything he could to help me get clean. But nothing worked, the addiction was too strong. I became a danger to you and Anastasia. And I was no good for your dad." She was broken too. I feel it now.

"But he loved you." I swallow thick. "He loved you every day since you left. Every day until he died. He loved you." I force the lump down my throat, holding back the tears burning behind my eyes. Anger trying to flare. "You broke his heart. He could've helped you get better."

She shakes her head with a pained smile. "He couldn't help me. He tried. I was dragging him down. I was destroying our family. He deserved better. You all did." When she looks down, a tear drops into her cupped hands. "I knew that if I was going to let the drugs kill me, I was going to make sure none of you had to be the one to find me." Another tear slides down her cheek as she raises her head. "So, I left." She confesses her darkness. Lays it out for me to judge. Regret streaks down her face.

"And you're clean now?"

"I am." She pushes a faint smile to her lips.

My chest tightens, making it hard to breathe. Anger trying to creep in again. "Why didn't you ever come find us? Or at least contact us?"

The corners of her mouth turn down as her brows pinch together in agony once again. "I was ashamed. I thought I'd lost the right to be in your lives." Her body curls inward, like forcing out the words was excruciating. "How could a child ever forgive a mother who abandoned them?" She hangs her head, releasing soft, whimpered cries. Her raw heart splayed. Nothing concealed.

My mother sits before me, frail and hunched over, crippled with regret, plagued by remorse. With an understanding of why she left us and why she never reached out, the constriction in my chest loosens. Years of pain, torment, and suffering begin to fade. Anger shifts.

I lean toward her. She looks up into my eyes, tears streaming down her timeworn cheeks.

"I came here to find you." I brush the tears from her wrinkled cheek. "To get answers to questions that have haunted me for years. Thank you for telling me all this." Two souls tattered, seeking comfort, yearning to be loved.

"You deserve answers." She sniffs. "I don't expect your forgiveness," she says, shaking her head gently. "But if it's okay with you, I'd like to be part of your life."

We've missed so much of each other's lives; I don't want to miss any more. "I'd like that a lot."

"Would it be okay to hug you?" She asks, her soul begging for atonement.

The boulder lodged so tight in my throat; air barely squeezes by. Tears threaten the corners of my eyes. I stand, holding my arms open. Practically collapsing into me, her body trembles. I hold her as time ticks, unable to erase lost years.

My soul in need of its own deliverance, I whisper, "I forgive you." Resting my head on top of hers, solace flows.

She convulses in my arms as sobs pour out of her, hugging me so tight, like she's trying to make up for twenty-five years of missed hugs.

Her crying subsides and we sit back down in our chairs. I take a few napkins out of the holder on the table and hand them to her. She dabs her cheeks and under her eyes.

"There's someone I'd like you to meet if you're up for it."

"Yes, of course." She perks up and straightens her posture.

"Give me a minute?" I get up and step away, calling Candi. "Hey, how far away are you?"

"Just around the corner, a few blocks down," she says.

"Do you want to meet my mom?" Outside of Anastasia, these are the two most important women in my life, and I want them to meet.

"Yes, I'd love to meet her. See you in a bit."

I return to the table and sit down.

"She'll be here in a few minutes. She's just down the block."

A smile lifts her cheeks and there's a twinkle in her eyes. "You're married."

Heat rushes through me. "No." A chuckle shimmies out of me. "We're not married."

"Oh. I never see any women on your Instagram so I figured you just keep your private life off of there."

"I do. I don't want all those strangers knowing my personal business. But no, Candi's...we're..." What are we? We haven't started using titles, but I know we're exclusive to each other. "We're seeing each other."

"Oh. I don't understand the terms you kids use today." She stands. "Let me get us some waters. I'll be right back. I should probably clean up my face a little before meeting her."

Candi arrives while she's gone and I pull over a chair for her.

"How did it go?" she asks.

I open my eyes wide and blow a puff of air, exhausted from all the emotion. "Good. Tough. But good."

Mom comes out with a tray of bottled waters, immediately smiling. She sets the tray on the table and we stand up.

"Hello," she says, reaching out her hand. "You must be Lorenzo's girlfriend."

Candi takes her hand, wrapping it in both of hers. "Yes, I am."

"Mom, this is Candi. Candi, this is my mom, Despina."

"It's a pleasure to meet you," Candi says with that warm smile of hers that makes everyone feel comfortable.

"And you." My mom smiles with a hint of pride.

We spend the next hour telling Mom about our Gucci shoot and how we met and she tells us a little about her life here in Greece. She never remarried. I think she never stopped loving Dad.

"We're gonna get going and let you get back to your day. I'm sure you didn't plan on having your afternoon derailed."

"I'm so happy you derailed it. This was truly wonderful."

"We have each other's numbers and email addresses. You can reach me anytime," I say.

"Thank you, Lorenzo." She hugs me, then steps back and takes my face in her hands. The biggest smile spreads across her face.

The weight that's been lying on my chest, suffocating me for years, has been lifted. She didn't reject me. She didn't reject us. She thought she was saving us.

We say our goodbyes and Candi and I leave the café.

Candi slides her hand into mine and we walk toward the shops she found earlier.

"Girlfriend, huh?" she asks coyly.

"Yeah, sorry about that. That was all her."

"It's okay. I kinda like it," she says, squeezing my hand.

I kinda like it too. "Where are we heading?"

"Do you want to talk about it at all?"

"Not right now. I want to sit with it a while." I'm emotionally drained.

"That's fine. I didn't get to all the shops. How about we see if there are any we both want to check out."

"Lead the way."

We walk, hand-in-hand, down the street, looking in the windows of little shops. Buildings of stark white are adorned with brightly-colored shutters and doors. Many shops have their wares displayed on the sidewalks. Everything from handmade pottery and dishes in vibrant colors to paintings to clothes and food.

"This is the cute dress I got for dinner tonight." She says, pointing to a mannequin wearing a body-hugging black dress that goes down below the knees. The top part starts under the arm on one side and the pieces of fabric tie together on the opposite shoulder, leaving the cleavage area asymmetrically exposed from under one breast up to the knot on the shoulder.

"That?" My mouth waters. "I'm ready for an early dinner."

18

Candi

I'm thrilled that his conversation with his mom went well. I hope he opens up to me more about it at dinner tonight. I hope he knows he can trust and confide in me.

I put on my lipstick and check my look in the full-length mirror. Satisfied, I go out to the living area of our suite. He's out on the veranda, overlooking Petra, where we're about to go eat. Wearing black jeans and a vertical-striped copper, black, and light gray shirt with the sleeves rolled up, he looks handsome.

"I'm ready."

Turning around, he looks me up and down. "Whoa. We have different definitions of the word cute. Maybe we should order room service instead," he says, rubbing the scruff on his chin.

I laugh, taking his hand and tugging. "Come on."

When we get to the restaurant, we're brought out to an intimate two-person table overlooking the Aegean Sea. Greece is breathtaking. Oia is built on the slopes of a cliff, facing a volcano, and the panoramic view is nothing short of majestic. From the angle of where we're sitting, we can see dozens of lighted homes and buildings that appear to be stacked on top of one another. A handful of boats are docked in the calm water below.

The tiny lantern with a tea light in it provides a warm, romantic glow over our table that's adjacent to a short stone wall. Traditional Greek music carries subtly on the gentle breeze. Within minutes, the waiter comes by to take our drink order and Enzo orders a bottle of Henriot champagne. When the waiter returns with our bottle and glasses, we place our food order. Enzo gets côte de boeuf and I get the cod fricassee. Having inadvertently skipped lunch, we're both starving.

"You look beautiful tonight." Where he was being playful earlier, his tone is now earnest.

"Thank you." His compliments are a soft caress.

He leans his body forward a little, focusing his gaze on my face. "You're a beautiful person, Candi. Thank you for encouraging me to come here and find my mom. Thank you for being here to support me. If it wasn't for you, I don't think I would've ever come. You changed my life. And I'm grateful for you."

When Dom died, I closed off my heart. Locked it up and threw away the key. No one could ever replace him or be to me everything he was. And now, I sit across from a man who's loving, thoughtful, passionate, and so much more. A man who's seeping into my heart and making me feel things I never thought I could feel again.

"*You* had the courage to do it. This took a lot of guts, to be vulnerable and take the risk. I'm just glad I could be by your side to support you."

"Heh," he chuckles under his breath, leaning in more with his elbows on the table and clasping his hands. "You see a version of me I can't even imagine."

I lean forward, mirroring his body language. "I see the true you. A man who just took a chance of having his heart crushed in a vice, not knowing what he would hear or how painful it could be, and did it anyway. I see a brave man."

"Thank you for this gift you've given me." He lifts his glass toward me and I meet it with mine.

"Do you want to tell me what you learned? It's okay if you don't."

"No, I do." He takes a drink of his champagne then shares the highlights of their talk.

"I hope this helped you heal a little bit. I know it doesn't erase years of pain and heartache."

"It doesn't. But, it's good to have answers and to know it wasn't because she didn't love us. My heart hurts for my dad." A mist coats his eyes as he squeezes his lips together and traces the bottom of his glass with his finger. "I wish he could've known she got clean before he died. Maybe they could've rekindled their love and he'd still be here today."

I reach my hand across the table and clasp my fingers around his, wanting some of his heartache to flow to me, so I can hold it for him.

"Maybe someday you can fix your relationship with your dad. He's still here and you have that chance," he says gently.

My heart stings a little. "Maybe someday." I don't know if that'll ever happen.

Our delicious dinners arrive and we lighten our conversation as we eat.

"Wanna grab some whiskeys and take in the view from our veranda?" he asks after we finish our meals.

Looking forward to spending the rest of the evening with him, I offer a silent nod and smile. My mind reels with vibrant flashes of last night, our kisses, his touch on me, the way he felt inside me. Craving percolates.

Back in our suite, we both take our shoes off and bring our whiskeys out to the veranda. I take a sip of mine and set it on the little iron table. Looking up at the sky, I walk to the railing and he joins me. Warm air strokes my skin.

"It's so beautiful," I say. Suspended in the dark blue sky that's speckled with tiny white stars, the moon glows, lighting the surface of the sea below.

He tucks in behind me, his strong chest touching my back, and looks up into the peaceful, mammoth sky.

"I get to travel to amazing places, but I'm usually in and out so fast, I don't get to truly take them in. I'm glad I got to work on the pictures from the shoot on the flight over so I can relax while we're here. This is a nice change of pace."

"This *is* nice," he says, circling my waist with his arms, spreading warmth through my body.

I rest my head back on his chest and lay my arms on top of his, sinking into the tranquility.

"Last night was nice too."

"Yes, it was," I agree, my body tingles, remembering how amazing he felt.

"I have to confess; I'm not used to a woman taking control. Not that I minded. It was pretty damn hot actually."

"Well, we have that in common. I'm not used to a man taking control."

"Maybe it's time we change that." The seductive current in his tone caresses my body in sheets of silk.

Moving an arm from my waist, he sweeps my hair over to one side, giving him access to my fully exposed shoulder. Dropping a soft kiss behind my ear, he continues down my neck and out to my shoulder with the same feathery kisses. Working his way back, he lingers his lips in the hollow just above my collar bone. I release a whimper.

"I love kissing this spot right here." He kisses again. "The little sound you make, telling me you like it." He kisses again, longer, holding my waist tighter.

Releasing my waist, he grabs our whiskeys from the table, handing me mine. We stare at each other, electric energy heating the air between us. I take a swig; he takes a gulp. Then he takes my glass and puts them both on the table. Returning to me, he takes me in his arms and kisses me so deep, I don't even know whose air I'm breathing.

As he kisses me, he turns my body to face outward again. Taking my hands, he places them wide on the railing. "Don't move them. Close your eyes." His whisper is hot against my ear.

I suck an inhale at his directions. Desire curling.

Placing his hands on my hips, he slides them up the sides of my body, gliding his fingers along the outer edges of my breasts. Traveling back down my body, he moves his hands down my outer thighs.

"You're not wearing panties," he growls, low and deep, sending a shiver down to my toes.

"I didn't want any panty lines with my dress," I say on an exhale.

He heaves a loud breath near my ear, looping an arm around my waist and hanging his head over my shoulder. With his other hand, he traces the seam of fabric from the top of my shoulder, down my décolletage, and over the exposed skin of my breast. Following the seam, he continues up the other side grazing my skin with a delicate touch. My chest rises and falls with my breaths.

His lips are on my neck again, sucking gently. I don't feel his hands. I lift my chin. "Where are your hands?" I whisper, awaiting his next scintillating touch on my skin.

"Keep your eyes closed."

I feel him. He circles my nipples with his fingers. My grip tightens on the railing. Inhaling sharply, my body responds, my back arching against him. He continues circling as my body continues responding. Then he cups my breasts and pinches my nipples, not too hard. Just enough to make me flinch and moan. A tingle rushes between my legs.

Suddenly, his hands are gone again. My breathing increases, anticipating his next touch. I start moving my hands from the railing and he grabs them, putting them back, and tilting his hard-on into the top of my butt. He slides his hands down my thighs again, taking the fabric in his grip on the way back up.

With the lower part of my dress hugging my hips, he slides his hand between my legs, dipping between my lips with his middle finger. I whimper.

"I love how wet you are," he says as he moves his other hand under the fabric covering my breast. Squeezing my breast, he dips his finger in me again and drags it out. Back in as he squeezes my breast. In with two fingers as he kisses my neck. Out and in again as my body lights with fire and starts writhing against him, my grip so tight on the railing.

He pinches my nipple, sucks gently on my neck, and rubs his finger against my nub, sending a shockwave through me. My whimper is loud, my breaths are erratic, my blood gushes hot through every vein.

"Enzo," I say, desperation in my voice as I heave a breath. "I — "

He sinks his fingers back in, tugging on my nipple.

"I want to see you."

"Patience," he breathes against my neck, stroking my nub with the length of his finger as he withdraws it.

Releasing my breast, he puts both hands on my hips and turns me to face him, moving my dress back down. I open my eyes and he weaves his hands into my hair then kisses me. Tasting like whiskey on my tongue, he teases me relentlessly. My heart pounds against my ribs. When he breaks our kiss, he tosses back the rest of his whiskey and hands me mine. I take a gulp.

"Come here," he says. "I'm not done with you." With the glass still in my hand, he picks me up and brings me to the bedroom, laying me on the bed. Then he takes my glass and puts it on the night stand. Grabbing the remote, he turns on the TV and mutes it, then he pulls out his phone, hits a few buttons, and seductive music ribbons through the air.

Propped on my elbows with one knee bent I watch him.

He unbuttons his shirt, revealing his toned torso that my eyes feast on. Pulling it off, he tosses it on a chair. Unbuckling his belt, the metal clanking, he unzips his jeans, letting them drop to the floor with a thud. Still wearing his boxer briefs, he walks to the bed.

"If I'm going to worship you, this has to come off." He holds out his hand and I take it, standing up from the bed.

Squatting down, he slips his hands under my dress. Keeping his eyes on mine, he maintains contact with my skin as he moves my dress up my legs and over my hips. The higher he goes, the faster my breaths leave me. I raise my arms above my head and he moves the dress over my breasts, pulling it off and dropping it on the floor.

"You're so beautiful, Candi." He sweeps his eyes across my body. Stepping in, he puts his arm around my lower back and cradles my head with his other hand. His kiss is gentle, loving. "Lie down," he hushes. "It's time you feel what it's like to have someone be attentive to your magnificent body."

My heartbeat picks up. As I lie back on the bed, he climbs into the center, tucking himself close to me.

"What do you like?" he asks, the curiosity in his eyes burns with greedy mischief as he awaits my answer.

"I don't really know. No one's ever touched me the way you do." My breaths heavy, begging for him to touch me, consume me.

"Then we'll explore together." He vows. "If there's something you don't like, tell me."

I take a breath and nod, lost in his kryptonic eyes.

He reaches over to my whiskey glass and takes out the ice cube. "Hands up here." He taps my pillow and props himself on his elbow.

I rest my hands above my head, anticipation pumping ferociously.

With the ice in his fingers, he touches it to my décolletage. I gasp, grabbing my elbows with my hands above me. He looks down at me with a wicked smile. At a glacial pace, he slides the ice down the center of my body. It's so cold, I flinch, moving my arms.

In one swift movement, he pops the ice in his mouth, straddles my body, and holds both of my wrists in one hand above my head. My breaths are heavy as I look up into his eyes. Locking his eyes on mine, he holds the ice cube between is teeth. Then he leans down, placing his lips over my nipple. My back arches in response as a loud gasp bolts out of me. The ice, freezing cold, his warm tongue circling my nipple, it's an intense sensation of pleasure with a hint of pain.

Taking the ice in his fingers, he moves it around my nipple as he takes my other nipple into his still-frigid mouth. Whimpering louder, I tug my wrists against his hand. He presses them harder into the pillow. Within seconds, his mouth is hot on my nipple, the stark change in temperature sweeps a rush of desire straight to my core. I squirm beneath him, needy and panting.

Giving my nipples a small reprieve, he glides the melting ice down my stomach, around my navel, and through the top of my landing strip, lifting off of me and letting it drip down between my folds. I moan at the sensation. Popping the small chunk that remains into his mouth, he crunches it.

Releasing my wrists, he focuses again on my nipples. Cupping my breasts in his hands, he alternately sucks on them. Moving his lips down the path of melted ice, he lifts off of me and slides his body between my legs. Tugging me closer to the edge, he kneels on the floor. Roving his lips leisurely across my flesh, he drops light kisses inside my hip, down my inner thigh, holding my knee out to the side. Licks of lust and fire follow his path.

Bringing my knee back in, he lifts the other one, looking up at me from between my thighs. He runs his tongue across his lips, a rapacious riot in his eyes. Placing his hands on my stomach, he stares at me. Holding my gaze, he opens his mouth, dips his head slightly, and slides his tongue between my folds, making my inner thighs tingle and tremble. He goes again, a little deeper. And again, deeper still. With each probe of his tongue into me, my breathing increases, my body rages with heat.

Inserting his fingers, he focuses the tip of his tongue on my nub, flicking it. I cry out, grabbing the sheets beneath me and closing my knees around his head. He presses one knee down while I try to relax the other. Wrapping his arm around the top of my thigh, he continues, increasing the rhythm of his fingers sliding into me and intensifying the pace of his flicks on my nub.

"Enzo," I say, breathless. Tilting my pelvis up, I'm desperate, rabid. I grab his hair as I moan. He moves his tongue so fast it vibrates my nub. I pant as my heart pounds with fury. "Enzo. Oh, God."

The wave of orgasm builds inside me with his unrelenting fingers and tongue working me into a wild frenzy. Tension amplifies between my walls as tiny electric shocks intensify. I'm panting so hard, my mind is simultaneously empty and frantic, and finally, it hits me like a tsunami. My walls clench, a million pins and needles spread through my core, and my legs seize shut around his head. My entire body stiffens as I cry out again then hold my breath, letting myself feel every sensation in this hazy bliss.

He wasn't lying when he said he was going to worship me. *Holy fuck.* When my body finally relaxes and my breathing begins to slow, I unclench my thighs from around his head.

"Powerful one, huh?" A smile oozing of victory splashes across his face.

"Uh-huh." Is all I can get out.

"We're not done yet," he says, standing and sliding his boxer briefs down his legs before climbing onto the bed.

"I don't know if I can take any more." I chuckle softly as my legs tremble.

"All right. We can stop," he says, lying next to me.

His dick pointing to his nose, he's ready to stop because I said so. His respect for me edges him deeper into me.

"Maybe just a break."

"Whatever you want. I'll never push you," he says, then kisses my shoulder. "I'll be right back." He climbs over me and goes to the bathroom.

When he comes back, I go and quickly brush my teeth and wash off my makeup.

He's under the covers when I return.

"Come here." He holds open the sheets.

I get in and snuggle into his chest, draping my arm across his stomach and sliding my leg between his. He rests his hand on my hair. We listen to each other breathe.

"What was Dom like?" he asks, his voice calm.

What?! The walls in the room start closing in as a burst of heat spreads through my chest. "Why do you want to know about Dom?"

"It's tough not to wonder about the man who still has your girl's heart," he says, stroking my hair.

My chest fists. Though his delivery is tender and curious, his statement smashes me in the face. I'm a mixture of grief, thinking about Dom in this moment, and hopefulness, as his words, "your girl's heart" drift into me. Goose bumps coat my skin.

"But my heart doesn't belong to him. Not anymore." Hearing myself say the words stings.

"You might not think so, but it does. You wear him around your neck, clinging to his ghost." He pauses. No accusation. No judgement. "I get it." His tone still gentle, he takes his Superman pendant in his hand. "We both know the pain of loss."

The parallels that connect us, reach deep into my soul. I place my hand on his, still holding the pendant.

"He was important to you. I want you to know it's okay to talk to me about him. It's not like we're on a first date and you're endlessly carrying on about an awful ex-boyfriend. I really want to know. What was he like?"

As uncomfortable as I am, I admire his openness and invitation to share something so intimate with him. This is going to be tough.

I take a slow, deep breath. "He was an architect. So talented and skilled at his job, plus he loved it. He was a very positive person and looked for the good in everyone. One of those people who would drop what he was doing to help you. He got along great with my parents and they loved him." I pause, reminiscing. A chuckle rustles out of me. "He'd sit through any TV show or movie I wanted to watch, even if he didn't like it and we'd seen it a hundred times. He'd watch it with me because I liked it." I shake my head. "And when I'd get home from a long day of traveling for work, he'd rub my feet." I sigh. "He had a lot of integrity. Did the right thing when no was watching because that's just who he was. We had similar values, respected each other, and shared some of the same desires for our future." I stop, my heart hurting.

"He sounds like a great guy. Like he deserved you." His tone is gentle, heartfelt.

"He really was." A stuttered breath leaves me. "They were together when they died. My mom and Dom. He wanted to take Destiny with him, but she was away with her mom for a few months doing research for a book while her mom was directing a film, and he didn't want to wait." I pause to fill my lungs. "At least they were together." I say with a sigh. "After they passed away, I didn't want to get close to anyone, ever."

"Why?" After his own loss, I know he knows why. With his own delicacy, he invites me to open myself to him. His desire to hear my answer embraces me.

"I got it in my head that the people I love get taken away from me. I don't think my heart could survive losing another person I love." Wrapped around him, my heart fists.

He tilts his head, looking down at me tucked into him. "Are you going to let that stop you from — falling in love again?"

My rib cage constricts, unbearable. "I…I don't know."

"Please don't let your pain drown you. You have so much life to live and so much love to give. I know your heart hurts. But, don't deprive yourself of the chance of having love again." Locking his tender eyes on mine, he tucks my hair behind my ear and brushes my cheek with his thumb. "I want a chance to earn your love, if you'll let me." He breathes, the air between us fills with hope. "Let me kiss away your pain." His words make a promise to my heart. His eyes shift between mine, waiting...

Shivers streak across my flesh.

Without another word, I lift my chin, offering my lips, accepting his promise. He lowers his face, claiming them, his touch sparking new life into me. My rib cage loosens, making space for him in my heart. *I'm falling.*

His kiss is deep yet gentle, slow and passionate.

Taking his time, he savors my mouth, moving my body to lie flat. He breaks our kiss, leaving my mouth wanting him. With a feather-light touch, he skims his hand with slow, calculated movements, heating my skin beneath it. Running his fingers from behind my ear, he trails them down the side of my neck, across my collarbone, and over my shoulder. Moving down my arm, he turns my hand to face up and lightly traces each finger then makes circles in my palm. Retracing his journey back up, he follows the same pattern on the other side. Everywhere he touches tingles.

Like he's painting a canvas with his fingers as the paintbrush, he glides them down the center of my chest, letting them curve under one breast and round up to the top of it. Making circles inward toward my nipple, he doesn't touch it. He mimics his pattern on my other breast, tantalizing me. Blood churns. While his touch is calming, what he's not touching is torturous. When he gets below my breasts, he flattens his hand against my stomach, grazing my skin on his way down between my legs. My breathing picks up as I close my eyes, waiting impatiently for his next movement.

Dipping his finger into the wet paint, he doesn't stay there long. Just enough to taunt me and make me gasp. Moving his hand, he wraps his fingers around my back as he presses his thumb lightly into my abs, traveling back up my body.

Hovering his face above mine, his eyes flicker with fire. The air between us simmers. Rolling on top of me, he slides himself into me, then moves his body high up on mine, his chest above my face. Body pressing against body, my senses ignite everywhere our skin meets. I've never had a man go so high above me. Then I feel it.

His dick facing down inside me, he gently begins grinding himself into me with a steady rocking motion. Every up and down stroke is slow, deliberate, and hyper-focused on my nub. I nearly buck beneath him. As he moves, he gazes down at me with his mesmerizing eyes, pulling me deeper into the intensity of the moment. Locking me in our ethereal chrysalis, his hot, controlled breaths float into my open mouth.

Rather than the rapid, shallow, panting breaths that usually fly out of me, my breaths are deep, and slow, following his unhurried rhythm. A contradiction to my racing heartbeat. Ensnared in our web spun of passion and tenderness, our esoteric connection brings me the most euphoric high I've ever experienced. Imprisoning my eyes, worshiping my body, capturing my heart, he rubs against me, embedding himself into my soul.

Neither of us says a word as our bodies speak a language our minds can't comprehend. Several more pleasure-serving rubs and my entire body explodes into ecstasy, every nerve-ending aflame as I tremble, heat blazing through me. He intoxicates me.

Within seconds, he pulses inside me, moaning, his body shuddering on top of me. Groaning over and over, he buries his face in the pillow above me. When his shudders subside, he lets the weight of his body drape over me, cradling me in his arms.

19

Enzo

Still deep inside her, I lift my face so I can look into her eyes. Silence fuses us, body and soul. Her mouth open, her heart pounds against my chest. Her breaths give me life. Her heartbeat is my bloodline.

My body drained, I roll off of her, keeping contact with her skin. *Holy fuck.* Though I've done coital alignment before, it was never so visceral.

"That was intense," she says, blowing a soft puff of air.

My eyes closed, I pull her into me and kiss her forehead.

"I'll be right back," she says, getting up and going to the bathroom.

Lying in my post-ecstasy bliss, I can't remember a time when I was so connected to someone. I don't want to know a time that she's not in my life.

My mind returns to her telling me that her mom and Dom died in the same car accident. Agony shreds my heart, gutting me for the pain she endured losing two of the closest people to her at the same time. Without a good relationship with her dad, I'm glad she has Destiny. I can't even begin to fathom what she went through.

Returning with a warm washcloth, she wipes me off. She takes the cloth back to the bathroom and returns to me, nestling her body into the side of mine again.

"Candi?"

"Yeah." She tilts her head to look up at me, still resting on my chest.

"I can't tell you what's going to happen tomorrow or next week or next year. But I can tell you I'm not going anywhere." I pause to emphasize my next words. "Nothing will take me away from you."

She squeezes her eyes shut, curling her body into me and holding me so tight.

I stroke her hair until we fall asleep.

With our flight not until early evening, we sleep in, have a leisurely breakfast, and find another nearby village to wander around.

Walking hand in hand, the sun warming our faces, we approach a tattoo parlor. She looks at me and tilts her head toward the parlor with a mischievous twinkle in her eyes, little vixen.

"What, now?" I ask.

A laugh spills out of her. "Yeah. To remind us of our trip," she says with a wink. "It's a better souvenir than a trinket that just needs to be dusted."

We walk into the parlor, the air alive with a high-pitched buzz and the smell of green soap.

"Na eísai sostós mazí sou," says the tattoo artist who's working on a customer.

We have no idea what he said. Probably something like, "I'll be right with you." considering he's working on someone.

"What are you going to get?" she asks.

"I don't know yet. You?"

"Me either. I don't want anything big and it has to be somewhere discreet. While I don't mind tattoos, I also don't want my skin covered in them," she says.

Considering she only has one and she's not looking to get all inked up, I have a feeling she'll pick something that has a lot of meaning.

We roam the parlor, looking for ideas in the images covering the walls to the ceiling and in binders overflowing the counters.

She stops on a page in a binder and looks up at me, pupils wide as a canyon.

It's an antique-looking heart lock with flowers and filigree on it and an ornate matching key. The epitome of her. Tough as steel on the outside juxtaposed against the fragility of her wounded heart.

"They remind me a little of the patterns on your mom's oil lamps you have in your house."

A bright smile lifts her cheeks as she nods in agreement. At the end of the nod, her head tilts slightly like she appreciates my remembering the lamps.

I get my phone out of my pocket and take a picture. "This way we'll have it to compare with in case you find something else you like."

She continues flipping through binders when the artist comes over.

"Hello, do you speak English?" I ask.

"Yes, no good, but yes." He smiles.

"We want tattoos. Can you take us?"

"Yes. I can. Only me today."

I show him the picture on my phone and Candi joins us.

"How long will this take?" I ask.

"How big you want?"

"One inch?" Candi suggests.

"Mm." He tips his head from side to side as the corners of his lips turn down, pondering. "Two hour I think."

I look down at my watch. "That might be cutting it tight with our flight." I look at her, not wanting to see disappointment in her face.

"How long for only the heart lock?" she asks him, covering the key with her hand.

"One hour?" He lifts his shoulders. "Maybe little more." He holds up his hand, pinching his thumb and pointer finger close together.

"But you won't have time to get one." She looks at me with puppy-dog eyes.

I chuckle at how adorable she is. "I have enough. Besides, I won't be forgetting this trip." I look her square in the eyes so she can feel the depth of my gratitude. "Come on, let's get you in the chair."

She sits back in the reclined chair and slides the waist of her black leggings down to the top of her pubic bone. Then she points to a spot that's three and a half inches in from her hip bone and about three inches down, centimeters from the top of her landing strip, ensuring it'll be covered by a bikini bottom. My mind jumps forward to licking that spot when it's healed.

"Here?" she asks him.

He nods.

"Can you make the lock open?" She gestures with her hand, opening the shackle from the body of the lock. When she looks up at me, vulnerability and anticipation coalescing, her unspoken words float into my heart.

In that instant, our energies intertwine, the promise of hope tangling between us.

"Yes. I can." He nods with a smile then looks at me and back at her. "I agápi sou?"

Shaking her head, she shrugs and smiles at him.

"Eh, hmm," He rubs his chin, his brain searching for the translation. "Your love, yes?"

Her cheeks turn a soft shade of pink as she looks back up at me. I grab a chair to sit with them. Putting the chair next to her, I hold her hand. As he begins his artwork, she squeezes my hand, but keeps her body still.

She winces, sucking air in through her teeth. "I forgot how painful these are."

"You did pick a sensitive spot." I wink, rubbing her hand with my thumb.

We get to the airport with just enough time to get to our gate before boarding begins. Though in discomfort from her fresh tattoo, once we're in the air, Candi opens her laptop and continues working on her images for the Gucci campaign. I start reading the book I brought, *I Am Watching You*, and fall asleep.

When we land in L.A., she lets me know she got an email about a track event this weekend at Willow Springs Raceway and invites me to join her. Excited to watch her drive, I accept. It's a two-day event, but I can only go the first day because I have to get back for work. We set our plans and head home with a couple busy days ahead of us.

I've been avoiding calling Anastasia to tell her that I went to see Mom. With her being a little older, I think she was angrier than I was. I don't keep things from her. I need to tell her. I pick up my phone and call her.

"Hey, how are you? I've been waiting to hear how things turned out with Candi. Are you two okay?"

"Yeah, we're good. Really good actually. I have so much to tell you." I sit on my sofa.

"I'm all ears." Her excitement reverberates in my bones.

"She finally let me talk to her and I apologized. I wasn't sure she was going to accept my apology, but she did. I ended up staying the night in her room and —" I hesitate and take a breath. "She pointed out that we were close to Greece and suggested I try to find Mom."

Silence pierces through the phone.

"She came with me and —" I swallow. "I found her, Anastasia. I went to the café where I told you the private investigator found her working. I saw her. I talked with her."

"What did she say?" Bitterness bites her tone.

"She was addicted to drugs and knew her addiction was putting us in danger and destroying Dad and our family, so she left. She said she thought if the drugs ended up killing her, she didn't want any of us to find her." I pause, harnessing myself for her reaction to my next words. "She's clean now."

"She is? Then where the hell has she been? Why didn't she come back to us?" she seethes. "Daddy died still loving her," she chokes out, her pain penetrating me.

"She was ashamed. She didn't feel she had the right to come back to us. I think she felt like she fucked us up enough already." I pause, bracing again. "She's following us on Instagram. Said she's been watching us grow up."

"She *missed* us growing up, Enzo," she scathes. Her stilted breaths come through the phone, anger rumbling through her. The broken heart of a child.

"I know she did." I drop my forehead into my hand, rubbing it. "I'm not saying what she did was right. She regrets it. In her mind at the time, she thought she was doing the best thing for *us* by leaving."

"But we were so little. We needed her. Daddy needed her." Soft sobs drift into my ear, tugging at my heart.

"I'm sorry. I didn't mean to upset you. I just thought you should know I went to see her." I pause, needing her to hear what I say. "And I wanted to make sure you knew that she didn't leave because she didn't love us."

Her whimpering sobs lodge a knot in my throat. I want to wrap her in my arms.

I try to swallow down the knot. "Maybe someday we can go see her together or have her come here." I offer, giving her a moment. "I think it would be good for you to see her. It helped me feel a lot better."

She sniffs. "I don't know. Maybe someday, but I just don't know." A mix of defeat and defiance color her tone.

I understand her resistance. "If you ever decide you want to,

I'll go with you. I know I never would've done it if Candi hadn't suggested it and gone with me." I shake my head, almost in disbelief of how lucky I am. "She's incredible."

"So, things are okay with her?" The heaviness in her tone lightens.

"Yeah. We stayed together in Greece. It was, I don't know. I've never felt so connected to a woman before. Not even just physically. It's, I don't know how to explain it. All I know is what I feel on so many levels when I'm with her." A core need, a desire, a longing stampede inside me.

"When it feels right, it doesn't need explaining." That hopefulness wraps around her words.

"Hmh. I guess so." It does feel right. Everything feels right when I'm with her.

"I gotta go."

"Okay, I'll talk to you later."

"Enzo?"

"Yeah?"

"Thank you for telling me about Mom." Her voice is soft and low, bruised. "I'm glad you went. And I'm glad it helped you. Maybe someday I'll be brave enough."

"I love you." Though I know she'd feel better, I can't force her to see Mom.

"I love you too. Bye."

I know she's still angry, but I hope what I told her helped her to heal, even if only a little bit. She deserves that.

I meet Candi at her place at four forty-five AM and follow her in my car to the racetrack. About two hours later, we pull up to a gate at the entrance of a parking lot where she signs something. When I pull up, the guy hands me a clipboard with an insurance waiver to sign. She drives further into the lot toward rows of car trailers and sports cars, and pulls into a spot. When I get out of my car, the potent smell of high-octane fuel drifts through the air, stinging my nostrils. She comes over to me, taking my hand in hers.

"I gotta go check in. There's a driver's meeting at seven-thirty. They're usually about half-an-hour." She leads us toward a group of about seventy people, all men. On our way, we pass a variety of different cars from Corvettes to BMWs to Porsches and Audis. Black rubber burn-marks on the pavement show evidence of celebratory donuts.

As we approach the group, a few of the men notice her, turning and calling out her name in a welcoming greeting. Small cheers of, "Ay!" as they spread their arms for hugs.

"Been a while, Kitten. Good to see you." A grizzly-looking man embraces her with a husky pat on her back.

"Yeah, work's had me traveling a lot so I've missed a few this year," she says, turning to me. "Joe, this is my boyfriend, Enzo."

I like the way, "boyfriend" smooths off her tongue. I puff my chest with pride and shake his hand. As she introduces me to a few more people, she works her way up to registration and more people arrive behind us. Once she's registered and I have a visitor's badge, we step out of the way.

"The meeting's going to start soon. There's some food over there." She points to a concession window in a small blue building. "You can walk around and check things out until we're done." She steals a kiss and joins the group that's grown to about a hundred and thirty people, including a few more women.

Wandering, I look around the track until she's done. What's not pavement is dirt. A small set of stands shows its age with chipped white paint. Clusters of low mountains keep watch in the distance.

After the meeting, she finds me. "I have to go back to my car to get my bag so I can change into my fireproof gear."

"All right," I say as we walk toward our cars. "You're quite popular here." With her personality, I'm not surprised. And as feminine and sexy as she is, she somehow fits in.

"Yeah, this is like a little family. When you come to the events regularly, you get to know each other and then meet up at the different racetracks. They used to give me a hard time in the beginning because I'm a woman, but I put them in their place," she says, confidence rides her tone as she swaggers her body.

Out of her trunk, she gets two magnetic signs with the number *2* on them and hands me one. "Will you put that on my door?" she asks, as she goes around to the passenger door and sticks hers to it. Then she grabs her bag and we make our way back to the trailers where she finds Joe. Roaring engines boom and echo around us. A couple guys are there, sitting in lawn chairs that form a semicircle, talking about engines. In the middle sits a Yeti cooler filled with waters, sodas, and beer. It's like a tailgating party.

"Can I get changed in your trailer, Joe?" she asks.

"No need to ask, Kitten. Go on in. You know where everything is," he gruffs, taking a swig of water from his bottle.

She disappears into his trailer.

"You ain't drivin'. Want a beer?" Without waiting for my answer, he reaches into the cooler and grabs one.

"Thanks." I take it from him and crack it open, taking a gulp.

He angles his head toward his trailer. "Don't let her nickname fool ya. She's a damn cheetah, that girl o' yours. She'll race the pants off any man out there. Girl knows how to handle a car. Needs a little help with the mechanics from time to time, but shit, that girl can drive." He takes another swig of water, spreading his legs in a protective, fatherly manner, folding his arms across his chest. "She's damn good," he says, stroking his hand down his beard. "We tried to get her to be an instructor, but her job threw a wrench into that." Respect coats every word he says.

Impressive.

She comes out of the trailer in a black racing suit that has a pink stripe down each side. Matching black shoes and gloves with pink stripes. So damn cute and sexy.

"Come on, boys. Who's ready to race?" Playfulness bounces on her words as a sassy smile lights up her face. Joy sparking in her eyes.

"We're comin', Kitten. Go git your car." He nods toward her car.

"Get ready to kiss my ass as I fly by you," she says, then kisses her hand, turns around, and places it on her sweet ass-cheek as she starts walking away.

Joe hurls a low, gurgling laugh.

I turn and walk next to her back to the car, taking her bag from her and holding her hand. "You really love this." Her energy is lit up.

"I do," she says brightly. "They're good people and it's a fun time. Exhausting, but fun. I haven't raced in a while so I'll take it easy on them the first couple laps." A frisky, wicked grin smears across her face. "I'm in the black group so we get to go out on the track during the education meetings because we've already been through them."

"What's the black group?" I ask, curious about this interesting world she's part of.

"We're advanced. The highest level before being an instructor. Each skill level has a group color and we go out on the track in our groups."

She unzips her suit and twists her long pink hair into one thick strand, tucking it into the back of her suit and zipping it up again. Opening her door, she gives me a kiss, gets into her car, and straps on her seatbelt. "You can try different spots around the track to watch us. The bleachers are there if you want to sit. Or you can stand on the top to try to get a better view, although they're not too high. We're out there for about twenty-five minutes each run." Donning her black helmet with a pink stripe, she fastens the strap under her chin, and starts her car.

With a wink, she blows me a kiss and shakes her hand with a hang-ten sign as she sticks out her tongue. "See ya in a bit," she says, then drives off.

As she goes to take her place in line, I walk to the bleachers and climb to the top. She's right, the view's not great, but it's a little better than standing on the ground. I'm able to see them start down the straightaway and round the first turn, then they're out of sight until they come flying back down the straightaway again.

She was full of shit when she said she was going to take it easy on them. I didn't think it was possible for this woman to turn me on any more than she already does. I was wrong. She's schooling them out there and it's sexy as fuck.

Her group comes in and she pulls her car back into her spot next to mine. Still in her car, she takes off her helmet and unzips the top of her suit.

"Wooow!" she exclaims, getting out of her car, triumphant energy emanating from her. "That was a good run."

"You were amazing. How fast were you going?" Her exhilaration bounds onto me.

"On the straightaway, you can usually get up to one-sixty, one-seventy sometimes. It's a rush." Her smile stretches across her face, dewy with sweat.

"Holy shit." She's one sassy firecracker.

We approach Joe's trailer and he spins around, whistling.

"Hot damn, Kitten. Great run. I'll git you on the next one."

She checks her time and does a little victory dance. We hang out with Joe at his trailer and a few of the other guys from her group join us. Joe takes out two lawn chairs from inside his trailer for us.

"Whaddya think, Enzo? You gonna start joinin' us? It's a helluva good time," he says, handing me a beer and sitting in his chair.

"I don't know, I might have to." Watching them for only a short time, the energy speeds through my veins.

I listen while they talk about cars, racing, lap times, and their families. She was right, there's very much a family feel here. After her second race, it's time for me to head back home. I say goodbye to everyone at Joe's trailer and she walks with me back to our cars.

"Thank you for bringing me here," I say. "This was fun and your friends are really nice. And I loved watching you kick their asses."

Playfulness tickles her laugh. "I'm glad you came with me," she says, leaning against my Jeep, eyes sparkling in the golden sunlight.

Standing close to her, I lean in. "Watching you race your car was an unexpected turn on. You can't imagine how badly I want to unzip your suit right now."

With that, keeping her eyes on mine, she tugs the zipper on her fire suit lower, giving me a better glimpse at her cleavage with her breasts packed into a low-cut, cotton sports bra. As my eyes follow her unzipping, my dick twitches. I strain to hold myself back from sticking my face into her breasts.

"You're trying to kill me." My hard-on presses against my jeans.

"No, just tease you a little." She winks, little vixen.

"Another success for you today," I say, my balls aching for her.

Pressing into her, I slide my hands through her hair, and lower my lips to hers. Releasing her lips, I brush a kiss to her forehead. Leaning back, I look her in the eyes. "Be careful out there."

"Always." Her smile holds her promise. "Be back home tomorrow," she says as she zips up her suit.

"Let me know when you're home safe."

"I will."

On my drive back to L.A., she's all I can think about. She's climbing deeper into my heart.

20

Candi

I haven't had a chance to talk to Destiny since we got back from Greece. There's so much I have to catch her up on. Back in my hotel room after the race, I shower and call her.

"Hi. I've been waiting to hear from you. How did the rest of the shoot go?" She always makes me feel like what's going on in my life is important.

"I know. I'm sorry. I've been swamped. I had to finish up the campaign and get it back to them. And then I've had some smaller shoots the past couple days."

"Were you finally able to enjoy yourself? Please tell me you were."

"I did. I shook off being mad at him and got in my zone. It was *awesome*. I felt so good and so excited. The campaign turned out so awesome and they loved it!" I shriek out the last few words in excitement.

"Yes! That's amazing. Oh I'm so glad, Can. And, how about you and Enzo?" she asks, her voice calmer, hesitancy coating her words.

"We're good. He apologized…when I finally gave him the chance to say something." I chuckle, only feeling slightly bad that I pretty much shut him down the first night. "He realized he shouldn't have done it even though he meant well. You're right, men just don't think."

"They don't," she confirms.

"Then after he apologized, I basically jumped him." I bust out a laugh, recalling how I straddled him.

"What? What happened?" Her tone escalates with excitement and curiosity.

"Honestly, I don't know what came over me. Every time we're together, I feel closer to him. Our energy is so strong, like this pull that just keeps magnifying. Our attraction, Des? I just couldn't take it anymore. It's like my body took over and I couldn't stop myself. And then I told him we should go to Greece to find his mom."

"You did?" Surprise jumps in her voice.

"Oh, I did. He said okay, and we went. Oddly enough, our schedules worked out that we could, so we went. She works at this cute café and she was there when we went. He saw her and they talked and it went really well. I mean, she lives in Greece so it's not like he's going to be able to see her all the time, but at least they opened the door to each other's lives again. It was so nice."

"Wow. That's great. Had to be a tough conversation."

"I'm sure it was. But he has answers now instead of the wondering eating away at him. And I'm happy I could be there with him. We went to dinner after visiting with her and he told me a little about their talk. Sounded like a huge weight lifted off him. And *after* dinner —" I raise my voice with a hint of tease.

"Yeah?" She raises hers, taking the bait. "Tell me." She begs, boiling over.

"Des, I have *never* had sexual experiences like this. The way he looks at me and touches me and just savors everything. He *told* me he was going to worship me. Used that exact word. And let me tell you, that man worshiped every inch of me. Oh and that's not all. I think he did that coital alignment thing. Des, it was fucking mind-blowing. I'm talking out-of-body experience."

"Ahhhh!" She squeals and we both erupt into bubbled-over laughter.

We calm ourselves, sucking in breaths.

"Seriously though, I haven't ever felt, you know, connected to a man during sex. I mean, it always felt fine with Dom, but it wasn't ever like this. Not even close. It was like he reached in and touched the heart of my soul." I inhale a warm breath that fills me, shaking my head. "It's so much more than that. It's everything about him. I can't believe I'm about to say this, but..." I pause at the weight of it. "it, kind of feels like, little pieces of my soul are coming back. Is that crazy?"

"No. It's not crazy. It's not crazy at all. It means you're alive and you're letting yourself feel again. And that's good. It's *so* good." Her hopefulness soothes me.

"I think I am. Speaking of, I got a tattoo."

"You did? Of what?"

"It's a heart lock. And the arm-part is open. I got it to remind myself to open my heart. I...I want to open my heart to him. I think I might be ready."

I hear her tiny gasp through the phone. "Can, I'm so happy for you." She says softly. "You know, letting Enzo in doesn't erase your love for Dom." Her loving words wrap around me like a hug.

"I know." Her words are what I've been warring with. I kept thinking that if I let myself feel something for Enzo, it meant I didn't love Dom anymore.

"Hey, you want to get together for dinner this week? The four of us?"

"Yeah, that'd be fun. He came to a race with me today and I know he has a gig tomorrow, but I think he's in town."

"He did? Did he like it?"

"Yeah. He said he did anyway."

"Well, that's great. Okay, I'll send a group text."

"Sounds good. I'm going to go. I need to get some sleep. You know how exhausting these are."

"Okay. Yup, I have a book to write."

We hang up and I receive her group text.

Destiny: Who's in town? Dinner Wednesday night? Meet at Taylor's Steak house, 7:00?

Me: I'm in.

Enzo: I'm in.

Nicco: See everyone there.

I receive a separate text from Enzo.

Enzo: Can I have you to myself after dinner? I have a surprise for you.

Me: I'd like that. A surprise?

Enzo: Yup. No questions.

A surprise? Hmm.

Enzo picks me up at six fourteen, one minute before he said he'd be here. I smile every time. As soon as we're in his Jeep, I have to ask.

"Can I have my surprise now?" I've been so curious since he texted me.

He chuckles, almost evilly. The sound makes me smile. "Not yet. After dinner."

"But why can't I have it now?"

"Because you can't."

We've both been so busy and our texts have been short. We take the ride to catch up with what we've been doing since coming back from Greece. Arriving at the steak house before Destiny and Nicco, we order drinks at the bar. They're not far behind us. Destiny's little belly is growing and I'm so excited to be his godmother.

We get seated and place our orders. During dinner Enzo and I share about the Gucci shoot and how beautiful Greece was. We don't dive into the visit with his mom to keep things a little more lighthearted. Nicco just got back into town after filming a movie and he shows us the gash on his arm from one of the scenes he was in that didn't quite go right.

"They stitched it pretty well. Said there shouldn't be a scar, but it looks nasty right now." He rolls up his sleeve to show us.

"Ew." Both Destiny and I groan in disgust as the guys chuckle at us.

"Enzo," he says. "I keep meaning to ask you about the scar above your eyebrow. How'd you get that?"

He touches his eyebrow. "That, yeah. It was July four years ago. There was a huge pileup on PCH."

Every hair on my body snaps to attention as my skin cools.

"An oil tanker jackknifed spilling oil all over the place. Cars were everywhere, slipping and sliding. We were all out of control."

My breaths shallow, my ears start ringing, my hands go clammy.

His attention focuses on Nicco. "I couldn't control my car and hit another car, then went tumbling off the highway. Landed completely upside down. I was so freaked out. I think I was in shock. I was trying to climb out of my car, but I was stuck. Couldn't get my seatbelt off. Next thing I know, the damn tanker explodes, blowing up the cars around it. I thought I was next. Then this guy comes running over."

His voice echoes in my head. My heart races in my chest as my breathing quickens and my stomach coils.

"He somehow pulls me out and away from my car. I'm lying in oily, chunked-up grass, covered in blood that I wasn't sure was mine or his. In seconds my car catches fire. He shouts and asks if I'm okay. I didn't know at that point, but I knew I was alive, so I said yeah. He tells me he has to get back to his mother-in-law and turns to leave. Out of nowhere, a car comes flying off the highway and hits him."

In that second, the car smashes into me. The cool of my skin suddenly ablaze, pulse battering violently in my veins, stomach churning acid. I catch Destiny's eye, barely able to breathe. Everything around me blackens to a tunnel as his voice morphs into a muffle.

"I found out later at the hospital that he didn't make it and neither did his mother-in-law. I felt so bad. Guy saved my life. All I have is this scar. I'm very lucky and very grateful."

I'm trembling, struggling for breaths as the air thickens on its way down to my vibrating lungs. My head shakes involuntarily in disbelief. My heart clamors wildly against my ribs. My mouth parched, I gasp for air. Enzo turns to me.

His eyes fly open as his skin pales. His voice, his movements, everything is in distorted slow motion. "Candi, what's wrong? Are you okay?"

Rage fumes hot in my eyes. I crank my head toward Nicco and Destiny, my body a flaming inferno, my head dizzy. Destiny's eyes wide, she pulls out her phone, furiously scrolling, then turns it to Enzo.

"Is this the guy?" she asks hurriedly.

Enzo looks at me, eyes narrowed and squinting, confusion glossing his face. He looks back at Destiny, to her phone she's holding out.

"Yeah." He shakes his head, puzzled. "Why do you have a picture of him in your phone?"

Short breaths rush in and out of me as my limbs shake and beads of sweat coat my skin. "I…I have to go." I blurt, the words scraping my throat on their way out. Grabbing my purse, clutching it to my chest, I run. And run. And run. Hot tears burn down my cheeks. Breath sucks out from my lungs. Heavy and vacant, my body drags.

I'm numb.

Enzo

"Candi!" Adrenaline tears through me as my body responds, darting up to chase after her. *What the fuck is happening?*

"No," Destiny says sharply, jumping up and holding her hand out to stop me. "I'll go."

Panic stains their expressions.

"Oh, fuck," Nicco says, dropping his head.

Devastation swirls in the air.

Destiny leaves and I return my focus to Nicco.

"Dude, is she okay? What did I say? What the fuck is happening?" My heart jackhammers between my ears.

"That's fucking Dom."

His words crash into me like a freight train. Everything goes black.

I'm a tumultuous mix of confusion, nausea, heartache, and fear.

What the fuck?!

How is that even possible? How is this happening? Oh, my God, Candi.

Destiny returns. "She's not in the bathroom. I don't see her outside." Her words rush out. "I'm going to take the car and go to her house. Nicco, you go back to our house in case she goes there. Enzo, you stay here in case she comes back. Group text with*out* her when she turns up."

Nicco hands her a set of keys then grabs her hand. "She'll be okay. Be careful. I love you."

Destiny takes a deep breath and nods. Then the split-second of calm is gone in a flash.

I hand him my cars keys. "We came together. I'll get an Uber. Go."

He scurries to his feet and leaves.

Alone, my thoughts are frantic, trying to piece together what just happened. The reality stunning me nearly immobile.

The waiter comes by and I toss my credit card into the leather billfold, not even bothering to look at the check.

Then I sit…waiting.

My mind frenetic, my body rattling, my heart crumbling…

21

Destiny

I wobble to our car as quickly as I can, knowing I need to manage my tornado of emotions for her. I beeline for her condo and pound on the door. Nothing. I call her. Nothing. I text her that I'm at the door. Nothing. I know she's hurting, but she would answer the door for me.

Me: She's not at her house.

Enzo: She didn't come back here.

Nicco: I'm not home yet. Let you know.

I pace outside her door, stopping every few seconds to knock again, in case she didn't hear me.

Nicco: She's not here.

"Where are you?" I whisper to myself as my heart aches knowing she's alone right now. Then it hits me. "Of course."

Me: I know where she is.

I get back in the car and head to the cemetery. As I drive, the bright blue sky abruptly shifts to an ominous charcoal gray, rolling thunder and throwing rain-darts. The traffic makes me impatient. I need to get to her.

Finally, I pull through the iron gates, rain-water running off of them creating a gully. Winding down the path to Dom's grave, I see her in the distance. I know you're supposed to be respectful and drive slow through a cemetery. Right now, no one is here. No one but my shattered friend who needs me. I accelerate to get to her.

Stopping the car, I get out and slowly approach her up on the hill, keeping a little distance. I know she's safe. And I know she needs to be here.

Rain pelts harder and faster. Slumped over Dom's grave, her rain-soaked body convulses mercilessly. Pink hair drenched and tangled down her back. A thunderous wail stops me in my tracks and goose bumps prickle across my body. I suck in a breath as tears sting my eyes. Her arms are wrapped around his tombstone, like she's wrapping them around his body. Her legs curl in as the rain beats down on her battered body, magnifying her torment.

Another torturous shriek that sets me back on my feet, piercing me. I can't take any more. I waddle to her as quickly as I can, managing to maneuver myself onto the soggy ground, close to her.

She gasps, startled, and whips her head toward me. Mascara streams down her pained face. Eyes pinched together, agony screams on her skin as her mouth gapes open. Unwrapping from the gravestone, she rests her head in my lap. The rain continues assaulting us. Thunder roars angrily. Holding one of her hands in mine, I carefully move her matted, soaking hair from her face with the other.

Tucking her into my body, I rock back and forth as she howls and sobs and mourns. Squeezing me so tightly, her body tremors in my arms as her frail heart relives Dom's death. My heart cries for her.

What feels like an hour passes. Her trembling subsides and her sobs temper.

I stroke her hair. "Come on, let's get you home and dried off," I shout above the roar of the storm whirling around us.

She looks up at me from my lap and squeezes her eyes shut, ignoring the water that's ricocheting off her face. Opening her eyes, lethargy in her movements, she rises from the ground and tucks her arms under me.

"You shouldn't be out here in this," she shouts with a loving scold, helping me to my feet as thunder claps and crackles above us.

"You're my best friend. I couldn't let you be alone right now."

Rain pouring down in buckets, she wraps her arms around me, squeezing.

A boom of thunder shakes the earth beneath us as white-hot lightning streaks across the dark sky.

"Come on!" she shouts, grabbing my hand and running to the car, rain teeming down on us.

I pop the hatch and throw the two blankets toward the front seats. We both hop into the car, shivering. Wrapping a blanket around myself, trying to dry off and warm up, I grab my phone to text the guys.

Me: I found her. She's okay. Taking her home.

Nicco: Are you okay? This storm is nasty.

Enzo: Thank God. Thank you.

Me: Yes, I'm fine.

Nicco: Okay. I love you.

Enzo: Glad you're both safe.

I start the car as Candi wraps a blanket around herself then gazes out the rain-streaked window at Dom's grave. I pull away and drive down the path. She's quiet the entire drive back to her house. From time to time, I peek over at her. She stares out the window, vacancy veiling her expression. Empty. Void. Detached.

I'm helpless. There's nothing I can do to fix this for her. Nothing I can do to take away her pain. All I can do is love her and watch her suffer. And it kills me.

Candi

Wild emotions overwhelm me. Confusion. Rage. Pain. Sadness. Betrayal. Physically, I'm an impossible dichotomy of freezing cold and burning hot. Nauseous. Claustrophobic. Weak. Heavy. Numb. A strange rush of fear invades the air surrounding me.

How is this even possible?

Destiny pulls down the street from my condo to find a parking spot. The rain has tamed to a drizzle that feels like thousands of needles stabbing my skin as we get out of the car. Silent, we bring the blankets up to my condo. Going in, we remove our wet shoes at the door and pop the blankets in the dryer. Still not saying a word, we head to my bedroom, peel off our soaked clothes, and dig around in my drawers for warm, comfortable clothes. I pull out an oversized sweatshirt that will fit over her belly.

Dressed in warmth, we go to my bathroom. I sit on the toilet lid, shoulders hunched, brain foggy, eyelids heavy. Grabbing a towel, Destiny wraps it around my hair, trying to soak up the bulk of the rain-water still drenching it. Hanging the towel on a hook, she grabs my hairdryer from under the sink and turns it on low. Weaving her fingers through my hair, she focuses the warm air on my scalp. I breathe, letting her love and the warm air soothe me. When my hair is mostly dry, she wets a washcloth and wipes my face clean of haphazard makeup. Silent, I watch her, so attentive, so gentle, so loving.

Once she's done, she takes my chin in her hand, lifting my face to meet her eyes. The corners of her lips lift delicately. I wrap my hand around her wrist and close my eyes, grateful for her.

"Thank you," I say softly. "I'll be right out."

She turns and leaves. I stand up and stare at my reflection in the mirror. My face looks distorted, like puzzle pieces that don't fit together. I drop my head and release a breath.

When I go out to the living room. Destiny's on the sofa, sipping hot cocoa. There's a warm mug, overloaded with marshmallows, waiting for me. I take the mug in my hand and sit down next to her, curling my leg under me and hugging a pillow to my chest.

"I wish we had cupcakes right now," I say, half joking and half serious. My soul craves comfort.

She smiles a knowing smile.

Lifting the mug to my lips, I sip the warm cocoa, sucking in a few marshmallows. Then I set it down and look over at her, wanting her to give me answers she doesn't have, she couldn't have.

"This is fucking crazy, right?" I say, still in disbelief.

Her entire torso nods in agreement.

"Is it real?" I ask, rampant visions of what Enzo described vibrantly flashing through my mind, filling in the missing snippets of what I learned had happened from the doctor at the hospital.

She reaches out, taking my hand in hers. "I think so." Her words shards, cutting me with the truth. Her touch compassion, trying to erase my pain.

Confusion rattles my thoughts. Though I want to believe it's impossible, he saw Dom's picture on Destiny's phone and said he was the man who pulled him from his car, saving his life. *Only to watch him die.* Inexplicable rage blazes through me. Every word he spoke is seared in my memory, igniting imagery that suffocates me as I stand helpless in my mind watching the car smash into Dom. Overwhelmed, the sadness I'd buried resurfaces from the crater in my soul with insurmountable force. Guilt ravages my core as I'm consumed by the thought that Dom is dead because Enzo is alive.

"What —" I suck in a breath, the air sandpaper, scratching my throat raw. "What do I do with all this?" I choke out, flailing my hands up and down my body, unable to stop the whimpers strangling me. "He's here and Dom's gone." Hot tears squeeze out of my swelling eyes. "How is that fair?"

Her head pitches to the side. "Honey, it's not fair." She squeezes my hand with love. "It's also not Enzo's fault that Dom's gone." She pauses, letting me hear her words. "Of course Dom would do what he did and save a man's life, that's who he was. That's part of why you loved him." Her brows curl together. "It's not Enzo's fault."

"But I want to blame him. I want to be angry with him." Fire streaks across my flesh as I huff out the words.

"No." She shakes her head gently. "You don't want to blame

Enzo. You want to be mad at Dom for leaving you."

The sides of my mouth pull down, the gravity of heartache. The skin on my face tightens inward as my shoulders hunch forward, slumping my torso. "He left me." Uncontrolled tears pour out. My lungs burn as I gasp for breaths.

I roll into her lap once again, seeking solace, peace, healing I know she can't give me.

With a loving touch, she strokes my hair.

"I know you want to be mad at him. It's okay to be mad. He didn't leave you though. He was taken away from you." The words echo in my head, bouncing around like a pinball.

It's true, I've blamed Dom for leaving me. Leaving me here. Alone.

"The only thing you can do is forgive." Her angelic voice floats into my ears. "Forgive Dom. Forgive Enzo. Forgive yourself." She delivers each word with tenderness. "Forgiveness is how you'll get through this."

I manage to control my sobs though my stomach stings. Sniffing, I nod in her lap, knowing she's right.

"We don't know God's plan. Maybe Dom's death was God's way of bringing Enzo to you. So you could love again." Caution filters through her words. "Maybe *this* is where your love story truly begins. Dom will always be in your heart. Nothing changes that." Absolution laces her words, washing me.

I lift from her lap and drape my arms around her neck. "I love you," I say, my voice straining.

"I love you too."

We hold each other in an embrace of friendship, sisterhood, and unconditional love.

I edge back, looking at her face. "Wanna Instacart some cupcakes?" I follow my question with as much of a smile as my puffy face can form.

She giggles. "Absolutely."

While we wait, we fold her blankets and toss our clothes into the dryer. Once our stomachs are full with cupcakes and hot cocoa, she heads home, leaving me with my colossal mess of thoughts and emotions.

It's late and my mind, body, and soul are overwrought with exhaustion. I feel bad about running out on Enzo. I need to talk to him. I'm sure Nicco and Destiny told him the man who saved his life was Dom, but this is something we need to talk through together.

Though I know Destiny's right, and none of this is Enzo's fault, my heart's in a million pieces and I don't have it in me to talk to him.

I don't know when I'll be ready.

22

Enzo

Knowing she's safe, I Uber home, my mind hazy, my body exhausted. I'm still trying to process how Dom, *her fucking soul mate*, was the guy who saved my life and I'm now dating…*shit, have fallen in love with*…his almost-fiancée. This is fucked up on so many levels.

My rib cage clenches tight around my heart. I can't even imagine what she's going through right now. It's unfathomable to me. I want so badly to hold her in my arms. To comfort or console her in some way. To take away the hurt that's imprisoning her and has been for years.

She probably wants to throw me off a roof, lighting me on fire on the way down. Obviously, I didn't kill the guy and she knows that, but the anger combusting behind her eyes and the ferocity reddening her features when she looked at me, bared the depth of pain consuming her soul. I know displaced anger and blame well enough to know she hurled them onto me the instant she connected that he saved my life. I'm here, he's gone.

What the fuck do I do now?

The next morning, my phone chimes.

Candi: I'm sorry I ran out last night. Can we talk?

Me: It's okay. I understand. Yes. When can I see you?

Candi: Tonight? My house?

Me: Be there around 5:00?

Candi: Okay.

I hit the gym, run my Saturday errands, and toil for much of the afternoon, trying to figure out what to even say to her. There are *no* words for this situation. Sadness weighs heavy in my heart, ripping me apart inside.

Do I let her go? If we try to stay together, will she always see a reminder of her dead boyfriend when she looks at me? Will I ever live up to him? Could I ever be enough for her? Or will our staying together only cause her pain?

Maybe it would be better for both of us if I just walk away. *Can I walk away?*

I love her.

I fucking love her.

I arrive early, as usual, pacing until it's time, nerves getting the better of me. At four fifty-nine, I ring her bell, my stomach twisting in knots. I take a deep breath before she opens the door, trying to prepare myself for a conversation that's going to destroy me.

When she opens the door, her essence strikes me in the face, knocking the air from my lungs.

"Hi," she says sweetly, then opens the door wider for me to enter.

"Hi." I bow my head and walk in, moisture coating my palms.

Tension looms.

Closing the door and locking it, she walks toward the kitchen. "Want something to drink?"

"No, thanks." As much as a drink would probably settle my damn nerves, I need to have a clear head right now. I walk to the sofa, my legs dragging, and sit down.

She follows me and sits next to me, curling her leg under her. "I'm sorry I ran out like that last night," she says, sorrow lining her beautiful features. "I —" She shakes her head, dropping her gaze to her lap. "I freaked out." She lifts her face. "I've been having all these strong feelings for you and it's felt so good and then, boom, hearing you say that Dom saved your life right before he got hit and died —" A sharp exhale releases from her. "It felt like a bomb imploded and exploded inside me at the same time. Everything just…crashed in around me."

My insides twist into a thousand shard-covered knots, cutting deeper the tighter they twist. I bend my knee up onto the sofa and lean toward her. "I can't imagine what you're going through." Looking into her solemn eyes, staunch reality rears its ugly head. "I also can't change it or undo it. I wish I could somehow. All I want to do is hold you and make it all better. And I can't. And I don't know what to do." I pause, my heart pounding violently.

Her body shrinks back as her eyes pull tightly inward and her lips draw down. Gravity tugs.

"He may not be alive, but he exists in the space between us." Anguish engulfs that space. "He always has and now he always will." My words haggard and weary. "I love you, Candi. But I can't compete against a ghost." I drop my gaze to Dom's ring around her neck. Dense air locks in my lungs. "I'll lose every time." A boulder expands in my throat, closing off the oxygen.

Her gaze follows my eyes to the ring.

"I want to be with you, more than anything I've ever wanted in my life, but how can I be with you and not wonder if I'll ever be enough? Me." I point to my chest, wincing at my own touch. "Every time I look in your eyes, I'll see his shadow. And every time you look in mine, I'll wonder if you see his ghost." My throat steals my voice as it cracks out of me. "I won't put you through that pain. And I don't think I could survive it. I have to love you enough to let you go." The words slash brutally at both of us as I force a swallow around the unyielding boulder.

She searches my face frantically like she's trying to decipher what I'm saying.

I take her hand in mine. "Thank you, for changing my life. For making me want to be a better man. You helped me see that I have the capacity to love. Because of you, I have my mom back in my life. Because of you, I've been able to heal. Because of you, I'm the man I am today." Hopelessness consumes the atmosphere. "Dom may have been your soul mate, but you're mine." Pain lances my heart as the words drop out of my mouth like bricks of granite.

I lean in, hold the back of her head gently, and press my lips to her forehead. It takes everything in me not to wrap my arms around her and never let go. "I love you." My words a pained whisper against her soft skin, I close my eyes, drawing out our inevitable end, coveting every last, precious second.

Standing up, I walk to her door and let myself out, not looking back…knowing it would kill me.

23

Candi

He's gone.

I didn't stop him.

I didn't say a word.

Nothing.

I let him walk out of my life.

He's right. Everything he said.

Fuck. I didn't expect him to say what he said and then walk out the door.

I didn't expect to lose him.

I don't know what I expected.

Paralyzed and stunned, each breath that enters my lungs burns my whole body.

I don't move. I can't.

What the hell just happened?

He said he loves me. He said it, right? I heard him say he loves me.

But he left. He left because he loves me. He left because I'm so fucked up.

But what if I love him too?

Just as I'm about to lose my shit, my phone rings, jolting me out of my hysterical thoughts.

"St. Agnes Medical Center, Fresno CA" lights on my screen. Adrenaline powers through me as my heart pounds. *Dad.*

"Hello?"

"Hello. Is this Candice Gamal?" A soft voice comes through the phone.

"Yes."

"Miss Gamal, I'm calling because your father has you listed as his emergency contact."

"What's wrong? Is he okay?" Panic threads through me. Though we haven't spoken in a long time and we don't have much of a relationship, he's still my dad.

"He took a pretty bad fall and hit his head. He's still unconscious and we're running some tests on him to find out more. He may have some broken bones. We'll know more in a few hours."

"What should I do? I can come stay with him. I'm about three and a half hours away."

"That's up to you. If you want to come, I'm sure he'd like to see you. If you want to wait until we run the tests and call you back, you can do that."

"No, I don't want to wait. I'll be out the door in fifteen minutes. If anything changes, please call me on this number."

"I will."

We hang up and I run to my bedroom to pack a couple days' worth of clothes, giving me no time for the all-out, self-pity breakdown I was about to succumb to.

Epinephrine pumping, fast and furious, through my veins, I jump in my car and head north. The first thing I do is call to reschedule the shoot I'm supposed to do on Monday, begging for forgiveness. Thankfully, it's a client I've worked with many times before and they're graciously understanding.

The second thing I do is call Destiny to let her know about what happened with Enzo and that I'm driving to the hospital to see what's going on with my dad.

She, of course, tries to encourage me and tell me it doesn't have to be over if I don't want it to be. But I can't disagree with anything he said. It was all true and warranted. The fucked-upness

I'm in right now? That wouldn't be fair for me to drag him into if I can't give myself, my whole self, to him. And I care about him too much to do that to him.

Hours of windshield time still ahead of me, I search my heart, with Enzo pervading every thought.

Around ten o'clock that night, I enter the emergency room. A nurse points me to curtain number three.

I push back the thick, blue-fabric curtain. Dad's eyes are closed, his hair grayer than I remember, his body frail beneath the cotton gown and thin, white hospital blanket. I stare at him, an ache throbs deep in my racing heart. *Please don't leave me too.*

Closing the curtain, I try to quietly drag a chair from the corner of the room over to his bedside. The drag is louder than I expected and he stirs.

His eyes blink sluggishly open. "Candi, what're you doing here? They didn't have to call you." His groggy words strain out as he tries to sit up and he ends up leaning back against the inclined mattress.

"I came as soon as the doctor called. Do they know what's wrong yet?"

"I'm fine. They didn't need to bother you. I just hurt my wrist a little is all." He touches his right arm that's in a navy sling.

"They said you hit your head too." *Is he brushing this off so I'll leave?*

He reaches behind his head. "Just a little bump. It doesn't even hurt."

Just then, a doctor comes in, holding a clipboard. "Mr. Gamal. I have good news for you. Your CAT scan is normal. I see nothing to be concerned about. And there are no broken bones, but you have a very bad sprain of your right wrist."

I heave a sigh of relief, drawing the doctor's eyes.

"This is my daughter, Candice." A weak smile spreads his cheeks.

"Nice to meet you, Candice. We'll get some paperwork together and then you can take your dad home. I hear you drove in from out of town. Will you be able to stay with him tonight?"

"Yes, of course. That's what I planned on. I can stay a few days if I need to."

"Good. If anything seems off, you bring him right back here to me." His encouraging, friendly tone eases me.

"Yes, I'll do that."

"Okay, let's get you out of here. Except for us doctors and nurses, no one wants to be in a hospital." His smile is warm and reassuring.

The nurse who checks us out gives us instructions for him to take it easy for the next few weeks and not doing anything strenuous that might delay the healing of his wrist. I pull my car around to pick him up and help him get in.

"Thank you for coming all this way. I'm sorry they bothered you." I can't tell if he thinks he's being a burden or he doesn't want me here.

"It's no bother, Dad." I look over at him. The strong, strapping, bullheaded man I knew growing up seems so meek and timid. It's been too long since I've seen him. That's on me.

I get him home and settled into bed. Then I go to my childhood bedroom, nostalgia wrapping around me as I look at my walls that are adorned with pictures I'd taken as a young, budding photographer. He hasn't changed anything since Mom passed.

I get washed up for bed then peel back my ruffled, lavender, twin comforter and slide between my purple butterfly sheets. Tucking myself beneath the covers, I'm too tired to cry and sleep takes me.

The night was restless as I woke every few hours, my mind reeling. Getting up before Dad, I make us coffee and get out mugs, my favorite purple butterfly mug is still in the cabinet. Looking around the kitchen and in the refrigerator, I don't see much food. Though I suck at cooking, I'm going to take him to the grocery store today and see what meals I can make for him to freeze and easily heat up over the next few weeks while his wrist heals. It's the least I can do.

Though he continues to reiterate that he's fine and doesn't need help and doesn't want to bother me, he agrees to go to the store with me and let me cook some meals for him. While he rests and watches TV, I try my hardest to cook half-decent meals, making him lasagna, spaghetti and meatballs, and stuffed shells. I'd picked up some containers at the store and prepare single servings so all he has to do is thaw them out and heat them up.

Lasagna being the last dish I made, I slice it up for us for dinner. Sitting at the aging walnut dining table, him at the head, me to his left, Mom's chair empty to his right, we eat quietly. I ask how his wrist is feeling and he says it's fine. Awkward silences still the air.

After dinner, I do the dishes and clean up the kitchen from my day of possibly-awful cooking. Then I join him in the living room, sitting on the gold, blue, and ivory floral-patterned sofa that Mom loved, curling my legs up onto the cushion.

He gets up from his worn-out blue recliner that matches the blue in the sofa and walks over to the bookcase along the wall to the left of the TV stand. Crouching down, he pulls out a large, tattered book and comes to sit next to me on the sofa.

The book in his lap, he pats my feet. "I want to show you something," he says, clutching the book with his hand, but not opening it. "I — I'm an old-fashioned man." A knowing smile warms his face as he shakes his head. "In my time, women weren't encouraged to pursue their dreams."

"I know, Dad. And I'm sorry I can't be who you want me to be."

"Et." He cuts me off, holding up his hand, looking in my eyes. A hint of sadness sits in them. "I'm the one who is sorry. I'm sorry I wasn't more supportive of you and what you wanted." His gaze drops, then he looks back up at me. "Time gives you perspective. I'm a stubborn man." Another acknowledging smile spreads across his face. "I'm so proud of you and what you've made of yourself and your life, luce dei miei occhi." The regret woven into his voice crushes me as a tear drops from his eye, traveling down into the crevices and up over the bumps of his weathered skin.

He'd never before used a term of endearment when talking to me. My heart splays open and falls apart simultaneously as tears threaten behind my eyes.

He opens the book in his lap, it's a scrapbook. "I have all your pictures from when you were little and up through today, when I could find them in magazines." His voice quivers as he looks down at the pictures in the book, touching a few of them, pride emanating from him. "Some are pictures I took of advertisements shot by you that were on billboards and signs in shops and malls. Your mom showed me how to use social media so I knew which ones were yours." He flips cautiously through the pages, taking care with each turn. Pages and pages of pictures I'd taken, pictures he'd taken, and clippings from magazines, all taped into this raggedy scrapbook.

A myriad of emotions pummels me as he flips through the pages. A lump lodges in my throat as tears brim in the lower lids of my eyes. He must've collected these pictures for the last twenty years.

Looking me in the eyes once again, he reaches over and takes my hand in his. "I know I've never told you before, but I need you to know, I *am* proud of you. Proud that you followed your dreams. Proud of the woman you've become." He squeezes my hand gently. "I want you to be *exactly* who you are. My feisty, driven, talented, tenacious girl. I don't want you to be anyone else. I want what every parent wants, for you to be happy." He tilts his head, raising his brows. "Are you happy?"

At that, I burst. Tears flow down my face as I hang my head. Holding my hand, he lets me cry. When I've pulled myself together, I tell him about Dom and Enzo and how twisted I am about it all.

"You can't blame this man. It isn't his fault. When your mom passed, I knew I'd never love another the way I loved her. No one has come along to sway that. You have many years ahead of you. You're being given a chance to love again." He pauses, narrowing his eyes. "Do you love him?"

The question holds the weight of osmium.

Without thought or doubt, my heart knows the answer. *Yes.*

Gravity tugs the corners of my mouth as I nod.

"Then let yourself love. Does he know how you feel?"

I sit, not knowing the answer. Have I let my fear mask my feelings for him?

"I don't know," I say, lifting my shoulders toward my ears.

"No one can know what's in your heart unless you tell them. I know this, I learned the hard way. I should have told you what was in *my* heart long ago." Another squeeze of my hand. "Fight for him." His gaze is more loving than any I've been on the receiving end of.

"Come, let's get some rest." He releases my hand, puts the scrapbook back on the shelf, and walks down the hall in his slippered feet to his bedroom.

I get washed up and lie in my childhood bed, replaying my dad's words in my head. My entire life, I thought he hated me for the simple fact that I wasn't a boy. I held such guilt that I couldn't be who he wanted. I harbored resentment and anger that he couldn't love me. And tonight, love swarmed my heart. His words, his scrapbook, his pride, his encouragement. Years of bitterness waning. Acceptance I've longed for.

This morning, he's up before me. The bold scent of coffee wakes me. We spend the morning talking about his daily and weekly routines and what adjustments he'll need to make. He and his next-door neighbor, Charlie, are good friends. Charlie called 911 when he slipped on his porch and fell. Dad said Charlie will be able to help with a few things until his wrist is healed.

Plans in place, meals in the freezer, he's pretty well set.

"Thank you for coming to take care of me. I'll be fine. Charlie will be able to help me."

With my bags packed and at my feet, I stand at the door. "Promise you'll call if you need me. I know it's a long drive, but I can come back if you need me to."

"I promise." He leans forward and bows his head a bit. "You get back home safely and go find your love." His lips draw into a smile.

"I will."

He cages me in his one arm and kisses the top of my head. "I love you," he says.

My heart swells, filling my rib cage, and I almost burst into tears again.

Releasing me, his hand remains on my shoulder as he gazes at me.

"I love you too, Dad." I stretch up and kiss his wrinkled cheek.

Back in the car, I think about Dom and Enzo, searching my heart.

It's time.

24

Enzo

I haven't heard from her. Did I really expect to? I said goodbye and walked away, never looking back. I guess something deep inside me hoped she felt...*something*. Something similar to what I'm feeling. She admitted she has feelings for me. Maybe whatever she felt wasn't enough. Wasn't strong enough to break her heart's grasp on the ghost of him.

I don't know that I agree with the saying that it's better to have loved and lost than never to have loved at all. Because this shit? This fucking hurts. The last few days, she's all I can think about. What's she doing? Is she okay? Is she crying? Is she hurting?

Or am I already someone in her past?

This is fucking brutal.

Wallowing in my mess, my phone rings, it's Nicco.

"Hey, man." My voice mirrors my torment. I don't even try to fake that I'm fine. I'm not.

"Hey. Just wanted to check in on you. You doing okay? That was some crazy shit." His somber tone matches mine.

"Yeah, it was. It's hard to even believe it's possible. Nah, I'm not doing okay. I'm sure Destiny told you I walked away." My rib cage closes in, clamping itself around my heart.

"She did. You sure, man? You two have something."

"What the fuck can I do? I can't be a daily reminder to her of her dead boyfriend and the fact that I'm here and he's not. I can't put her through that kind of pain. She's in love with a ghost she can't let go of. Where does that leave me?"

He blows a huff of air. "I know. I get it." The consolation in his voice doesn't soothe me. He sighs. "I have to tell you that her dad had an accident, fell or something, and she drove up there. We think he's okay, but we're not sure. She went straight to the hospital and we haven't heard from her yet."

"Oh, shit." My heart sinks with a thud in my chest. She's been through so much and now this. And I know she has a tumultuous relationship with him. God, I want to be there with her, for her.

"I know, man."

"Thanks for calling and checking in on me. And for letting me know about her dad. Let's get together for drinks soon."

"Yeah, that'd be great."

We hang up and I immediately text Candi, doubtful she'll respond.

Me: Just off the phone with Nicco. He told me about your dad. I hope he's okay. I hope you're okay. I'm here if you need me.

Delete, delete, delete. *She doesn't need me.* She's made that abundantly clear.

I'm here if you need anything.

A glimmer of hope sweeps through my chest when I see the three dots, telling me she's replying back.

Candi: Thanks for reaching out. I appreciate it.

That glimmer disintegrates at the sight of her impassive response. Can't really expect anything more. At least she didn't tell me to fuck off. Given that Destiny is her best friend and Nicco and I are friends, we're bound to run into each other at some point. Eventually, we'll figure out how to be near each other and be okay. Maybe even still be friends.

Friends.

The word spreads sorrow through my core, settling uneasily into my bones, sludging like quicksand through my veins.

25

Candi

Of course Enzo texted me when he found out about Dad. He probably would've come with me, to support me and to help. Because that's who he is. And let's face it, his meals would've been a hell of a lot better.

Dad's right. I need to fight for him.

But there's something I have to do first.

I unpack my bags, put away my toiletries, and throw in a load of laundry. Then I open my hope chest at the foot of my bed. Mom's wedding veil is on top, protected in a zippered, thick-plastic storage bag. Placing it on the floor, I take out the bag of seashells from the time Mom and Dad took me to the beach when I was around eleven. Mom was on the beach blanket napping and Dad walked along the water's edge with me, picking seashells. I was happy. It's the only happy memory I have with him. I vow to make more memories with him and see him a little more often.

Next, I pull out Jelly Bean, the stuffed, light gray rabbit they gave me for my fifth birthday. I slept with that thing through college. Peeking inside the chest, I take out my old Canon PowerShot point-and-shoot camera that Mom gave me. The camera that started it all. Lifting my purple butterfly purse off of the blanket my grandma had knitted for me, I put it on the floor. Then I pick up Grandma's blanket, underneath of which lies an old photo album I'd tucked away, thinking my heart had healed after Dom. I carefully lift it out and grab Grandma's blanket, then sit on my bed, draping the blanket over my lap.

Opening the cover of the album, I'm struck with the picture of my and Dom's first date. Heartache fists inside my chest. He took me to the zoo and we had the best time walking the paths and looking at the animals. Sentimentality pulses in my chest. I lightly touch his face.

"Sometimes I still see you here," I say to him. "Standing in front of me, looking at me the way you did on our first date. I close my eyes, shut out the world, and see you in my head. I walk down memory lane, so I can be with you again for a little while." I rub his ring between my fingers.

Flipping through the pages, memories inundate me, making me smile and making me sad. With each turn of a page, I relive the moment, trying to let go. Time passes as I'm lost in reverie. Coming to the end of the album, I close it and hold it tightly to my chest, letting my head hang over it.

I'm ready.

I get back in my car and drive to the cemetery, down the winding path I know by heart. My legs heavy, I climb the hill to his grave and sit next to him in the grass. A breeze caresses my face, gently blowing strands of hair.

I sit.

I breathe.

Silent.

Taking in a long, labored breath, I let it out slowly. With trembling hands, I weave through my hair to the clasp at the back of my neck. The arm of it under my nail, I pull it open, releasing the circle. Both sides of the chain in my hands, I lower Dom's ring into one hand. Closing my fingers around it, I hold it to my chest, staring at his gravestone.

"I'll never stop loving you." I inhale down to the crater, and let it out, releasing pain, releasing him. "But it's time for me to open up my heart to someone else and the chance to love again."

I close my eyes. The sound of my breaths fills my ears. The breeze wisps away his ghost from my soul.

Opening my eyes, I pull a pouch out of my pocket that I'd brought with me and tuck the ring safely inside, then return it to my pocket. Pressing my fingers to my lips, I kiss, and place my fingers on his gravestone.

"Goodbye, my love."

With a sigh, I get to my feet and go back to my car. When I get home, I go to my bedroom, open my hope chest, and put everything back in, adding Dom's ring.

Sitting on the floor at the foot of my bed, it occurs to me that I have no idea what to do to get Enzo back. I need to show him I'm ready. I'm ready to move on with my life. I'm ready for him to be in it, fully, completely. I'm ready to take a chance on love…with him.

Because she writes romance novels for a living and because she's my best friend, she'll know how to help me. I get my phone and call Destiny.

"Hey, how's your dad?"

"He's good, he's good. He gave himself a bump on his head, which is thankfully nothing, and he sprained his wrist. I made him some meals to heat and eat. God bless the poor guy. I hope they're edible." We both spit out a chuckle.

"Oh that's great to hear. I'm so glad he's okay." Her pitch shifts softer. "And, how're you doing?"

"Well, I'm thoroughly and completely exhausted. Mentally, physically, emotionally. But —"

"But?" Uplifted curiosity lifts her voice.

"I need your help."

"Anything."

"I said goodbye to Dom." I'm a strange mixture of melancholy and freedom.

"Okay." She gives me space.

"When I was with my dad, we talked like we've never talked before. Des, he has hundreds of my pictures in a scrapbook. He told me how sorry he was for not encouraging me. He told me he loved me. I never felt so seen by him." My soul fills with peace as I think back to our conversation.

"Candi, that's so great to hear."

"And I ended up telling him about Enzo. He asked me if I loved him." I take a breath, affirming what's in my heart. "Des, I do. I love him."

Her gasp lifts the tiny hairs at the nape of my neck. "Oh, Candi." Soft joy sits in her voice.

"So, I came home, went through our photo album I made, went to his grave, took off his ring, and…and said goodbye."

"Okay." Permission sifts through her single word. Permission to feel anything and everything I was feeling.

"I feel like this whole time, Enzo's put himself out there. Been vulnerable. Let me in. And, I couldn't meet him, not all the way. But, I'm ready now. I'm ready to fight for him. But I have no idea *how* to fight for him, what to do."

"We'll figure it out. Hmm. It'll have to be some kind of grand gesture. Something that'll let him know you *are* ready." Thrill threads through her gasp. "Oh, I have it. I know what to do!" Her excitement shrills through me, making me excited.

She tells me the plan. It's brilliant…and I'm going to be mortified.

Destiny: We're done with dinner. It's about to start.

Me: I'm almost there. I can't believe I let you talk me into this.

Destiny: ; -)

The Uber driver drops me off at Stage 2. Thankfully, someone's on stage singing. I scoot into the bathroom, not sure if I'm going to pass out or vomit…or both. Thankfully I don't do either. I wet my hands and spritz water onto my face, tapping my chest with the last droplets on my palms, glancing at the spot where Dom's ring used to hang. I smile. My soul at peace.

That peace is the calm before the storm. I'm a nervous mess. But, I'm gonna do it.

I exit the bathroom and sneak down to the platform, hugging close to the line of people facing the stage. The person singing finishes and walks down the steps off the platform. I'm up next. Trepidation moving me slowly, I walk up each step, my heart frenzied.

"Hi. What's your name?" the DJ asks when I reach him in the center of the stage.

I lean forward, putting my mouth close to the microphone. "Hi. I'm Candi." My voice echoes as a high-pitched screech flashes through the room.

"Ooooo." The crowd cries out in unison, holding their ears.

The DJ chuckles, pulling the microphone away from me. "A little too close." He smiles politely. "First time?"

I grit my teeth and pull back my lips into what I'm sure looks like a petrified smile.

"You're gonna do great. What song are you singing tonight?" he asks.

That's when I see Enzo, Nicco, and Destiny weaving through the small crowd. My heart pounds faster. I move the microphone away from my mouth and whisper in his ear.

"Here we go," he says with a dip of his head and hands me the microphone, gesturing where to hold it.

Yup, here we go. Music to *Hero* fills the room. As I read the lyrics on the screen, I change them.

Locking eyes with Enzo, I start singing. "Will you be my hero?" My vocal cords vibrate. "Will you dance, with me every night? Will you run, every day by my side?" Tone-deaf sounds attack the air. "Will you hold me, when I break down and cry? Will you save my soul tonight?" Missing every note, my voice struggles as he gazes at me, shaking his head and rubbing his smile with a curled finger. The microphone shakes in my hand as I watch him stepping toward me, people parting to let him through. Feeling like a fool, I let a small laugh slip out of me. The crowd cheers in encouragement. "You make me tremble, when you touch my lips. You make me laugh, I'm telling you this."

His lips pull into a tight smile, stretching his cheeks as he moves toward me.

My voice continues its assault on the crowd. "I would die, for the one I love. I want to be in your arms tonight." I sway my body, grabbing the microphone with both hands like I'm the lead singer in a sold-out stadium. "You are my hero, baby. You have kissed away my pain. Will you stand by me forever? You have taken my breath away."

I turn toward him as he steps onto the stage. He joins me and takes the microphone, continuing the song with the correct lyrics and perfect pitch. Facing me, he holds my hand, looking deep into my eyes. The room fades around us as he sings to my heart, affection rushing the warm air between us.

His beautiful voice sings the last note and he drops his head, touching his lips to mine. The crowd roars with applause, cheers, and whistles. Breaking our kiss, we buckle into laughter, then take our bows and exit the stage.

Taking my hand in his, so familiar, we make our way through the crowd to Nicco and Destiny.

"That was *painful*," Nicco says, holding his stomach and laughing heartily, then hugging me.

"Something tells me you two were in on this," Enzo says, pointing back and forth between them.

Destiny hunches her shoulders to her ears with a shit-eating, I-don't-know-what-you're-talking-about, grin on her face.

"You guys mind if we head out?" he asks, basically telling them we're leaving.

"Catch you later," Nicco says, patting him on the shoulder and tossing him a nod.

I hug Destiny. "Thank you," I whisper in her ear, then give

Nicco a kiss on each cheek.

The valet pulls up his Jeep and we get in. On the way home, I update him on my dad and our reconciliation.

He drives us back to his place. "Come up?" Endearing innocence a whisper on his tone, hopefulness perching his expression, like he doesn't know my answer.

"Mmhmm."

We go inside and he offers me whiskey which I accept, hoping it might help me figure out how to start this conversation. Handing me a glass, he walks to the sofa and I follow him.

I take a sip and sit down, curling my leg up under me and facing him.

"I'm glad your dad's okay and you had a chance to work through some things."

"Thank you. I am too." I take a sip of whiskey and set it back down. "Talking with my dad helped me think about a lot of things. See some things more clearly."

One foot on the ground, he raises his other leg to rest on the sofa so he's facing me. He listens, his body leaning toward me, his attention fully on me.

"I know that what happened, and this strange thing that now connects us, makes *us* pretty complicated." I pause, taking a breath. As much as he doesn't want to cause me pain, I don't want to cause him pain. "I heard every word you said the other night." I look down into my lap, then lift my head. "Honestly, I can't deny any of it." I push a weak smile to my lips. "You lit a light inside of me that died a long time ago. A light I thought was gone forever."

It's the first time his gaze drifts down to my chest, to where Dom's ring used to lie. Looking back into my eyes, he takes a full-body inhale, his eyes flitting between mine, quietly waiting for my next words.

"When Dom died, I closed my heart. Locked it. Threw away the key. I learned how to survive on my own. Never needed anyone. Never relied on anyone. And then you came along and, without being conscious of it, I relied on you, in the best possible way. From arriving at my house one minute before you say you will, every single time."

His lips crack into a bashful smile.

"To being there with a simple text when you knew I was hurting and you knew I was with my dad, knowing how hard that was for me. And deep inside," I say, touching my hand to my chest. "I know I can count on you to have my back and be there when I need you."

He reaches out, taking my hand in his, gazing into my eyes.

"I don't want to be alone anymore. I'm tired of worrying about being hurt. I'm tired of being afraid of losing another person I love. I'd rather love you and risk getting hurt than live another day without you. Because honestly, losing you would carve a hole in my soul." My voice strangles the words as tears brew in my eyes and I rub his hand. "I know I come with some wounds." I shake my head. "And I don't know what I can promise you, but I'm willing to try. I'm ready. And I'm hoping you could still love me." A tear leaves my eye. I swallow hard, knowing I'll have to accept his rejection if he can't get beyond the tragic reality that connects us. I'll respect it. And I'll leave knowing I tried. I fought. For *him*.

Moving his body closer to me, he tucks my hair behind my ear and cups my face in his hand, gently rubbing my cheek with his thumb, brushing away the tear. "I'll never not love you. I love you more than anything that could try to come between us. I'm here for you, Candi, forever." Releasing my hand, he cups the other side of my face and kisses me, long, slow, deep. Consuming me like I'm what's been missing in his soul.

Shivers lift the hairs on my body as my heart fills with his love. Breaking our kiss, he rests his forehead against mine, his eyes penetrating me.

"I love you, Enzo." Words I never thought I'd hear myself say again, flow freely with such fierce intensity and truth.

He heaves an exhale that sounds like the release of a breath he's been holding in the depths of his lungs since the first time our eyes met. Hunching his shoulders, he claims my lips again, affection shifting to need, hunger, desire…rooted in love.

His fingers pressing into the base of my neck, he deepens his kiss, devouring me. Breaths becoming rapid, heighten my desire. I grab the bottom of his shirt in my hands, tugging it up his body. He releases my lips and leans back. Raising onto my knees, I tug it off over his head. Before I drop back down, he weaves his arms under mine, clasping his hands on top of my shoulders, holding me in place before him.

He places kisses on the exposed skin of my breasts then greedily runs his tongue up through my cleavage. I grab his biceps, letting out a soft moan, causing his grip to tighten. With his teeth, he tugs at the tail of the bow tied at my chest, covering my breasts. Another tug until the fabric falls open. Releasing one hand from my shoulder, he takes my breast in his hand and holds it, closing his mouth over my nipple. I tilt my face toward the ceiling, arching into him. My pulse races as breaths pant lightly from my lungs, flames licking up my chest.

Sitting back on my legs, my nipple drops from his mouth. Greed laces his face as his open mouth hurls breaths. I reach for his belt buckle, metal clanging as I hastily unfasten it, eager for what's beneath. I pull open the button on his jeans and he raises onto his knee so I can unzip them. Then he stands in front of me and I shift my legs off the sofa, my feet meeting the ground. My hands on the waist of his jeans, I pull them down his legs, and he steps out of them. His erection bulging in his underwear.

He holds out his hand and I take it, rising from the sofa. Before I can blink, he hoists me up, wrapping my legs around his waist. I throw my arms around his neck. Holding my thighs, he lifts me up and down, pressing himself into me. My cotton pants are wet between my legs as he continues lifting and lowering me. I moan, closing my eyes and biting my lower lip.

"I want to feel you." I breathe, begging.

"Not yet. I'm going to take my time with you." His seductive growl runs the length of my spine.

My body wrapped around his, he walks us to his bedroom. When he sets me on the ground next to his bed, he slides my pants down my legs. I step out of each leg and he tosses them away. As he rises, he puts a gentle hand on the inside of my calf, gliding slowly up my leg until he reaches my wet lips. My inner thighs heat and tingle, yearning.

"Mmm," he murmurs, sliding his fingers back and forth on top of my panties, making me even wetter. Then he peels them down my legs and stands in front of me.

Now it's my turn. I sit on the edge of his bed and pull the waistband of his underwear over his hard-on, uncovering his mushroom-head. I tug it down just enough to take the velvety-soft tip into my mouth, eliciting a grunt from him as his hands rush to the sides of my head. Pulling the waistband farther down, I slide my mouth farther down his length. He heaves an exhale. Sliding my lips up, I go back down, taking him deeper into my mouth.

"Ah," he groans, his fingers pressing with restraint into me, resisting a forceful pull.

I glide off of his shaft and move his underwear over his butt, then tug them down in the front. That's when I see it.

Goose bumps scatter across me as I gasp. My neck jets forward on reflex as I inspect it, the intricate swirls on the bow, the teeth on the bit. It's a perfect match. Then I look up at him, his eyes watchful.

"The key," I say softly, warmth flooding my body.

Hypnotic, kryptonite eyes possess me. He hushes a soft stroke of his thumb across my cheek as the corners of his lips lift. "This was your surprise I never got to show you." His deep, low sound bolts up my spine.

I stand, looking up into his eyes. "But when did you get it?"

"When we got home." One side of his mouth curls higher.

"Why?" I search his eyes.

He pulls my body flush to his, our tattoos touching where our flesh meets. "So I'd know every time I hold your body against mine, I have the key to your heart and I'm opening it with my love for you in the space made only for us."

He *has* opened my heart. He's cradled my vulnerability and understood my fears, accepting me through it all. Loving me with all my fucked-upness. He's shown me his big, beautiful heart, blessing me with the miracle of a second chance at love. A love so deep, it's filled the cavern of my soul with the promise of eternity.

EPILOGUE 1

Candi

Arms filled with containers of s'mores-making ingredients, Destiny and I stand on her back porch watching our husbands play with our kids. Their little legs propelling them in circles around their daddies' legs, Lucia loses her balance and tumbles into the sand. Before Enzo can reach her, Angelo throws himself into the sand to help her up. Once she's to her feet, she brushes her sandy, dark curls from her face with the back of her hand, leans in, and plants a kiss on his cheek, swelling my heart.

After a day of making sand castles, kicking around a soccer ball, and collecting seashells, it's time to relax with a yummy snack. Gazing at each other, we smile then walk down into the warm sand.

We put the containers and extra-long forks on trays near the fire pit.

"Come on, kids," I call out. "It's time."

Their little squeals fill the air with joy as their tiny legs run through the sand, kicking it up behind them. Nicco and Enzo follow, looking more exhausted than the kids.

Destiny hands them each a long fork, already speared with a marshmallow. Nicco and Enzo sit in their chairs.

"Come here, Angelo," Nicco says, patting his hand on his inner thigh and opening his arms toward his son.

"Daddy, will you help make mine hot?" he says, bobbing his way into Nicco's arms.

"Yes, of course I will. I'm very good at it now. I wasn't always though."

Angelo looks up at him, wide-eyed, as though alarmed his daddy could ever not be good at something. "Really?" His intonation goes from low to high.

"No," Nicco says, shaking his head. "Your mommy had to teach me how. I burnt my first one and sent it flying into the sand." He motions the fling with his empty fork.

The adults bust into a chuckle as Angelo's little face fills with an incredulous expression of wonder, the firelight sparkling in his brown eyes.

Lucia's already taken to sitting on Enzo's lap, tucked into her daddy's strong arms, filling me with warmth. "Make it spin, daddy," she requests, her curls dancing around her cherub-face.

Enzo obliges, spinning the fork for the perfect toasting. Lucia claps her hands together with glee.

With s'mores eaten and bellies full, the kids are falling asleep on their daddies' chests. Nicco and Enzo bring them inside and up to the spare bedroom, where I used to sleep when I stayed over.

We toast our marshmallows and assemble our s'mores. Gobbling them down, we lean back in our Adirondack chairs and gaze at the stars above.

"We love these nights with you guys," I say, reaching out to hold her hand.

"We love having you come," she says, holding onto mine.

After a few minutes, Nicco and Enzo rejoin us, sitting back down in their chairs.

"They're out," Enzo says, taking a sip of his wine.

"*I* might be out soon," Nicco chuckles, picking up his wine and raising it toward the fire, indicating he's about to toast.

Destiny and I pick up our glasses from their spots tucked into the sand.

"To those who are gone. To those who are here. And to those who are on the way," he says, rubbing Destiny's belly and raising his glass in the air.

We raise our glasses and take a sip, Destiny drinking water.

In the peace of the moment, I breathe.

If I had to do it all again, I wouldn't change a thing. I'd go through the pain and the heartache all over. I'd suffer the agony of losing Dom, my loneliness, my empty soul, my broken heart, to get exactly here, to this moment, right here and now.

My career filling me up and continuing to be successful, the best friend a girl could hope for, a renewed relationship with my dad who's a huge part of his granddaughter's life, my loving husband by my side, and our daughter asleep in my best friend's house; I am unimaginably blessed.

EPILOGUE 2

Enzo

The warm, summer-night air stirs with the salty ocean breeze as we sit around the fire pit at Nicco and Destiny's house. Belly full of s'mores, sand between her toes, our little girl sleeps on my chest, dark curls snuggling her face. As precious and beautiful and loving as her mom.

The moment Candi breezed past me at Nicco and Destiny's wedding, sauntering her sexy confidence, something inside me knew she was going to impact me in some way. We came to each other flawed, battered by life, hurt bottled inside.

Together, we embraced each other's flaws, healed the wounds of life, and unbottled our hurt, setting it free. Together, side-by-side, day-by-day, loving each other.

Never once did she try to change me. Rather, her influence helped me see that I wanted to change myself. I learned to change my perspective about my resentment toward my mom. And I learned to embrace my worth in and of myself. Because of her, my life is enriched in ways I couldn't have imagined. She encourages me and supports me in every way, inspiring me every day.

I watched her crumble, and I watched her rise. She worked through her pain and healed, morphing into her majestic butterfly. She's the strongest woman I know and I'm proud and grateful to be her partner, knowing that whatever comes our way, we'll tackle it together.

Until Candi came into my life, my dream of having a family was only something I'd hope to experience through Anastasia and Gino. I'd almost given up on having it for myself. And now we have our sweet baby girl who gets to grow up with Angelo and her cousin Sophia, who Anastasia had a few months after our wedding, and soon another little Mancini.

My career is stable with money coming in and I'm surrounded by family and love. Mom comes in for visits from time to time and we go to see her once or twice a year. Having her back in my life is a true gift.

I would never have believed this could be my life. From the day Candi came back to me, there was never a doubt that her heart belonged to me. And every time I look in her eyes, no shadow exists, only her never-waning love…for me.

She's my rock, the foundation of our family. And every time I kiss her, she feels like breathing, she smells like comfort, she tastes like love…she is my home.

ARE YOU READY FOR ANGELO AND LUCIA'S STORY?

Turn the page to start reading.

Get the full book here...

https://books2read.com/SomeoneToWatchOverMeCromack

PROLOGUE

Angelo

Watching someone you love get their heart broken time after time and not being able to take away their pain is crippling. Yet, this is exactly what I've chosen to do.

When I was ten years old, my dad shared with me a piece of life-knowledge that I took to heart. He told me that your first love is never your last love. So now I suffer as I watch her get her heart broken and wait for the time to be right and for her to be ready for me.

And through my suffering, I try to remember the joy that will come when she's finally ready. This is my plan and what I've chosen to endure because I've been in love with Lucia since the day she was born.

One thing my dad didn't share with me is that plans can change in the blink of an eye. And nothing could've prepared me for the obliteration of my heart.

1

Angelo

I'm supposed to protect her, like a big brother should. I'm not supposed to fall in love with her.

I was two years old when I fell in love with Lucia Cipriani. I've known her since the day she was brought home from the hospital. Our parents are best friends. We've grown up just blocks apart and our families spend a lot of time together on weekends and even vacation together sometimes.

We've gone to the same schools our entire lives. Though she's two years behind me, she's always been smarter than me, something I've always admired about her. I've taken to being a big-brother figure and watching out for her, which frustrates her sometimes. It's the role I've assumed. One, because I *am* protective of her, and two, because both our dads expect it of me, and they've told me so. She's so damn pretty too, with a body any guy would masturbate to, including me — a fact she'll never find out about. Her physical appearance draws attention from a lot of guys — a lot of dirtbags.

I graduate from UCLA in a couple weeks and tonight's frat party is an epic celebration so far. Drinking with my friends, playing pool, and dancing sweaty bodies-smashed-against-sweaty bodies in the dimly lit basement. The floor and walls vibrate to the pounding music as the stench of stale beer and pot wafts through the air.

Then *she* walks in.

My Lucia...but not mine. I didn't know she was coming.

Though she's been here a lot, she's never come to a party. At least she's with her roommate-slash-best friend, Sherrie. Neither of them are party girls, quite the opposite, in fact. I wouldn't have had so much to drink if I knew I'd basically be on bodyguard duty tonight.

The theme of the party is, "boxer shorts and lingerie." Seeing my white dress shirt on her, now I know why she borrowed it. Thank God she's wearing it over her lingerie. Only two of the buttons are closed at her chest, and the boxers, also mine — little thief — cover her butt and tops of her thighs. Her long legs are accentuated by black stiletto heels. *Jesus, I want to know what she's wearing underneath my clothes.*

Trying not to ruin her night by stalking over and telling her to leave, I tuck into the hallway with the burnt-out light bulb, watching her like a hawk as drunk, hormone-raging turkey vultures sniff out her virginity and circle around her and Sherrie like they're prey. She shouldn't be in a place like this. My jaw tight, I grit my teeth, ready to pounce if any of them so much as thinks about touching her.

One of my sleazeball frat brothers, Joe, enters the circle and hands them each a beer. He's not necessarily a bad guy, he's just a man-whore, and *not* someone I want hanging around Lucia. With her still here two more years after I'm gone, I have no idea how I'm going to protect her from assholes like him. Irritation pounds at my temples to the thump of the music as I tilt my plastic cup into my mouth, letting the beer slide down my throat while keeping my eyes on Lucia.

The girls spot me, exchanging words as they look at me and back at each other.

2

Lucia

"Never?" Sherrie's voice rises as her brown eyes widen in disbelief.

"No, never. We don't think about each other that way." My heart sinks a little. The statement is a complete lie on my end. I say it to convince myself, knowing the effort is pointless. "Angelo just —" I shrug, "doesn't see me that way. He looks at me like I'm his little sister and that's all." He thinks he's being sly, tucked into the shadow of the hallway. But I feel his protective eyes watching me.

Outwardly, I'd always expressed my frustration with his need to protect me, but inside, I wondered if he intimidated any guy who even thought about asking me out because maybe he wanted me to be his and he was waiting for me to be old enough to tell me. That naïve thinking was of a hopeful, pitiful little girl.

I've been waiting twenty years for him to tell me he feels something more for me than just friendship. As we've gotten older, my innocent childhood crush turned, shifted, morphed into a deep love that intertwined with heated lust once my hormones finally kicked in. But as long as I've waited and hoped, there's never been any indication that he feels anything close to the need and desire I feel. It's painfully obvious that he doesn't feel the same way about me as I feel about him. *Felt about him.*

"Well, maybe it's time you show him you're not so little anymore. Day-um." She shamelessly roves her eyes up and down his body, sculpted muscles accentuated by the dim lighting of the shadowy hallway. "I know I'd be all over his fine ass." She snaps her fingers with a tilt of her head.

"Sherrie." A laugh slips out of my numbing mouth.

She's not the only girl who swoons over him. His dark, Italian features and lean, muscular body have always captured gawking glares from girls.

After several glasses of wine, Sherrie and I did a few shots of Chocolate Cinnamon Toast Crunch at our apartment before we came and they're kicking in. I briefly look over at Angelo, catching a glimpse of his perfect chest and abs hiding beneath his open, black, collared shirt. I've seen his body plenty through the years and his dedication to working out since he came to college is evident in his mouthwatering physique.

"I'm serious. He's so damn hot. If you two didn't have this weird relationship, I'd get after what's behind those black boxers." She spouts a playful roaring sound, making me laugh. "I don't see him with anyone." Swiveling her head from side to side, she continues the motion through her wiggling body. "Let's just test him and see what happens."

"What do you mean?" I ask, lifting my heels alternately from the sticky floor.

"I mean," she says, taking a gulp of her beer then handing it to me to hold. Her eyes focused and twinkling with mischief, she unbuttons the two buttons on his shirt I'm wearing. "Let's test him…and see." She winks at me and opens the shirt a little.

"What are you doing? I don't think this is a good idea. Maybe we should go home," I say, sensing eyes surrounding me like a pack of wolves as my head grows dizzier.

"Not yet. I want you to walk over there and lean against the wall next to him. See what his reaction is." She cocks her head in his direction.

"I can tell you what his reaction will be. He'll cover me up and tell me to go the hell home." I know Angelo. When he looks at me, he sees a ten-year-old girl with pigtails, not a fully-developed woman. It's a truth I've cried about many a night. It took a long time, but I finally let go of my crush on him when he came to college. *At least that's what I keep telling myself.*

"Go on," she says, nudging me. "I'll be watching and I'll tell you what *I* see."

I sigh and decide to appease her so she'll let it go. Tossing back the rest of my beer, I hand her both of our cups. Though it's pointless, I turn and start walking toward him. His dark hair is a little longer on top and perfectly disheveled. The scruff dusting across his jaw is hours past a five o'clock shadow, making him even sexier.

Each step toward him sends sensations through me that I shouldn't be feeling but can't stop. His gaze travels up my body and I practically hear his thoughts, *"Put some clothes on and go home."*

When his brown eyes lock onto mine, they level me, sending butterflies flitting in my stomach.

3

Angelo

Lord, have mercy on me. She's a tall, straight shot of silky-smooth tequila. Every step of her heels onto the concrete floor sends a shock straight to my dick. As I watch her beautiful breasts bounce behind her black lace bra, I'm wishing I was wearing jeans instead of boxer shorts. *Think of disgusting shit.*

"This isn't quite your scene," I say as she approaches me. "Didn't expect to see you here." Resting my arm on the wall, I try not to seem as drunk as I am.

She leans her back against the wall, standing close to me. "Sherrie and I were bored. I couldn't study anymore. We knew you guys were having a party so we thought we'd stop by."

I turn myself to face her, trying to block the view of her hot body from ogling, testosterone-filled, thirsty glares, and put my palms on the wall on either side of her. "You had to pick the boxer shorts and lingerie party to come to, huh?" It's taking all my willpower not to glance down at her full, succulent breasts. Instead, I bore my gaze into her hazelnut eyes.

"Yeah, why?" she asks, her tone bordering belligerence.

I fucking cave, glancing down at her breasts then forcing my eyes to return to hers. "Do you want a sweatshirt from my room?" It comes out more like a command than an actual question that would imply she has a choice. I'm not trying to be an asshole. I'm simply trying to prevent her goddess-like body from being visually defiled by every guy in the room.

Her eyes darken, darting back and forth between mine as I

take a deep, heavy breath…trying not to visually defile her myself.

She heaves a disgruntled sigh. "You can't protect me from everyone forever," she says, a hint of venom rides her tongue as her eyebrow raises and she sasses her head from side to side.

I lower my face, inches from hers. "Wanna bet?" Provoking her, I raise an eyebrow right back at her.

A line dents her brow as her chest rises and falls with hot breaths that sweep across my lips. *What I'd do for just a taste.*

She's a wicked temptation who's becoming harder to resist. *Fuck. Get a grip on your drunk ass.*

She growls at me, frustration seething steam from her ears. When she tries to duck under my arm, I scoop her up and throw her over my shoulder, causing laughter, hoots, and howls from the surrounding sea of bodies.

With eyes on us, I start walking up the stairs as she pounds on my back, yelling, "Put me down!" So feisty.

I head straight for my room, close the door, and put her on her feet, holding her until she's steady in her heels.

"What's wrong with you?" she shouts. "No guy on this entire campus will come near me because of you." Eyes squinched together and pointing her finger into my bare chest, she takes a step toward me like she's ready to rumble and it's so damn cute. "You're *not* my brother and you're *not* my boyfriend." I can't tell if her voice is laced with anger or hurt…or both. Then she softens. "You're my best friend, Ang." Her yearning eyes are killing me.

I say nothing. Hunger boils my blood. It's taking every ounce of restraint to not throw her sexy ass on my bed and put my mouth on every part of her body I've wanted to taste for as long as I can remember. I keep my secret hidden. Hidden under layers of steel. I can't let her know until the time is right.

Throwing both arms in the air, she growls again and tries to get past me. I reach out my arm and stop her, pinning her against the wall.

Startled, she looks up at me from between my arms. So…

fucking…beautiful. Her long dark waves hug the sides of her luscious breasts as her eyes spit daggers at me from beneath her thick lashes.

We stare at each other, breathing the same air. The dulled pounding of music filling our ears.

"Why do you put me on this pedestal so no one can reach me?" Her feistiness shifts to confusion, grasping for answers. Answers I'm not willing to confess. She belongs on a pedestal. There's not a single guy on this campus who's worthy of her.

"None of the guys you pick are good enough for you."

Fury returns to her as she puts her hands on my chest and pushes me away. "No one is, Angelo, according to you! Who *is* good enough for me?" she blasts, getting up in my face, glaring at me. "*You?*"

The question smashes me in the face. Nope, not even me. My heart fists in my chest, pounding.

I step back to prevent myself from grabbing her and kissing her. "You've had too much to drink. I'm not letting you go back down there dressed like this and drunk."

She slams her arms by her sides. "You can't stop me," she fumes, making another attempt to leave.

Without much effort, I grab her again and toss her onto my bed. "You'll stay here tonight so I can look after you. I'm not letting you near those vultures. Take off your shoes and get under the covers."

She squints her eyes, resigning to the fact that she's lost this battle. "You're infuriating. You know that?" Standing up, she starts taking off my boxers.

I quickly look away, wanting to watch every move she makes. Listening for the sound of my sheets, I wait. Trying to distract myself from picturing her, I stare at the painting of the flaming guitar on my wall. Dad gave it to me on my thirteenth birthday. It's my favorite piece of art. And it's also a reminder that'll I'll never be anywhere near as musically talented as him.

"Are you in?"

"I'm in, bully."

I take off my shirt and shoes, and shut off the light before getting into the bed, turning my back to her. Wanting to do the exact opposite, and knowing that's a bad idea. She's been in my bed plenty of times, usually crying on my chest about some jerk who stood her up or getting a B on an exam. This is uncomfortably different, I've never been drunk with my self-control compromised.

Her soft hand is on my shoulder, tugging me.

I lie on my back, gazing at her beautiful, moonlight-kissed face, restraining myself and trying to ignore the flames licking my dick. *Give me willpower.*

Thank You!

Thanks for reading Kiss Away Your Pain. Your support means so much to me. I hope you loved it!

If you did enjoy Candi and Enzo's love story, please take a moment to leave your honest review on Amazon, GoodReads, and/or BookBub. Thank you!

WHAT TO READ NEXT...

Someone to Watch Over Me (Book 3 in my Wounded Hearts series)
https://books2read.com/SomeoneToWatchOverMeCromack

AN INVITATION

This is a special invitation for YOU. Yes, you. I know you can join thousands of authors' newsletters and I know that can be overwhelming. The readers who choose to join my free newsletter are friends to me, people who actually want to be with me in my little corner of the world.

Of course, I share updates about my books, and I also share personal stories, tough times, funny times, goats/chickens/bunny pictures, do special giveaways no one else gets, give you the first look at covers and chapters, and more.

So, this is my personal invitation to you to jump into my world and join my free newsletter. When you do, you'll receive free chapters of some of my books and a fun Book BINGO Challenge printable PDF.

HEAD HERE TO JOIN:

https://debbiecromack.com/newsletter/

WHERE DID THE IDEA FOR THIS BOOK COME FROM?

Kiss Away Your Pain was born because my readers loved the secondary character of Candi in Someone Exactly Like Me so much that they requested her story.

My muse for the character of Candi is my friend, https://www.instagram.com/jameslee4/. When we first met, she had mermaid-long, pink, curly hair. She's sassy as anything with a huge heart and is fiercely loyal.

I'm going to be honest; I was terrified to write this book. For my first two books, the stories came to me and I was basically just the person jotting them down. For this one, I had to CREATE the story, hoping I could deliver to my readers the story they want to read.

The stories I write are first for me because if they're not coming from my heart, you, my reader, will feel it. Second, they're for my readers because you keep me writing. So, this one being requested by my readers, I put quite a bit of pressure on myself because I didn't want to disappoint you or let you down.

As I'm quite vanilla when it comes to things in the bedroom, I decided to binge-watch Sex/Life on Netflix, not something I'd normally watch, but it did give me some really good inspiration. If you've watched it, you may pick up on some of that inspiration. In full confession, I must say, my, that man has a big ding-dong! LOL!

I hope you enjoyed reading Candi's story. Be sure to check out my other books!

MORE BOOKS BY

Debbie Cromack

Standalones

Untouchable Zane

Wounded Hearts Series

Someone Exactly Like Me

Kiss Away Your Pain

Someone to Watch Over Me

Coming Soon

Broken Billionaire Brothers series

A SPECIAL THANK YOU

A.L. Jackson. Where do I begin? My gratitude spills out of my heart for your love, care, and time. Thank you for always being there for me with your encouragement, kindness, thoughts, and suggestions. You help me remember to be free with my writing and strategic with my business decisions. You're always there with a virtual hug when I'm about to have a meltdown and there to cheer me on and celebrate my little milestones. I'm blessed in that God brought you into my life and we've become friends. I cherish the friendship we're building. Love you!

K.G. Fletcher. Thank you for being you! Thank you for your kindness and teaching me so many things, helping me along this wild path of self-publishing. I'm grateful for your tips, suggestions, support, and friendship. Let's keep sharing our love stories with the world.

C. D'Angelo. What would I do without our daily chats? I'm happy our life paths have come together. Your friendship means so much to me. Girl, we'll never have things figured out, but we'll keep going anyway. Thank you for your friendship and support every single day.

Julie Soper. My sweet friend. My mental health hug. My character medical adviser. LOL! Thank you for always checking in on me to see how I'm doing. You have this beautiful, uncanny way of knowing when I'm struggling. Your words of love and virtual hugs mean so much to me. Thank you for your friendship.

ACKNOWLEDGMENTS

My readers thank you for choosing to be in my world and for your support. Your excited and loving messages keep me going and make my heart smile. Thank you for telling your friends to buy and read my books. I appreciate you so much!

The writing community and my author friends, I appreciate you. I love this community! You're there with me through tears when the words aren't coming and my story is poop. You're there for me when I'm trying to figure out strategies for my business. You're there with me to celebrate my releases and when things go well. I thank you with all my heart. Thank you for all your sharing, all your kind words, and all your love. You mean so much to me and I'm grateful for you every day.

My wonderful beta readers, **Courteney Tunstead, Melissa Johnson, Colby Bettley**. My books always improve because you give, so lovingly, of your time and your thoughts. I appreciate you so much!! Thank you for making this story better than I could've done on my own!

My ARC and Street teams, bloggers, and bookstagrammers, THANK YOU so much for your devotion and dedication to help spread the word for me and all the authors you help and support. I could never reach new people without all of your time and effort. You are the heartbeat of this community and you help me keep writing books for you.

I'd like to thank some incredible women who I've never met, but who love and support me pretty much every single day: **Julie Soper, Robin Buck, Jen Chiola, Heppy Jael, Michelle Mastandrea, Suzie Cloen, Kait Miguel, Cheryl Herrman**. Thank you for the laughter you share, thank you for drying my tears, thank you for your support and guidance when I'm ready to pull my hair out, thank you for your love. You're a warm blanket around my heart.

And **YOU, my new reader**. Thank you for taking a chance on reading my book. I hope you loved it!!! Without you, I wouldn't be able to do this amazing work I love and bring you stories to escape into. Thank you!

ABOUT THE AUTHOR

Hi! I'm Debbie and I write contemporary novels that are romantic, sexy, and emotional with a lot of heart and worth-the-wait steam. I've been called the Master of Slow Burn, a title I happily accept.

I write realistic, flawed characters you'd want to get to know in real life. My heroes are virile and also broken. They have huge hearts, respect their women, and have a hidden romantic side. My heroines are often awkward, feisty, and embody everything the hero never knew he needed.

After spending 25+ years in corporate America, being the CEO of an event decorating company, and then an online business coach, I tried my hand at writing romance novels, publishing my debut novel at the age of 50, and have been writing ever since.

I live in an old farmhouse where I care for a dwarf bunny named Nutmeg, two Nigerian dwarf goats named Patches and Tiny, and lots of chickens. I like my book boyfriends how I like my cocoa: hot and yummy! With my knack for decorating, I tend to go all-out for each holiday. And I'm a total sucker for the Hallmark Channel…especially at Christmas.

CONNECT WITH ME

Come connect with me on my **social media accounts.**
Here's my Linktree link where you can find **ALL** my links:
linktr.ee/Debbie_Cromack_Author

Printed in the USA
CPSIA information can be obtained
at www.ICGtesting.com
LVHW050816290723
753809LV00043B/773